PELT OF THE

RED FOX

A NOVEL OF THE WEST

TWO BLANKETS · BOOK THREE

PELT OF THE
RED FOX

A NOVEL OF THE WEST

R.L. ADARE

HAT CREEK

HAT CREEK

An Imprint of Roan & Weatherford Publishing Associates, LLC
Bentonville, Arkansas
www.roanweatherford.com

Library of Congress Cataloging-in-Publication Data
Names: Adare, R.L., author.
Title: Pelt of the Red Fox/R.L. Adare | Two Feathers #3
Description: First Edition | Bentonville: Hat Creek, 2025.
Identifiers: LCCN: 2021948626 | ISBN: 978-1-63373-643-6 (hardcover) |
ISBN: 978-1-63373-644-3 (trade paperback) | ISBN: 978-1-63373-645-0 (eBook)
Subjects: BISAC: FICTION/Native American & Aboriginal |
FICTION/Westerns | FICTION/Coming of Age
LC record available at: https://lccn.loc.gov/2021948626

Hat Creek trade paperback edition June, 2025

Cover Art by Casey W. Cowan
Cover & Interior Design by Casey W. Cowan
Editing by Dennis Doty & Amy Cowan

*So many women have suffered in the Old West, so many forgotten,
so many who should be honored for their valor and strength.
I dedicate this novel to you.*

ACKNOWLEDGEMENTS

M Y ETERNAL THANKS FOR this novel go out to my two supportive beta readers, Kathy Ann Trueman and Kerri O'Donnell, PhD. without whose assistance this book would never have been written in its present form. I also want to thank my editor, Dennis Doty whose skill shaped this book. As well, immense thanks to Oghma Creative Media, and Casey Cowan, its C.E.O. and guiding light. Thank you all.

GLOSSARY

NEZ PERCE

háma: man

he: yes, the affirmative

ilekíuzitske: to feel hot, as to sweat

kine: here, at this place

máma: wife's brother's child

názog: salmon

Nch'i-wána: The great river, The Columbia River.

Nimi'ipuu: The Real People, the Nez Perce.

Pike: mother, pronounced *pee-kay*

taz: good

weyekin: spiritual guide, or spirit animal

CHINOOK JARGON OR TRADE LANGUAGE

camas: a starchy bulb eaten by many different tribes and the white pioneers, creates gaseous condition when undercooked.

cultus: weak, useless, small, frequently used in the negative as in cultus whiteman, useless white man, but used also as a positive as in cultus potlatch, a gift where, unlike normal Chinook custom, no reciprocal is required."

dentalium: shell used as jewelry as well as used as a money trade item.

mistshimus: slave.

nika: mine.

potlatch: gift, gift giving ceremony.

skutch: vagina

tatoosh: breasts

tenino: vulva, pudenda.

Tyee: local clan leader of Chinook, they had no overall chief.

whiteman(s): used as a referent to Caucasians.

wootlat: penis.

PELT OF THE RED FOX

A NOVEL OF THE WEST

SMALL WILLIE,
PICKLES & WHORES

CHAPTER I
MAY TO OCTOBER, 1857

THERE WERE SEVERAL events, or rather chains of events, which served as reminders to Two Blankets that she couldn't plan a life if she didn't know what the determining factors would be. Perhaps it was because she was used to the way the clan worked. In the summer, one primarily worked gathering food and hides for trade as well. Every day one gathered root vegetables or fished for salmon if that were the assigned task. The herbs used by Stinging Nettle and Bone Rattler were picked in the appropriate season. Of course, there was also the daily cooking and food consumption. Life had a pattern, a natural flow that could be depended upon season upon season, year after year. People grew older, had children, and raised them. Occasionally, they died of old age, and it was not a surprise, but a cause for ritual celebration of their life and achievements. Sometimes, a person died of accident or disease, and this was a cause for grief and sadness.

But life with Marshall was different. Perhaps it was because Two Blankets was not privy to his long-range plans or perhaps only because his ways were incomprehensible to her.

She had spent five weeks soliciting his sexual attention. She expected to have to taper that back now that she was pregnant, but in fact, his interest in her seemed to vaporize now that she was with child. It didn't evaporate immediately but seemed to diminish rapidly.

She teased him about it one day a couple of weeks after he had 'discovered' her condition. It was mid-afternoon when she approached him.

"So, husband Marshall, do you have an hour free this afternoon?" He had his plans spread outside the trading post on the large table, the usual half-full whiskey glass weighting one corner of the detailed map, the bottle weighting another against the afternoon's rising wind.

"What? Oh, Two Blankets."

She wrapped her arms around him from behind and pressed against him. "I just thought it has been almost a week since we..." She let her voice trail off suggestively.

"That does feel good. But you are with child now."

"That didn't stop you two weeks ago." She stroked his chest.

"I didn't know that then. My Mama always said my Pa had to keep his distance when she was with child. It was women's business, and her two sisters backed her up. Pa always gave way when she was with child, and he taught us boys to as well."

"Are you sure of that? I never heard about it in the clan." She slipped a hand into the waistband of his trousers.

Marshall squirmed away. "Now, don't do that. You might need it, but I ain't risking my cock taking a pregnant woman. It's despicable. I got to go up to the main building and consult with Haroldson." He rolled up his map and left quickly.

Two Blankets watched his back as he walked out. "That was as strange as strange could be."

Every time I think I am beginning to understand him, he does something that tells me I will never understand.

Gray Wolf rolled in the dust in comment.

The work on the settlement progressed at a faster pace as the days lengthened during that summer. The flooring was in in the former *Tyee's* house, now the main house of the Johnston's Trading Post, and the siding was up on both floors. Marshall made a trip to Portland and returned a week later with tubs of paint. The men went to work painting the building red, and when the windows went in two weeks later, they painted them blue.

At the beginning of September, he made another passage to Portland. This time, he returned with two women.

"Wonder of wonders again, Gray Wolf. Will you look at that?" The two women were just getting off the steamboat, awkward in fancy shoes and their flowing satins and petticoats. One was a plump blonde who might have been pretty once, ten years before. Now, she looked worn and tired, and her laughter was falsely gay. The other was a few years younger, less worn looking, yet she seemed to carry an even harder look about her. Their trunks were unloaded, and the men carried them up to the red and blue building. Behind them stood Mr. Shales, looking dapper as usual, his eyes taking in everything. Marshall escorted him up to the main building, following the two women.

Two Blankets shifted her weight from one aching foot to another. "Why is Marshall bringing two women here? They don't look like wives, though I don't know if I would know. Maybe they are accompanying Mister Shales. But they don't look like the type to be his companions either."

She walked up to the main building. To Two Blankets, it looked garish, bright red with blue window trim with the words "Johnston's Landing" written large across the false front of the third story. Of course, she hadn't seen many *whiteman's* buildings, and what she had seen at The Dalles were at a distance. Maybe they all looked like this. The windows across the front were stunning, like vertical pools that one could look through, with only a slight distortion, clearer than water. She stepped up onto the little porch, that ran across the front, and through the door. A rough bar ran with a polished hardwood rail along the right side. A narrow set of stairs ran up the left-hand side, and the men were dragging the trunks up to the second floor.

"Goddammit! Pick those up and carry them. We just built them stairs, and you're going to scar them all up." Marshall seemed almost like a hen clucking over her chicks. "Alton, come over here for a drink while the pretty ladies get themselves situated."

"Marshall, you been out here in the woods too long if you think they're either pretty or ladies. They're whores and almost as rough as your men. I think the dark haired one even has a beard."

"Now, Mister Shales, this here ain't a big city like Portland. This is Delores Sue." The blonde smiled showing yellowed teeth and held out her hand. Alton took it.

"Pleased, I'm sure." Delores Sue's voice was mellifluous, a dulcet, flute-like tone.

"This beauty is Aimee. She's French—or at least of French extract—from the grand city of San Francisco."

Alton smiled uncomfortably and wiped his hands surreptitiously as he held his handkerchief to his mouth.

"You, sweet ladies, get yourselves settled upstairs in your rooms. Got a feeling your services will be in demand tonight. Some of these men ain't seen a bush the whole winter and spring. Might have to reacquaint them with what one looks like."

The blonde, Delores Sue, giggled as they turned to the stairs.

"This is what you have been buying with my money?" Alton absently twisted his waxed mustache into a new point. "Red paint and a couple of worn-out whores?"

"Now, you think about it, Alton. The red paint is to make a point. *Ad-ver-tis-ing.* Johnston's Landing is a big deal, not just another trading post among a hundred other shabby posts. And the whores? I'm paying the men a dollar or dollar twenty a day. I get back half of whatever they make from the whores, Pay out with one hand and take it back with the other. Makes good business sense, I'd say."

"Oh, all right, Marshall. I take your reasoning."

"In compensation, as a part owner, you are welcome to partake in the pleasures, on the house." He slapped Mr. Shales on the shoulder.

Shales stepped away with a disgusted look. "I have women I can see in Portland that aren't likely to give me some disease. That sort of thing is fine for the employees. They can always be replaced. We are management, Mister Johnston." He turned to Two Blankets. "And this must be your wife. Missus Johnston."

Two Blankets noticed he didn't offer his hand. "Hello, Mister Shales. Always a pleasure."

"My, oh my, Marshall didn't tell me she was with child."

"Yes. A few months now. We are pleased."

"I'm sure you are. And you, too, Marshall."

"What's that smell?" She sniffed the air as she wandered toward the bar.

"I don't smell nothing," Marshall said, "nothing unusual, anyways." His look, and Mr. Shales', as well, followed her progress.

"It smells strong...sour-like...and a little bitter." She approached a small barrel of pickles on the bar. "There, in that jar. Those huge green things. If they are to eat, can I have one?"

"Them's pickles." Marshall unscrewed the lid. "I get them from Portland. I don't think you'd like them." But he handed her the most massive, bumpiest pickle he could fish out.

Two Blankets took a small bite and then a larger one. "Oh. I never realized. Now, this is a whiteman's food that tastes delicious. Can I have some more to take back to the longhouse?"

Marshall fished out a jar from the back of the bar and loaded it with six or eight pickles.

Two Blankets took the jar. "Thank you, husband Marshall." She turned away toward the door. "These are really good. I mean really."

"Pregnant women, what can you do?" Marshall said to Alton.

ALTON SHALES ONLY stayed a couple of days. "At least you ain't leaving us this time with your balls swollen like grapefruits."

"I didn't need the reminder, thank you. Sometimes, you are a very crude man, Mister Johnston."

"I don't have the pleasure of working with the likes of your kind every day, Shales. Some of us gotta get our sleeves dirty."

"As you say, Mister Johnston. Some of us do have to get down in the dirt and work."

"I think that's what I said. Have a good trip. We're going to make some money now."

The steamboat's whistle blew. The stern paddles churned the water, and the boat pulled away.

Two Blankets munched on another pickle. "Are you coming up to the hut for lunch, husband Marshall?"

"What's that? Oh, no. I've got a lot of work to do up at the Landing. You don't need to worry none about me. Might be late in, as well."

"All right. Would you get some more of these pickles for me?" She bit off a hunk. "They are delicious."

"I'll order you a barrel next week, and I'll send you over another jar for the time being." Marshall turned away and yelled at a worker, then stalked up to the Landing.

It was an odd feeling, but Two Blankets almost felt abandoned. She had never thought she might miss Marshall's attention. She shook her head. *When I think about it, it seems silly to miss something I never wanted in the first place.*

Gray Wolf looked up at her. *I don't waste any time with human thinking, but maybe you should be thinking more often, then.*

I know, darling Gray Wolf. I am slow sometimes.

A couple of months later, in October, Two Blankets woke early. Though she could not tell, it was two or three hours before dawn. She automatically reached to Marshall's place in the sleeping furs, but he hadn't shared her furs for a week.

She lay very still and listened. She could hear her own breathing, which she stilled back into a sleeping pace. Slowly, she extended her senses outward.

There. Is that a breath? She heard nothing, then she heard another breath, and that, the squeak of leather? A boot, perhaps?

A full moon outside shed some light within. As her eyes adjusted to the meager light available, a shadow moved across the doorway.

Suddenly, the steps moved toward her. She reached for the knife she kept under the furs. It was slapped immediately from her grasp and flew across the bed. Two Blankets had time to get one loud yell out before a huge hand clamped over her mouth. She squirmed and fought. She bit the hand that held her down. His other hand slapped her down into the bunk and stunned her.

"Now, you be real quiet here, and maybe I won't kill you right away. Maybe I'll wait a bit. Gilly, check the door. Look outside. See if anyone noticed or is coming."

Gilly opened the door flap and looked toward the village. "I don't see no lights or hear nothing, Small Willie. Nothing."

"Okay. Come back in and light the lamp."

Gilly fumbled for his flint and tinder and lit the lamp.

"Keep it shuttered fool, so no one sees."

Two Blankets came out of her unconsciousness and stared up at a face she thought never to see again. The fear in her eyes turned to anger. She struggled, and he balled his over large right hand into a fist.

She subsided.

"Better. I been looking forward to this day a long time now. You know, I only got partial use of my left arm since you stabbed me. You cut a nerve or lifting muscles, or something. I am only half a man now, or so the hirers say down on the docks. Oh, they'll give me half-pay. Half-pay for half a man." He spat into the sleeping furs. "Am I supposed to kiss their ass for that? I figure you owe me—you and Marshall both."

"Hurry up, Willie. I don't like it here."

"So, where does Marshall keep his money?"

He eased the hand off her mouth. "He only keeps about a hundred dollars here. It's in the cash box." Two Blankets waved a hand toward the bar.

"Gilly, check it. A hundred dollars. I didn't come all the way out here, get off the boat twenty miles downstream and ride around the forest for a day and a half, then sneak down the stream for a hundred dollars. Even with you in the bargain, that ain't worth it."

Gilly opened the cash box and turned the money out. "She's right. Just over a hundred here. Let's get out of here. I don't want to get shot for a hundred dollars. I don't want to get shot no ways."

"Where's the rest of the money, bitch? Marshall don't run a place like this on no hundred dollars. Not with payroll and shipping."

"He keeps the rest up at the Landing."

"What do you mean? This *is* the Landing."

"He doesn't use this longhouse for trade anymore. He has a big new building for that."

Gilly looked out of the door flap toward the Landing building again. The sky was graying a bit and the stars fading. "Come on." His voice was fearful. "Let's just take the money and get out of here. There might be twenty men up in that there bunkhouse, getting up anytime now."

"Get a grip on your cowardice. We're going up to the Landing and collect some real money." He stood with his left arm around Two Blanket's neck, half-choking her. "My lifting muscles might be damaged, but I'm plenty strong enough to lift you once I get hold."

Two Blankets squirmed in his grip. His other hand brought a large skinning knife up to her throat. She stilled.

"Good. I'd love to cut you, but not yet. Now, walk little girl."

Outside, she could see the smoke coming from the bunkhouse. Someone was up. *What can I do to change this? Should I yell again? No, the knife is too close.*

White Mouse whispered in her ear. *When a snake has you by the tail, be still. Be very still.*

The White Mouse is right, for once. Be still and compliant, for now. Patience is key. Wait your chance. Gray Wolf growled deep in her throat.

They crossed the creek at the bridge and walked up toward the Landing, three people with their shadows looming out before them, long and almost black.

"I don't like this. Not at all."

"Shut the fuck up, Gilly. You were all fired up when we was in Portland."

"That was when you said we'd just sneak in and steal the money."

Small Willie shifted his arm around her throat. "Goddamn arm. Seems like you're a bit heavier than you were before." He looked down at Two Blankets. Her rounded naked belly protruded in the stark moonlight. "My gawd. You're pregnant. Marshall's gone and got his Indian whore pregnant." He laughed. "Well, don't that beat all."

He prodded her up onto the porch with the skinning knife and looked through the window. Except for the strips of moonlight passing through the windows, all was dark within.

They crept in through the door and stood in the doorway, just listening.

Small Willie's lips touched her ear. "Where's ol' Marshall sleep when he's up here?"

Her whispered voice barely penetrated the silence. "He has a cot in the back. I don't know, really, but I expect that's where he'd be if he is not with one of the whores."

"Ha-ha. He's got an Indian whore wife and couple more up here. Business is good." He propelled her onward with the knife. "To the back, then."

Quiet as mice, wary of the cat, they moved toward the back room. Small Willie opened the door and edged in behind her. The knife point brushed her throat as a reminder not to make a sound.

Be still. White Mouse hid beneath her hair.

Patience. Not yet. Now is not the time. Gray Wolf said. *You will know the moment.*

Shush. I will know.

The room was deep and narrow. This was the first time Two Blankets had ever been in here, and she looked about furtively with only her eyes, not daring to move her head. It was lined with shelving, and the shelving was packed with supplies. From whiskey, a lot of it of different types, furs, nails, a few boxes of bullets, foodstuffs, to every other sort of supply a trading post might carry. More than could be cataloged in one short look, but she did see that everything was shelved carefully and in its own place. At the very back, below a small window, was the cot. Upon the cot, with a half-bottle of whiskey on a barrel next to it, lay Marshall, snoring and oblivious.

Small Willie chuckled under his breath. They slipped up to the cot, and he nudged Marshall with his knee.

"Go away." Marshall turned over and covered his face with his arm.

"Good morning, *Mister* Marshall." Small Willie spoke in a polite, but sarcastic voice.

Marshall drew back his arm and looked up through one bleary eye "What the fuck do *you* want?"

"Wall, I got part of what I want already." He shoved at Two Blankets. "But, unfortunately, you don't keep the cash in the longhouse anymore."

Marshall blinked away his drunk and hangover.

"Light that lamp there, Gilly," Small Willie said.

Gilly lifted the glass and fumbled a flint and steel a few times until he finally caught a flame.

Marshall rolled to face the two men. "Maybe you should think about leaving while you're still alive. You got my woman, after all."

"He's letting us leave, Willie. Let's go now."

Two Blankets couldn't see Gilly, but she could hear his agitation. Upon Marshall's face, she saw a quiet recalculation.

"I told you to shut up. After all this work I gone to, I think I'll want your cash, too. Don't try to tell me you ain't got any."

"I wouldn't think of it, Small Willie. I always thought you was a smart one. It's in the lockbox, about two thousand."

"See, Gilly, I told you." Small Willie stooped and moved his grip on Two Blankets. "Real easy, open the lockbox. You keep a pistol in there?"

Marshall eased up into a sitting position and moved slow-like to the lockbox. "No pistol, just the cash, and some important papers."

Small Willie edged up on Marshall and put his knife against Marshall's throat. "Just to keep you honest."

"I ain't gonna trade my life for a couple of thousand, or for my wife either." He spun the combination and opened the door, stepped back with his hands up and in the clear. The stack of bills was in a neat bundle with a tin of coins. Keeping one arm firmly around Two Blanket's neck, Small Willie gathered the bills and stuffed them into the pocket of his trousers, then took the tin, as well.

"It has been nice doing business with you, Mister Johnston." He nodded to Marshall. "Back out, Gilly."

Not time yet. Gray Wolf said.

I know, dear one.

Two Blankets looked Marshall in the eye and saw recognition there. At that moment, she knew he would shoot her before letting these two get away. He would avoid it if he could, but Small Willie MacKenzie was not leaving Johnston's Landing—not alive, anyway.

They backed out of the storage room and through the bar to the front door. Once on the porch, Two Blankets caught a glimpse of Marshall quietly and patiently pulling down his Mississippi M1841 from its place of honor over the bar. In no hurry at all, he began to load it.

"Back across the bridge, Gilly. Just stay calm, and we are in the clear."

Gilly hunched down behind the bulk of Small Willie, who was in part protected by the body of Two Blankets.

"I don't like his calmness, Small Willie."

"You'd be scared of your own shadow."

Marshall Johnston strode onto the porch of the Landing. He glanced at the sky which was just lightening and scattered with a few clouds. The moon was still up, and the wind was nonexistent. The range, a hundred yards or less.

"Gilly."

"Mister Johnston."

Marshall walked slowly toward the bridge. "I'm only going to say this once. Small Willie ain't walking away from this, not unless he throws down his knife now."

"You know that ain't happening, Marshall. Seems like I got a pretty good shield here, in your pregnant wife."

"I figure I got one minie ball for him, ded-i-ca-ted, you might say. If you don't want the second one, get down flat in the dirt right now, and you might live."

Gilly spared one look to Small Willie. "I'm getting down right now. Don't shoot me." He lay flat in the gravel and the dirt. "I'm down. I'm down."

As they approached the bridge, Small Willie spared Gilly a kick to the ribs. "Coward."

The bunkhouse door opened and several of the men piled out carrying cudgels and knives, into the clearing and spread out.

"Just stay back men. This is between Small Willie and me, and it is about over." He raised his rifle and took aim.

Just before he put his eye to the sight, though it was just shy of a hundred yards, Two Blankets saw what she thought was a nod of recognition from Marshall.

Small Willie took an awkward backward step up onto the bridge across the stream.

Now, said Gray Wolf.

Two Blankets let all her muscles go slack and swooned. For a moment, Small Willie looked down and readjusted his choke hold, then lifted his head before pulling her back up off her feet. Her feet never left the ground. The sharp crack of the rifle echoed across the Landing. The sound seemed to take seconds, though she knew that was an illusion. Small Willie just stood there for what seemed like minutes before dropping the knife and collapsing over her.

Marshall strode up to the pile, the two hundred-twenty-pound bulk of the dead man laying atop Two Blankets. He handed his rifle to Big Ed and reached down to pluck his stack of bills and coin box from Small Willie. Then he rolled the body off of her. The left eye looked out in surprise.

The right eye was just a bloody hole.

Two Blankets looked up at Marshall appraising him. Strange that he had made the shot, one that few would believe, but between them, she had won some ground. She smiled. "Got a pickle? I'm hungry."

He reached out his hand, and she stood up. "You took a chance there."

"I knew you would shoot, and, husband Marshall, I have seen you shoot." She looked down at what remained of Small Willie. Ten minutes before he had been alive and demanding, vibrant even, though undoubtedly, he was an evil man. Now, there was just a shell. "I'd like to keep his knife..." she rubbed her neck "...as a memento."

Marshall stooped and picked up the skinning knife with a blade one could shave with. "This is a wicked blade for a bitty little thing like you." He handed it over.

"Maybe I ain't so bitty after all, husband." She bent and stripped the sheath off his belt.

Marshall eyed her with his calculating look. "Maybe you ain't. I can see you're naked. You better go back to the longhouse and get some clothes on." He looked around. Most of the men were out now watching him and his naked and very pregnant wife.

Two Blankets straightened her back and marched off toward the long-house slow enough to listen to Marshall and Gilly.

Harry Everton looked down at the body. "We're going to have to have an inquest here."

"An inquest, Harry?" He screwed up his face and thought about it. "I suppose you are right. Price of civilization when you can't shoot a thief on your own property, but we brought some of this government crap on ourselves. Talk to Captain Ainsworth when the steamboat comes by. Should be long about eleven o'clock."

"I will. Meanwhile, we'll store the body in the shed. You, men, drag this body over to the storage shed." Four of the men watching grabbed an arm or a leg and dragged Small Willie MacKenzie over to the small fur storage shed.

"Let's see about Gilly, here." He strode back and kicked Gilly back prostrate. "What shall we do with you?"

"Whatever you want. Just don't shoot me. I'm sorry. I was mad, and I did want to rob you, but the rest was all Willie. Goddamnit, I think I shit myself."

"Well, that part I do believe. You're either too cowardly or not foolish enough to try what Small Willie did. But what to do? I should hold you for the judge, and maybe you'll get a couple years in the prison."

"That's fair for what I did. You ain't gonna shoot me?" Gilly sat up. "I did. I went and shat myself."

"Or I could fine you myself and avoid all that judge stuff. Say thirty days free labor for what you did? These would be the worst jobs Mister Everton can come up with. You do that, and we are square. You complain once or come out late one time, and I call the judge."

Gilly didn't even take the time to compute. "I'll take the work. You'll see, Mister Marshall. I'll be the best employee you ever seen. I promise."

"All right, we'll try it. Get over to the creek and wash your pants. Then go up with Big Ed and fetch back that horse, my horse now, and whatever gear you left up there."

"Yes, sir. Right away, Mister Johnston, sir."

Two Blankets walked into the longhouse and slipped into her dress. It was tight across the belly but would do for another month. She looked at the blade she had appropriated from Small Willie's dead body. A large blade, it had a deadly appeal to her. Many women of her clan and tribe could defend themselves, though most would be uncomfortable with a weapon like this. But there were some who were just as adept as any warrior man. She suspected she was one of the first group, now, but fully intended, after her recent experience, to become one of the second. She slid her belt through the slots in the sheath and tied it up so that it rested easy on her leg.

She looked about the longhouse. It was time to make her presence known at the Landing. Marshall was somewhat in awe of her for the moment, though this new-found respect would not last long if the past were any teacher.

She brushed her hair and put on a pair of moccasins. Satisfied with her appearance she marched out of the longhouse and walked up to the Landing. Pushing through the door, she saw Marshall, Harry Everton, Henry Haroldson, the carpenter, and a couple of the older labor crew at the bar. The bottle was passing almost as quickly as the good fellowship. At a table, looking disheveled and sleepy, sat Delores Sue and Aimee, drinking coffee.

Two Blankets walked up to the pickle jar and fished out a juicy one. She crunched down on it with evident pleasure. She looked up to see a dozen puzzled eyes watching her. "Harry, could I have a cup of coffee, please?"

"Yes'm. Sit down, you look a might worked over...well...you don't look it. But you should if what I hear be true."

"Thank you, Harry." She took her coffee. "It be half-true if men's talk is like usual." She sat down with the two women.

The dark-haired whore, Aimee, perused her speculatively, as if sizing up competition. "I hear that, Missus Johnston, what you said about men's talk. I saw the last, and it was right brave of you. The way you faked that swoon, must've took Small Willie completely by surprise, leastwise for a second."

"A second was all Marshall needed for his shot."

"It was a mighty shot. Not hard to hit a target at that distance, but right through the eye with his pregnant wife in the way."

Two Blankets spared a glance toward Marshall. Impatience was showing on his face. "We've most of us seen Marshall shoot before. Remember

Henry, at five times the distance. I wasn't worried about my warrior hus-band Marshall's shot." She spread a "hero-worship" smile across her face toward Marshall.

Marshall turned back to another glass of whiskey pressed into his hand.

"So, you Marshall's Indian whore?" Delores Sue lifted her coffee cup and took a drink.

"No, Miss Sue. I'm Two Blankets, his wife. Tribal folks don't really have a tradition of whoring, at least not where *whitemans* aren't around. Mind you, I don't have anything against it. It's your body, after all."

"No tradition of whoring." Aimee laughed. "Never heard it spoke of that way before."

Delores Sue pursued the topic. "Marshall ain't selling your services?"

"No. I would leave him, or cut him if he tried."

"I believe that. Didn't see it myself, but I heard you was pretty courageous out there." Delores Sue brushed the hair out of her eyes.

Aimee elbowed Delores Sue. "He certainly hasn't been shy about using ours."

"I knew he would take the shot. All I could do was give him the best chance. As far as him using your services, that is a warrior's right, to take another woman if he is so inclined. My right, too, for that matter."

Aimee looked quizzically at Two Blankets. "Well, we can't be not in-clined, being his whores and all. But he is hardly worth a sigh if you know what I mean."

Two Blankets blushed, though it hardly showed. "I don't gossip about my warrior husband. I thank you for your kind company, ladies, Delores Sue and Aimee."

Aimee reached out her hand. "I thank you, as well, Missus Johnston," and then broke into a paroxysm of laughter.

Delores Sue looked confused, then took Two Blankets hand as it was given. "Thank you, Two Blankets, truly."

The steamboat whistle broke through their conversation. From the Landing porch, Two Blankets could see the *Jennie Clark* nose up to the dock. She saw Captain Ainsworth descend to the deck and Harry Everton gestic-ulating and talking. Ainsworth nodded, and Everton hopped back onto the dock. Ainsworth gave a signal, and the *Jennie Clark* puffed smoke and began backing away from the dock.

Harry Everton walked at his usual measured pace up to Marshall, who waited in the clearing fronting the Landing.

"Well? What's the news, Harry?"

"Ainsworth says, if the judge ain't busy, he'll bring him up tomorrow around this time and take him back on the next afternoon if we can get this cleared up quick like."

"Simple enough. We should be able to do that if the judge is amenable to sense."

"Ainsworth asked if we could box up Small Willie, too. The territorial government will pay the cost, three dollars, I believe."

Marshall spat into the yard. "Put one of Haroldson's apprentices on it. Small Willy don't deserve no better."

Harry Everton went off to see the coffin built.

It is odd how a man's life, like even Small Willie's, as bad as he was, is just a subject for an official investigation to justify the killing and a pine box. Among the *Nimi'ipuu,* he would be thought of as a brave warrior, if foolish and stupid. We would have held a ceremony even for an enemy.

Two Blankets got up the next morning, as usual, just before dawn. When she woke, she felt different, not as much physically as emotionally. It wasn't a significant change, more like a shift in perception.

She built up the fire and went outside into the wisps of fog to take care of her personal needs. She stretched and looked about the Landing. Gilly was sitting on the ground next to the big table. He saw her and got up. He shivered from the cold and droplets of the foggy moisture dripped from his hair. He stretched and shook himself.

"Good morning, Missus Johnston, if I may call you that."

"Good morning. What should I call you? Everyone calls you Gilly."

"Gilly is fine, ma'am."

"But what is your last name?"

Gilly looked down almost ashamed. "It is Gildschwarzwalden, ma'am. Please don't put that about."

"That is a mouthful. What does it mean? I will call you Mister Gilly. You can call me Two Blankets."

"No, no, I don't think I could, Missus Johnston. That wouldn't be polite. Mister Johnston said I gotta be polite. The first thing he said when he gave me his instructions was, 'Be polite.'" Gilly twisted his cap between his hands. "It means something like, gilt black forest. My grandpa come from Germany."

"All right. What are you doing here? Mister Johnston want something? Or want you to do something?"

"That's the thing, Missus Johnston. He said I was to put myself at your disposal, first thing before you even got up. I gotta do it every morning, begging your pardon."

"What's he mean at my disposal? You mean work?"

"Yes, ma'am, work. That's it. Whatever you got. Collect eggs, feed the chickens, milk the cows, care for the pigs. After that, I can go and clean the outhouse at the Landing and the slit trench by the bunkhouse. Then maybe eat, if'n nobody's got nothing else for me to do."

"I see. You got any writing? Can you count?"

"I can't write. No, ma'am, I can't. But I got counting. Well, up to a hundred, leastwise."

Two Blankets thought about it. *So, Gilly is mine, at least for now. Marshall means to foist this man off on me, the man that just tried to rob us.*

He is afraid of Marshall. Gray Wolf looked at the shivering Gilly. *May be the best is to make him a little afraid of you, too.*

Two Blankets scratched Gray Wolf behind the ear. "Well, let's see how you do, Mister Gilly. Take this box and collect all the eggs. Don't miss or break any. Then count them and put them on the table here."

"Oh, yes, ma'am. Right away, ma'am." He took the tray and jogged over to the chicken pen.

Two Blankets wandered back into her lodge. She found a half a pickle left and munched it. Such a strange sour taste. She had never liked this flavor before. Thinking about the flavor of pickles, she wanted coffee.

Even yesterday's coffee, strong and bitter, I want it. I never liked that before.

She went back out and saw that Gilly was done with the eggs and squatting, waiting for her. "How many eggs, Mister Gilly?"

"Eighty-seven. I counted them twice."

"Where is your count sheet with your marks?"

"I counted them in my head. I got this many." He made some marks on the ground.

"Just a minute." Two Blankets went back in the lodge and fetched out her count sheets. She brought the sheet back to the table. "Now, how many?" She began her count and tedious marking of four downstrokes and one cross stroke.

"Pardon, Missus Johnston, but you are doing that the hard way." He wrote the marks "87" on the paper. "Eighty-seven."

"That's eighty-seven? Just those two marks like snakes?"

"I told you I knew my numbers."

"You will teach me."

"Me, teach you?"

"Yes, but not today. Do you know how to make coffee?"

Gilly looked surprised. "Of course, I know how to make coffee."

"Show me."

"There should be some coffee roasted and ground in the bunkhouse."

Two Blankets built up the fire while Gilly walked over and found some spare coffee. "Normal-like you gotta roast the green beans and then grind them up, but I found a little with that part already done." He put the rough ground coffee into the pot and the pot onto the fire. "Now, you just let it boil a bit, kinda slow like. What you want me to do now?"

"Thank you, Mister Gilly." Again, he seemed unaccustomed to being thanked. "You know farm animals? Pigs and cows?"

"I grew up on a pig farm. We had cows, too."

"Well, the chickens, pigs, and cows need to be fed. The cows need to be milked if you know how to do that. Then, that's all for today."

"I'll do it right away." He turned to go, then turned back to her, "And thank you."

"No more than you deserve. Tomorrow, you start teaching me numbers."

Two Blankets eyed the sky. The fog was burning off, but it looked to come on cloudy later. A day or two and it would rain again. She poured her coffee into an old tin cup and walked up to the Landing with her cup and pot. As she climbed the stairs to the porch, she glanced about the camp— the Landing, as Marshall called it. She remembered how it used to be when the clan was here. Men, women, and children, all going about their business. Now, it was one man directing it all to his shape, or the shape of it in his mind.

"This might be *Tyee* Marshall Johnston's clan now, but I am the first woman of the *Tyee*. It will take my shape as, well."

But carefully. White Mouse said.

And quietly. Gray Wolf added.

"Yes, dears, quiet and careful. Quiet and careful."

She opened the door and entered the Landing. Not a soul stirred here yet. Not a lamp burned and the fire in the stove was banked down. She set her pot and cup on the table, then stirred the fire back to life and added some sticks of wood. She fetched out two pickles for breakfast, sat down, munched a bite of the pickle and took a swig of coffee.

She looked about the Landing and noticed the dirt in the corners, the bar that was only partially wiped down, and the windows that were already dirty.

Yes, there are things I could do here.

THE INQUEST

CHAPTER 2
OCTOBER, 1857

THE NEXT MORNING, Two Blankets saw that Gilly was waiting in the predawn fog as he had the day before. He was shivering, but he was there.

"Good morning, Mister Gilly."

Gilly took off his hat and said, "Good morning, ma'am. I hope everything I done yesterday, I done good."

"Well enough. Do the same today. Then you to show me numbers."

"Numbers, ma'am? I ain't no teacher."

"You did say that Marshall said you were at my service?"

"I did, ma'am. I don't know if that is what he meant."

"Seems to me, at my service means exactly that."

"Yes, ma'am. I'll be counting the eggs then."

Two Blankets made up the last of the coffee and sat drinking it. Sat, drinking, and planning. She wasn't sure where her plans would lead her, but she was sure of the first steps.

She brought out her egg records and some extra paper. When Gilly told her the count today was "eighty-three," she made him write it on the record, "83" and made her own four straight marks and one slanting mark count. It came out the same.

After Gilly had finished the normal morning chores, she asked him, "Now, teach me some numbers."

Gilly thought about it. "I don't know if I can."

"Do you think I am too stupid to learn, Mister Gilly?"

"Oh, no, Missus Johnston, that ain't it. I don't remember how I learned. My ma taught me my counting numbers."

"Show me like I was a child, then. Show me the first five."

"Well, all right." He wrote on the paper, "1, 2, 3, 4, 5," and then said the words as he pointed to each snake-like scrawl.

Two Blankets repeated the words. "Now, I will have to practice these. Thank you, Mister Gilly."

"Yes, ma'am. Pardon, ma'am, but why you call me Mister Gilly? Everybody else just says, Gilly."

"Out of respect, Mister Gilly."

"Respect? Huh. Respect." He turned away to his day's chores. He seemed to be churning the concept of respect over in his mind.

Two Blankets filled her page with practice numbers. After the first column, she shook out her hand. "This writing numbers hurts." Then she remembered the first hide she had scraped. "That used to hurt too."

She examined Gilly's numbers, then her own efforts. Several of her "5s" were backward, and all looked awkward. She started another column, this time, when she finished, they were a little better. She remembered Standing Bear's efforts at beading, and her eyes became moist. She patted her stomach and went on.

"This is a skill, just like beading, then. It is hard at first, but I will get better." She filled two more columns and looked again at her work, then turned the page and filled the other side. Her labor was so intense that when she looked up, she saw it was a handspan before noon. Downstream, past the bluff behind the Landing, one stream of dirty smoke rose from the approaching steamboat. It was still occluded by the cliff, but she would soon be visible, likely the *Jennie Clark*.

She thought of something. She looked at the egg count for today, "83" and there was "3" on her practice sheet. That made her smile. She looked at yesterday's count, "87," but she had no "7." It was just a line at the top and a slanted line going down. She practiced it until she got a good approximation.

"But what about the 'eighty' in the eighty-seven and the eighty-three?" It seemed to be just two circles, one atop the other, but maybe she would have to learn a whole bunch of new numbers for twenty, thirty and so on. "Well, I will just have to ask tomorrow."

———————

AS THE BOAT came into sight and maneuvered to the dock, four men left the storage shed with a raw pine box across their shoulders.

The remains of Small Willie were just a box of dead flesh. Maybe the *whitemans* don't have a spirit carried in the body? Maybe that's why they bury them in the ground.

She saw Marshall making his quick way to the dock, and two men on the foredeck of the steamer. The crew ran out a gangplank, and the two men walked precariously across it to the dock.

Two men among several. Yet, no one could mistake these two, erect and officious, uncomfortable, but commanding. All around her, men were making their way up to the Landing. Though they might have no business there, curiosity demanded they be there. She didn't see Ike, the sawyer, or Frank Milson, his helper, but of the rest, it looked to be the full crowd.

The four men set Small Willie in his box down on trestles in front of the Landing and stood back. Marshall, the two suited officious men, and Harry Everton entered the Landing followed by the rest.

Marshall took charge. "We've put you up here behind the bar Judge Ambercrombie, if that'll do you, and your clerk at the end."

The whip-thin judge looked about him as if judging already. Perhaps, he never stopped. "It will do." He sat upon a chair set up on a box behind the bar. He checked his watch. He opened a box and took out a gavel, looked at it with a moment of affection. He rapped it on the bar.

"All stand," the clerk said, then noticed that everyone was standing. "This inquest is now in session, Judge Ambercrombie of the Territory of Oregon presiding." He sat in only the third chair in the place, with the second on the right hand for witnesses.

"This inquest is convened to determine the manner of death of—" he looked down at the paper before him "Small Willie MacKenzie."

"Marshall shot him," said one man, one of the new laborers, Two Blankets thought, to the laughter of some of his compatriots.

"Shot him right in the eye."

The gavel hit the bar once with a resounding clap. "This may not be a court of law, but it *is* a legal proceeding. There will be respect shown for the proceedings."

"Your honor, would you like a drink before we get started?" Marshall asked.

Ambercrombie stiffened. He twisted his black mustaches and leaned forward. "There will be no drinking while the proceedings are in session. This may be the frontier, and you men may find this amusing, but I did not make the trip from Boston to Independence to the Oregon Territory just to give up civilization."

"Well, maybe in fifteen minutes, when we get done, then."

"The proceedings may find a reason to arrest you, Mister Johnston, and hold you for trial, for murder. Let us get this started. Who first encountered Mister MacKenzie?"

The men looked around. Even the two whores sought her out.

Two Blankets stepped forward.

"I am not going to take testimony from an Indian in the shooting of a white man."

"Your honor, you asked who first come across Small Willie. That would be Two Blankets."

"An Indian?"

"And my wife."

"I don't like this. Step forward and take a seat, then."

Two Blankets sat in the witness chair.

Judge Ambercrombie leaned forward. "Do you, uh... talkee the English? You speakee?"

Confusion glanced across her features. "I am *Nimi'ipuu,* so I speak that language, the language of the People. I speak the Chinook Jargon and some Chinook, as well. I know some English, but not as much as the other three.

I do not know the meaning of *talkee* and *speakee*. Maybe my English is not as good as I thought."

Many of the men and the two whores laughed at this.

The gavel rapped. "Quiet. Are you making a joke of this court? Or of me?"

"No, sir. I did not say it to make a joke."

"Speakee— Ahem... Tell the court your name."

"Two Blankets Johnston."

"You are Mister Marshall Johnston's wife?"

"Yes."

"That official or do you just say that?"

"We have a piece of paper from the Territorial Governor, and we were married with Chinook ceremony as well. I'd say it was official two ways."

He pulled down on his vest. "Please tell the court how you met Small Willy MacKenzie."

"Well, I first met him when he worked for us several months ago, and he tried to rape me. So I stabbed him."

There were chuckles spreading, and Judge Ambercrombie lifted his gavel. The laughs died under his stern gaze. "I meant *this* time."

"Oh, I am sorry. I thought you meant how we met. This time, I woke in my sleeping lodge and he clapped his hand across my mouth. I tried to knife him again, and he slapped me." She showed her bruises.

The judged examined her bruised face. "Mister Murphy, note that the Indian woman—Missus Two Blankets Johnston—is bruised about the face." To Two Blankets, "Continue."

"When I came back from being knocked out, he wanted all our money."

"So, you don't sleep in the Landing? With your husband?"

"My husband Marshall Johnston was not there. I don't talk about our sleeping arrangements with strangers, no offense intended."

"All right, and what did Mister MacKenzie want?"

"He wanted all our money, and he wanted to have sex with me."

"Did you give him the money there?"

"We only had about a hundred dollars there, and he told Gilly to get it."

"Gilly?"

"Mister Gilly. They came together, Small Willy and Mister Gilly."

"Why didn't you tell about this Gilly before?"

"I am sorry, sir. You didn't ask."

Ambercrombie blushed a bit, and Two Blankets saw that he was younger than his clothing or his pretensions.

"Then what happened?"

"I told him that Marshall kept all the extra money up here at the Landing. We came up into the Landing and into the back room where Marshall was asleep."

"Thank you. From here on, we have the testimony of a white man, so we will not have to depend on Indian testimony. You are dismissed."

"Thank you, Judge Ambercrombie." Two Blankets smiled her widest smile and noticed he blushed a second time. She looked up and saw the older whore nodding.

"Mister Murphy, call Mister Marshall Johnston."

"Mister Marshall Johnston."

"I'm right here." Marshall sat down.

"You are Mister Marshall Johnston?"

"I think I just said that."

"Respect the proceedings of this court. You own Johnston's Landing?"

"It's got my name on it. Yeah, I own it."

"You are fined fifty cents for disrespecting the proceedings."

Marshall stood up. "This here is my place. I am Marshall Johnston, and I ain't paying no fifty cents. What's more, I'm feeling powerful dry right now." He reached behind the bar, grabbed out a bottle, and took a big shot, then another. "Go on Judge."

Judge Ambercrombie schooled his features. "Tell us what happened."

"He asked where we kept the money. I told him, and he got the two thousand dollars. I told him not to do it, and he said he was having the money and my wife and I better not pursue. He backed out of the office and then out of the Landing. Some of the men was getting up and gathering by the bunkhouse. I got down my Mississippi rifle and loaded it. I stepped out onto the porch."

"Where were Mister Gilly and Mister MacKenzie at this time?"

"Let's step out there, and I can show you."

"Mister Murphy, note that the court has stepped out to view the scene and that we will take the rest of the testimony out there."

"Yes, sir."

Everyone filed out of the Landing and spread out beyond the door.

"I was about there, just past the coffin box, and Small Willie was up at the bridge. He had Two Blankets—Missus Johnston—about the neck with his left arm and a knife at her throat with his right hand."

"So, that's about a hundred yards."

"Just shy of it, I'd say. About ninety."

"Where was Mister Gilly at the time?"

"I was hiding behind Small Willie."

"Mister Johnston was testifying. Mister Johnston?"

"It's like Gilly said. I told him to toss his weapon and drop to the ground."

"And I got down right away, just like Mister Johnston said."

"Gilly dropped like he said. Small Willy took a step back onto the bridge, and I nodded to Two Blankets. She swooned, and I took the shot."

"You fired even though you might hit your wife?"

"He would have killed her, anyways. Like you said, she's only an Indian."

"Hmm. Right. Let's see the corpse."

They walked over to Small Willie's box, his new home, and lifted off the lid. "Let the record show that Mister MacKenzie was shot in the right eye. Note also, his boots are missing."

"They fit one of the men. Didn't seem like ol' Willie would be needing them anymore."

"I should look at this knife. I suppose it was a small knife?" Mister Ambercrombie couldn't take his eyes off Small Willie.

"About as small as Small Willie was." A few of the closer men chuckled. Two Blankets noticed there was a sound of pride among them. "Two Blankets, the knife?"

Two Blankets stepped up and slid the knife from its sheath, flipped it over, and handed it hilt-first to Mr. Ambercrombie.

Mr. Ambercrombie took it from her tentatively, examined the long, wide blade. He tested the blade with his thumb.

"Careful there, Mister Ambercrombie."

A thread of red welled up from his soft white thumb. "Sharp." He reversed the knife awkwardly but with care and handed it back to Two Blankets. She slid it back into its sheath without looking.

"You give a weapon to an Indian, Mister Johnston?"

"After what she went through, I figured she deserved it."

"Hmm. True, too true. Let's go back in, and I'll make my ruling." They filed back into the Landing. Once everyone was inside, Mr. Ambercrombie rapped his gavel once. "Having seen the evidence, it seems very clear that the shooting and killing of Mister MacKenzie were justified." There was general cheering to this pronouncement. "I further rule that absent any claims here, any property of Mister MacKenzie shall go to Mister Johnston." His gavel had to rap twice to quell the disturbance. "Now, as to Mister Gilly."

"Me, sir?" Gilly said.

"Yes, you. You came here with the express purpose of robbing Mister Johnston. Is that not true."

Gilly looked at the judge and then at Marshall. "Yes, it is true. But I never meant to hurt anyone. Small Willie said it would be easy. When Mister Johnston here said to get down, I laid myself right down. Didn't I Mister Johnston?"

"Hmm. That true, Johnston?"

"It is true. Gilly and I got an agreement. He works for thirty days for free, and we call it square. Absent anything the court says, of course."

"That may be true. I commend you for your patience, Mister Johnston."

"I don't 'spect no more trouble from Gilly, here."

"In that case, I fine Mister Gilly ten dollars for troubling the court."

"But I got a deal with Mister Johnston here."

"Unless you want to go back to Portland and stand trial."

"No, sir. I'll pay the ten if Mister Johnston will advance it. I'll work it off, I promise." Gilly gave a pleading look to Marshall.

"I'll stand the ten."

"Then, this inquest into the shooting and killing of Small Willie MacKenzie is concluded." He rapped his gavel three times to make his point.

"There's a small drink all around, then it's back to work. We got two hours to make up. Now that you are officially off the books, I take it you could stand a drink or two, Mister Ambercrombie?"

Ambercrombie thought about it, but only for a moment. "I will take that drink, Mister Johnston. You lead a rough life here, but I can see the value in it."

Marshall poured the first drink for Ambercrombie. "We are a little rough here, but not like it was just a few years ago. When I came here and married Two Blankets, I was the only white man here. We didn't mean no offense to you or to the promise of civil-i-zation."

"None meant. None taken, Mister Johnston." He choked down his first drink with some back slapping by Marshall. Marshall poured him a second which he drank more slowly.

When the *Jennie Clark* whistled her down-river stop the next day, Marshall escorted Mr. Ambercrombie to the steamboat along with Small Willie in his box.

———

WHEN SHE SAW Gilly the next morning, she showed him her practice sheets. He seemed unimpressed, but wrote the next five numbers at the top of a new sheet, "6, 7, 8, 9, and 0" and read them off.

"I know seven from yesterday, and eight is like what you wrote for eighty, what is this zero?"

Gilly scratched his head and screwed up his eyes. "I'm trying to think of how my Ma explained it, but I can't quite. What number comes after nine?"

"That's easy, ten."

"This is how you write it, 1 and 0. That's ten."

Two Blankets wrote it in her scrawl. "10, ten."

"That's how Ma explained it, one bunch of tens and no ones. It will make sense after a while."

"So, this '83' you wrote yesterday means eight tens and three ones?"

"Yes. That's right."

She looked at her hash marked sheet. She had sixteen sets of five plus three, but she knew that was eight tens and three ones. "That's the same as my marks on my counting sheet. See. I have eight tens and three ones."

"Can I go to work now, Missus Johnston?"

"Yes, go ahead. But after you get done and have had breakfast, I want you at the Landing."

"I can't go in there without Mister Johnston's permission."

"You can go with mine, if I am there."

"Yes, ma'am."

Two Blankets filled her page on both sides, examined it, then filled another page with the whole set of ten numbers. When Gilly brought up his egg count, she looked at it, ran through the numbers in her mind, and said, "Seventy-nine?"

"That's right, ma'am. Ma'am?"

"Yes?" Two Blankets looked up.

"About that word you used yesterday. Respect?"

"Yes, respect."

"Did you mean it? You weren't just saying it to be nice?"

"I meant it."

"Thank you, ma'am. I'll see you after I eat and do my outhouse and slit trench duty."

Later, when she was up at the Landing, Gilly came in. Marshall was up and about and gave Gilly a foul look, then ignored him when he went to Two Blankets.

"Ma'am. You wanted me to come here. Marshall—I mean Mister Johnston—ain't too pleased."

"You are assigned to me until I release you?"

"That's what he said, yes, ma'am."

"Then, take this broom and sweep the floor clean. Don't do it like they've been doing it. Clean every bit you can see."

"Yes, ma'am." Gilly took the broom and began to sweep in the middle of the room.

"No, Mister Gilly. Begin at the back corner and sweep toward the center. Use the broom as a tool to get every bit of dirt."

Marshall eyed Gilly suspiciously.

She got up and poured a cup of coffee. She approached her husband. "Husband Marshall?"

"What do you want, Two Blankets?"

"You said you would order pickles?"

Marshall looked his surprise, but tried to cover it. "I ordered you a whole barrel. Be in next week. What you doing with Gilly, here?"

Gilly was now sweeping with such care it might take him an hour to sweep just this room. "I'm training him to clean. The Landing should shine, and you are so very busy, my husband."

He took a sip of coffee and looked about, really looked, and nodded. "True, Two Blankets. I can see that."

"I would like to get a calendar and a clock, if I can have one."

"A calendar. What would you want a calendar for? Or a clock?"

Two Blankets felt shame overcome her for a moment. *Yes, Marshall asks the question. What do I want them for? But, is that what he really means?*

He means, what does a stupid woman like you want with these things? White Mouse said. *That is what he means.*

Gray Wolf spoke from her lay-down near the door, as far into this domain as she would come. *Shy White Mouse is correct—*

White Mouse chittered and nodded her head.

—I am surprised to say. This is the beginning.

"I wish, husband Marshall, to learn my dates from the calendar and time from the clock. These are important things in your world and in my world now."

Marshall's ego was stroked a bit. "Well, it is true, Two Blankets. If you think you can learn dates and time, I see no reason for you not to try. If you cannot, do not feel frustrated. It is a hard task." He got up and went to the back room. "Here is a calendar from my whiskey supplier."

The calendar had twelve sections and was stained from coffee cups and liquor bottles. It was torn on the corner but would do. "A clock costs too much money. I don't even have a pocket watch. Maybe we might get a clock for the Landing."

"Thank you, husband Marshall. I did not know that."

"There is a lot of things you do not know, Two Blankets. But it is good of you to try and learn. If it turns out too hard, don't worry. Learning ain't for everybody." He turned to the door and just before he got there he said, "You do what Two Blankets says, you hear, Gilly?"

Gilly nodded his head. "Yes, sir, Mister Johnston. I will, sir."

Later in the afternoon, Two Blankets entered the Landing. She saw that the two whores looking tired and bleary, and none too alert. She got a cup of coffee and sat down at the table. They looked at her. She saw dislike in their eyes.

I wonder how first wife Swimming Salmon or Bears-Many-Children would handle a situation like this. Probably with a stick. But it is the honor and reputation of the Tyee, *of Marshall, that is involved.*

"Good afternoon, Delores Sue and Aimee."

Aimee laughed as if at a private joke. "If it isn't 'we don't have a whoring tradition' in the clan.' You're an Indian. We're white. That is the difference."

Two Blankets directed her look at Aimee. "Marshall Johnston is the *Tyee,* the boss of the Landing. Do you agree that is true?"

Delores Sue and Aimee appeared confused.

"That's true enough," Delores Sue said.

Two Blankets took a long sip of coffee. "I never used to like this coffee. And I never thought to like pickles." She bit off a chunk and chewed. "This is delicious."

"Coffee and pickles?" Delores Sue said.

"I have been first wife to Marshall Johnston for three-and-a-half years. He has the title to this property because I became his wife. I have been true to him and carry his child. Do you understand me?"

"I'm starting to," Delores Sue said.

"I have a history with him. I helped catch two men who were trying to rob him. When Small Willie tried to rape me, I stabbed him. Later, when he tried to rob my husband, Marshall Johnston, I pretended to swoon, so my warrior husband Marshall could shoot him in the eye."

"So, you are his wife and cannot be challenged? Especially by two whores like us?" Aimee asked. "Is that it? We should fear you?"

"Yes, I am his wife and will not tolerate any challenge to that. But not because you are whores. I told you already, I do not care about that. Did you not believe me?" She sipped her coffee and smiled.

Delores Sue blushed, "Truthfully, we didn't believe you, Missus Johnston."

"Call me Two Blankets, if we are to be friends."

"I will be your friend," Aimee said. "I think you can be trusted, Two Blankets. But I have never heard of a wife who did not dislike a whore, especially one who had been with her husband."

"It is a tradition among my people not to be *jealous,* I think you would say the word is. As you say, it is hardly worth a sigh. But if you challenge a *Nimi'ipuu* over her warrior, you might find yourself facing this." She pulled out the skinning knife and lay it on the table.

Delores Sue edged away slightly. "I'm not sure I understand all your traditions, but I know what the knife means. I am pleased to meet you, Missus Johnston." She extended her hand.

Two Blankets took it. "Two Blankets."

"Two Blankets." Delores Sue gripped the hand and shook it. "We understand each other. Me and Aimee here thank you for straightening us out."

Two Blankets held onto the hand as she first looked Delores Sue in the eyes, then Aimee. As she released her hand she thought, *I believe I can trust these women,* at least to a degree.

You may trust their fear, Gray Wolf said.

Two Blankets walked back to her longhouse. After spending a handspan of the sun tidying, she looked about.

What do I do now? Gilly does my morning work.

She petted Gray Wolf absently and scratched his neck ruff. A surge of pleasure and a look of determination marked her face. She strode out of the longhouse and over to the old bunkhouse which had now reverted back to being a storehouse for hides and bulk items. She threw the door flap back and stepped in.

After her eyes had adjusted to the lack of light, she searched the rolled up hides. There were beaver and elk, many deer hides and various others. She pulled out a smaller elk hide, a female's, she thought.

Yes, this will do.

She fingered the hide, now stiffened from being rolled up for perhaps a year. She searched the rest of the hides, not sure what she was looking for, but confident she would know it when she saw it. Near the back, in a corner, she saw the yellowed teeth and small eye holes of a reddish pelt. Pulling it out, she saw that the claws were still attached.

The red fox, it will work very well.

She thought of her egg tally sheet and wondered if there were not one for hides as well. Tucked between a hide and the frame of an old bunk she found a sheet. She opened it and searched for a pattern. Though she could not read the words, she could see a pattern for withdrawals and deposits.

"Well, I will do as much as I can." She marked the number "2" in the withdrawals column. "Now, what for my name?" She marked a "2" and a square with the traditional four stripes of the Hudson's Bay Trade Blanket. "It will have to do."

She brought the hides back to the creek near her longhouse and placed them entirely immersed in water and weighted them down with rocks. Nodding her approval, she searched her longhouse until she found what she was looking for. Stacked in the back, amidst foodstuffs and old, occasionally used tools, was a clay jar as big as her chest, sealed with river clay and pitch. She rolled it outside next to the door. That was all she could do until the hides softened a bit perhaps by the next day.

The next morning, Two Blankets was not surprised to see Gilly waiting. He counted the eggs and wrote "91" as the count. Two Blankets had given up her tally system. She just traced the number with her finger and said, "nine-one, nine-one, ninety-one."

"Show me the numbers ten, twenty, thirty and on up to one hundred, Mister Gilly."

Gilly wrote in a column, "10, 20, 30, 40, 50, 60, 70, 80, 90 and 100."

Two Blankets looked at the pattern presented, then wrote next to the "10", 11 12 13 14 15 16 17 18 19, and named each number. "Yes?"

Gilly examined her numbers. "It is amazing how quick you are to learn."

"You have taught me much. Go ahead with your feeding chores." She deliberately filled in the rest of the matrix, then examined it and wrote it all again, and a third time. "You have taught me more than you can know.

She showed the calendar to Gilly when she finished her copying her matrix. "I want you to show me how to use this, Mister Gilly."

"Well, I can tell you two things about this calendar. First, it has all twelve months and all the days. For that it is useful." He pointed to the months and named them, "January, February, March..." and she copied him. "So, all twelve months on one page."

"That is good?"

"Well, that part. The second part ain't so good. This here calendar is from last year. See that there '1856?' That's the year, last year."

"1856. And that circled part in the middle? What is that?"

Gilly looked down where she indicated. "Well, that's June, twenty-five. Seems important." The wording indicated, *"the god damned Chinook gone— camp mine."* "I can't read the words. I never learned my letters."

"That's all right. Go about your duties. I will see you later at the Landing."

She practiced her matrix of numbers two more times, then, bored, walked up to the Landing, her calendar in hand. She poured a cup of coffee and sat down. Marshall stood there at the end of the bar, a cup of coffee in hand, a distant look on his face.

"Husband Marshall?"

"Hmmm? What, Two Blankets?" His answer was short as if she had interrupted an important thought.

"I do not like to disturb you."

"Then don't."

"You were kind enough to give me this calendar, so I could learn dates."

"I told you it would be difficult. No matter if you can't learn."

"It is not that. I think I can. But this calendar is from last year. I understand the calendar is different each year."

He came over and looked. "Yep, that is from last year." Walking back to the back room, he rummaged around on his desk for a couple of minutes, then came back and threw a rolled sheet down on the table. "Here. That should do you."

"Thank you, husband Marshall," Two Blankets said, but Marshall had already gone back to his ruminating.

At that point, Gilly came in. "I'm finished with my morning chores and all, Missus. Johnston."

"Good, Mister Gilly. Sweep the floor, as before. Then, I want you to clean up and polish the bar. All the dirt gone, and what is shiny, glowing."

"Yes, ma'am."

Marshall stepped past her with a look at Two Blankets. "You got him working like a lap dog. That what you're after, to make him your pet?"

Two Blankets looked up at Marshall. He was eying her suspiciously.

"No, husband Marshall. This is the Landing, the center of your property and activity. It should shine like a star on the *Nch'i-wána* for every steamboat and flatboat that passes by. Everyone should remember Johnston's Landing. Is that not true?"

"Well, that part is true. I thought it was pretty clean."

"Men do not see dirt. Look at these beautiful windows. Mister Gilly's next project."

He stepped up and examined the window and the trace of dirt already showing. "I see your point. Gilly, just keep on doing what Two Blankets here says." Then he stepped out.

TWO BLANKETS UNROLLED the hides in the creek. They were soft enough now. The hides were dirty from storage and had only been rough-scraped, but she was pleased to see no beetle damage.

No beetles. These hides must have been stored up in the smoky rafters. That is good.

She began by scrubbing the red fox hide with a piece of pumice stone, first on the fur side, then more intently on the flesh side. Laying the hide on a driftwood log, smooth and level, she scrubbed, allowing the waterlogged weight of the stone do the work for her. She had done every stage of the tanning process before but had never done one hide from start to finish. Two Blankets knew she was not a master tanner, but hoped to do a decent job of it.

Remembering the many times she had done this task made her tear up. The memory of Fox Tail and her exemplary tanning skills made the tears fall. Tanning was a clan task, a group task, where men and women worked and laughed together. Now, she was doing it alone.

"There is no help for it, worrying about what cannot be. I work alone. Sometimes, I cry alone. I am alone. But this is my choice, my choice." She wiped her eyes on her sleeve and continued fleshing the hide. Now she switched to a fleshing tool made from an elk antler. Stretching the hide on a flat beam with the fur side down, she settled into the repetitive work, taking off the leftover fat and meat, then the membrane below, until she could see the pores of the skin glistening through. The head and claws were especially difficult. She slowed down and spent the time necessary.

Finally, she judged she was finished.

Now, she washed the hide thoroughly and squeezed it dry, then washed it again. Then she placed it back into the stream to let the running waters wash it overnight. She weighted it with rocks and looked up at the sun. Wiping her brow, she saw it was already evening. The other hide would have to wait until the morrow.

Straightening up, she rubbed her back. Suddenly, she was exhausted and somewhat sick feeling. She walked back to her longhouse and took a bit of salmon to her furs. She lay down, nibbled on the dried salmon, and fell asleep.

The next morning, after her predawn work with Gilly, and his lesson on the calendar, Two Blankets walked up to the Landing. She had coffee and started Gilly on the windows. Marshall came in and barely noticed her. She walked back to the creek and washed out her red pelt twice more. She ran her hand over it and smiled in partial satisfaction.

"Fox Tail would say, 'Not bad, for a twelve-year-old.' Well, Fox Tail was a master tanner, I am an apprentice." She smiled, bittersweet, remembering similar remarks she had said regarding Standing Bear's beading techniques.

Punching tiny holes in the edges of the fur, she laced it to a drying rack and tautened the ties until it was like a drum skin. Now it would have to dry a few days before she could start on the next stage. She pulled the elk skin from the creek and noted this hide had better fleshing than the fox fur. On the other hand, there was all that hair to remove.

"Ah, well, the help arrives in one hand and leaves immediately in the other." She began working the hide with her antler scraper. There was an ease to this when the work had been partially done by someone else. Soon, she could see the pores of the hide on the underside, and it was ready to wash out. Another two handspans of sun passage and she had this skin stretched out on its own frame to dry. She stroked it with the pleasure of a job well done and well done by her alone.

Her dress was soaked to the waist, her moccasins sodden, and her hair tangled. As she walked up to the Landing, she wondered, *does a man worry about* his *appearance after a hard day's work? Alton Shales probably does.* But she knew what kind of respect Alton Shales would generate. Yes, they needed him, it seemed, and the money he could provide, but real men did not respect him.

She entered the Landing and took a bowl of stew from the communal pot that was kept simmering there, as well as a small loaf of bread, and coffee. She still desired coffee, though its appeal was lessening. Sitting at the table, she dipped the bread into the stew and chewed thoughtfully.

"Oh, my word. Two Blankets, what have you been into? A bear fight? Struggle with a giant salmon?" Delores Sue descended the staircase daintily in her pointy-toed shoes.

"If it were a bear, it was a bloody and dirty one. Don't get near me. You're filthy." Aimee sat away from her.

"I have been tanning hides. It is a messy business." Two Blankets took another bite of stew. "If we are talking about smells, Aimee, you might want to wash 'tween your legs. The smell of seed and sex is keen upon you." Two Blankets smiled to take some of the sting from her remark.

"Seed and sex? Well, I—"

"She's right, Aimee. You smell about as strong as a bear in heat."

"It's still a rude thing to say. But—"

"True," they both said together.

"All right, fine. I apologize for my remarks, Two Blankets."

"No, need. Every word you said was true. I was just wondering why a man who just finished working a dirty job felt no shame, but a woman is always supposed to look like she just bathed."

Aimee pulled out a pipe from a hidden pocket in her dress. Two Blankets had seen pipes before, but they were mostly of the crude 'corncob' variety. She knocked out the bowl and began packing it with tobacco which she drew from an embroidered pouch. The neck of the pipe was curved and looked, to Two Blanket's eyes, rather elegant. Her pipe lit, Aimee settled back in a wreath of smoke and pleasure.

"That is quite a pretty pipe, Aimee. I have never seen the like."

Aimee leaned forward conspiratorially. "Ah. A corncob actually smokes just as well." She took another puff. "But this looks rather more sophisticated. It is all part of the image. Image and style, that is what makes a difference with people."

"That's why you are a dollar whore here in the sticks, rather than a three dollar whore in a nice house in Portland?" Delores Sue laughed.

"It's the main reason." She puffed out a smoke ring.

Two Blankets looked in confusion between Aimee and Delores Sue. "But what about substance? Does that not make a difference?"

They both looked at Two Blankets. In an explosion of smoke, Aimee lost her composure first followed by Delores Sue's laughter. "Honey, when you take away all the other stuff, what Aimee calls 'image and style,' it's all the same, just a butter-churning paddle plunging into a churning-tub."

They turned back to each other in conversation, and Two Blankets took that as a dismissal.

The next morning, after Gilly finished his morning chores, she had him go over the months of the year. He didn't know the months either, but he did know their order on the calendar, and the fact that only two started with a "J." Also only one with an "F, S, O, N or a D." She could learn those by sight. March/May, April/August, June/July, would cause her problems, she knew.

Two Blankets also saw faint symbols on the calendar that somewhat resembled moon phases. "Are these the moon signs, Mister Gilly?"

Gilly looked close to where she pointed. "Oh, yes, this calendar has the moon phases."

"So, this month is October."

Gilly examined the calendar. "That there is an 'O,' and there is only one 'O' month on the calendar, and it's in the right place, so, yes, October."

"And this here is Saturday, the third?"

"This calendar's got Saturday as the last day each week, and that's the third."

"That is a full moon?"

"Yes."

Two Blankets sat back with a sense of pride. "According to the calendar, on Saturday, the third of October, in 1857, we had a full moon."

Gilly ran through the logic of it. He was tempted to just accept the information, but he was her teacher in this. "Yes, that's true."

"Next week, on Sunday, on the eighteenth of October, there will be an empty moon?"

"It is called a new moon in English."

"Ah, a new moon. Thank you, Mister Gilly. I think I have learned much today. Much that is special. When we meet at the Landing, we will work on the windows."

She found the quarter moon in April. About April 15 was the day of her catching the child from Standing Bear. She traced thirty-six weeks and ran off the calendar. Her child would be due sometime in the first week of January of the year 1858.

"A calendar can be a useful item. About three more months."

The child will come when you are too big to walk. What else do you need to know? Gray Wolf churned the air with her legs as she wriggled on her back.

She looked first to Gray Wolf, then to the sky. The morning fog was blowing off, but gray weather was coming in. It would rain in the next several days, and, Two Blankets guessed, it would rain strongly and for several days. She looked over at her hides. They were still quite damp.

At least two more days there. You can't rush a wet hide.

———————

TWO MORE DAYS drying, and Two Blankets judged it time. A glance at the sky, and she threw a canvas tarpaulin over the elk hide. It wouldn't hurt it at all if it were to get wet, but it would delay her. She carefully unlaced the red fox pelt from the frame. It was a little stiff, but not bad. She decided this process required her work cape, not any clothes that would be ruined. She fished out the red and white tablecloth and smiled as she pulled it over her head. This "tablecloth" dress had a lot of good memories in it.

She broke the seal on the jar and worked out the plug. The sight and smell of what lay within made her choke, and she could feel the bile rise in her throat. She forced it back down.

There is nothing like a jar of old brains to calm the stomach, but there is no way around it, not if I want this leather tanned right.

She scooped out an appropriate amount, about what she could have held in her hand, and plopped it into a stone bowl. Blending in about a cup of warm water, she stirred it until the brain mixture was a slurry. Then she put the mix back on the edge of the fire to warm it up again. She sat back on her heels.

"Image and style. Is there something to that? It is somewhat the same as I have been telling Marshall about the Landing. There is nothing to make the Landing stand out from other trading posts, except what people can see. Or what they think they can see."

She pulled the bowl carefully off the fire. The mix was warm to the touch, the bowl hot. Grayish pink in color, it still stank, but that was to be expected. She put another stone bowl full of water on the fire, then scooped up a handful of the glop and began working it into the hide. The whole hide she worked from the head to the foot until every section had been saturated. Then she put an old piece of cloth into the hot water and wrung it out. Placing the hide on the cloth, fur side up, she began working the brain mixture into the fur side. Finally, she had an entire hide sloppily coated with brain-mix. She rolled it up in the cloth and set it aside to absorb for a couple of hours.

Image and style. I will try it. I have no image or style right now unless you count a half-tanned wench as stylish.

Most of the men seemed to be at lunch now. She would take a chance and bathe in the creek, dress and all. She had saved her moccasins by leaving them off.

Once at the creek, she submerged. The water was cold now, in October, but she seemed to have a regulator in her body. After the initial shock, the water felt refreshingly cool. The brain coating flowed away with the water from the stream, and she scrubbed her entire body with sand. Two washings of her hair and two rinsings were enough, or she counted them as enough. She was cold to the bone now.

Hurrying, she danced her way back to her longhouse. She built up the indoor fire, stripped off the red and white cloak, and hung it up to dry. Rubbing her skin dry with an old cloth, she wondered what to wear. She finally decided upon an elkskin wrap from Warm Springs, one of her parting gifts. It had pretty beading and wrapped her whole lower torso. It would cover her no matter how pregnant she got. She slipped on the good calf-length moccasins from Warm Springs, as well, and laced them up. Finally, she combed out her hair with an old broken-toothed implement, something she had found after the clan had burned and left the village. Her hair was glossy.

She examined her softened hands. Brain tanning must be good for humans, too. That brought a smile to her lips.

She walked up to the Landing with that smile still warming her. When she walked into the Landing, she saw first Delores Sue and Aimee sitting at their usual table. Then she noticed Marshall, Harry Everton, and a couple of the other men at the bar. All but Harry had a drink in hand or before them.

They did not remark on Two Blankets, and she moved toward the table. Delores Sue indicated she should sit in her usual chair. Gathering up a cup of coffee and a bowl of the ubiquitous venison stew she sat down.

"Delores Sue. Aimee." She greeted them and took a sip of coffee. "What is wrong with this coffee? It tastes terrible."

"Two Blankets." Delores Sue lifted her cup and Aimee nodded. "The coffee tastes normal to me. May I?" She reached across and took a sip from the cup. "It ain't great coffee, but it's about average for this place. Try some sugar."

Two Blankets spooned a teaspoon of sugar into her cup and stirred, then tasted. She put in two more, hesitated, then added another spoon of sugar. She tasted and sat back relaxed. "Now *that* is good."

Aimee rolled her eyes. "She is well and fully pregnant."

"What do you mean?" Two Blankets took another drink and shook her head. "My, that is wonderful."

Delores Sue leaned toward her. "You got the craves is all. First, you don't really like coffee, then you do, then it is too bitter, and you want four teaspoons of sugar in it. I notice you ain't had a pickle for breakfast in the last week."

"That's crazy. I'll show you." She marched over to the pickle barrel and pulled out a monster and marched back, sitting down triumphantly.

"Well?" Delores Sue and Aimee leaned forward.

Two Blankets bit off a huge chunk and chewed. She spat the bite out onto the table. *"Blech.* There is something wrong with this."

"No. You just don't like pickles no more." Delores Sue laughed. "Just drink your sugar and coffee and be glad you can keep something down."

After a deep draught of coffee, Two Blankets said, "I notice you two look especially pretty this morning." Both had their faces made up and fresh dresses on. Their hair was brushed and shiny. True, the face make up was strange to Two Blankets, but it was applied artfully, like ceremonial paint.

"Thank you, Missus Johnston."

"Please, call me Two Blankets."

"Might I say your hair is really glossy, and your hands are simply amazing soft. You doing something special?" Delores Sue was truly curious.

"I've been brain tanning."

"Brain tanning? I never heard of that."

Two Blankets scooped up some stew on a piece of the loaf of bread on the table. "Well, it sounds really horrible, but it's great for the hair and hands, apparently. You take a hide, and then you mix up the brains of an animal and cook it down. Then you work it into the skin."

"Oh, stop. Now I want to puke, and my courses are on me, and I don't have cloths." Aimee turned her somewhat green face away and into her hands.

"You don't have moon cycle pads?"

"No, I forgot to pack them when I boarded the steamboat."

"Wait right here." Two Blankets jumped up and jogged to the moon cycle hut. She grabbed three pads stuffed with cattail fluff and hurried back to the Landing. Upon entering, she turned away from the men and surreptitiously approached Aimee. "Try these. This is how the *Nimi'ipuu* do it. When you are finished, throw the fluff away and wash out the covering."

"Thank you, Two Blankets. I am not used to people—even women—being so downright direct."

"That I cannot do much about. Many of the Chinook are the same."

Just then, Gilly entered the Landing and made for Two Blankets. Aimee tucked the moon cycle pads under her dress and sat down on them.

"Missus Johnston. Miss Delores Sue and Aimee." Gilly pulled his cap off.

"Mister Gilly, sweep, then the bar, then—"

"I know. Sweep, clean and polish the bar, then get started on the windows. Ladies." He put his cap back on and went for his broom.

"Why you uncommon hard on him? I mean, clean is important, but—"

"Image and style, Aimee. Image and style. Even here. I need to get back to my brain tanning."

"Eerp."

"It does sound bad, but wait until you see the red fox skin. Then you will understand why it is worth it." She got up, and with a nod, left the Landing.

Two Blankets checked the red fox fur and saw it was still a little stiff in places. It would need one more treatment. The elk hide was almost dry but could wait until tomorrow if need be. The sky was gray, and the slow build-up of clouds looked ominous. She might have another day outside to wait for the elk hide.

Within the longhouse, she changed back into her tablecloth cape. It was still damp from the morning's washing, but it was warm and clean. She added a few sticks to the fire, stripped off her moccasins, and left the longhouse. Once outside, she stirred the fire back into life and put the brain-mix back on the edge to warm.

Unrolling the red fox fur onto the table, she felt of its softness. This wouldn't be a perfect tan, maybe not even a good one by Fox Tail's standards, but it would be something she would be proud of. The stone bowl of water was still warm on the edge of the fire. She poured water onto the fur and began working it in.

Washing the brain solution from the skin took several wash and rinse cycles. Halfway through, she had to add water and wait for it to warm. When it was as clean as she could get it, she saw that one more treatment with the brains would finish the tanning, and she set to work. A handful of the grayish-pink mass and then she worked it into the skin. Another handful. Work it into the skin. Though the project seemed endless, she knew it was not. Each application softened and conditioned the skin. She turned the hide and began working the brains into the fur. This part seemed to go faster, or perhaps it was just the thought of the finished fur that made it seem faster. Either way, she soon was able to wrap the fur up in the cloth for the final wait.

After a couple of handspans of the sun's passage, Two Blankets unrolled the cloth. She wiped off as much of the excess brain-slurry as possible. The hide was still somewhat stiff to the touch, and it was still too wet. She knew she wanted it damp. If it went too dry, it would be impossible to work. If it was too wet, it would stretch and even get thin in places. She squeezed out the brain solution and hung the hide near the fire to dry a bit. It looked to be tomorrow's project.

The next morning, after her work with Gilly, she checked on her fur. It was just damp, but no longer wet. She gathered up the hide and lay it across her hide breaker, which was just a smooth, sturdy branch wedged into a crack in the longhouse on one end and a post with a "y" crotch driven into the ground at the other. Taking one side of the hide in each hand, she rolled it fur side in and worked it back and forth, keeping pressure on the hide breaker all the while. This produced a sort of friction and some small heat which helped soften and dry the hide. It was hard work, what people often call "back-breaking" work. To her, it was just work, and there was a joyful component to it ,as well.

About every finger or two of sun travel, she would check the hide and feel its softness. She pulled on the hide from different directions, head to foot, then turned the hide and worked in the opposite direction. From time to time, she pulled the hide from the hide breaker and stretched it in each direction by hand. She aimed to stretch every section of the hide, and she clung to this aim as she had to her trip up the river to Warm Springs. After two handspans of sun of this treatment, the hide was dry and supple.

She sat back and stroked on the hide which hung over the pole. But for the smoking, she was done with this hide, and the smoking process would involve little work from her.

Two Blankets loosely stitched up the sides with the fur side out, until it resembled a bag, closed at the head end. Then she sewed a piece of old canvas about a foot and a half deep to the bottom. A small hole in the ground and a few coals in it were all she needed. She knew she did not want a fire, only smoke. She built a small tripod over it and hung the skin with the canvas "skirt" just brushing the ground and her fur "bag" centered over it. Into the hole, she dumped several handfuls of punky and rotten wood. She sat back and watched. Just the right amount of smoke and no heat. It was perfect she judged. She pegged down the canvas skirt and let the red fox fur pelt fill up with smoke.

Smoke trailed from the mouth and claws, creating a fierce appearance. The sun was going down, and she went to the creek to wash up. She wasn't as dirty this time. It only took one scrubbing with sand to do the job. Her cape, she washed as best she could while it was on. There were men beginning to walk about the camp, though none nearby.

When she had finished washing, she walked back to the longhouse with a sense of achievement. Maybe this was a twelve-year-old's job, but she had done it and done it alone.

She pulled the skin down and removed the twine holding the canvas to the bottom and along the two edges of the hide. She felt along it, first along its edges, paying particular attention to the legs and paws and head, then along the body entire. Yes, she could feel some areas of stiffness where she had not worked enough brain-slurry, and there were two small areas where the skin was a bit thin, but all-in-all, she was pleased.

She held the fur before her, the yellow stained teeth smiling at her and the empty eye sockets staring into hers.

"You have sacrificed much, sister red fox, to bring us to this day. I hope

I have done you justice, done a tribute to your death. We honor you, my child and I."

You have done a tribute to sister red fox. I can feel a piece of my spirit residing within. Just a tiny one, but it is there. Gray Wolf sat and watched with deep green spirit eyes.

I am only White Mouse, no predator like Gray Wolf or this red fox, but I can feel the seed of it as well.

Two Blankets kicked dirt into the smoking hole and pulled the brain pot off the fire and banked the fire down. With one look at the now darkening camp, she entered the longhouse. The men were beginning to pass drink at the bunkhouse, and their coarse talk and laughter flowed about her. She stripped off the cloak and hung it up. Holding the fur close to her body, she crawled into her sleeping furs. She held the red fox close to her belly and felt the soft and fluffy texture against her. It was a good feeling, a sufficiency. It was a job well done and a completion. She fell asleep sensing only this completion.

EVENTS AT THE LANDING

CHAPTER 3
WINTER, 1857

THE NEXT DAY, about mid-afternoon, Two Blankets dressed again in her elk-skin wrap and good moccasins. She brushed out her hair. She wasn't sure why she clothed herself so, but it seemed necessary to make a favorable impact. Why should she worry about impressing Delores Sue and Aimee?

Have you contemplated that they are the only women at the Landing, the only persons you might share something with? Gray Wolf's question stirred her.

Have you been thinking, Gray Wolf?

That is a human problem. In my pack, the bitches run together. It is that simple.

I see. Mayhap you have been with me too long.

She picked up the red fox fur and walked to the Landing. Sitting down at what she now thought of as "their" table, at least for this span of sun's passage each day, she spooned sugar into her coffee.

"You are wearing your pretty dress again today, Two Blankets."

"It is almost all I have that will fit." She pulled at the wrap to cover her belly. "Hello, Delores Sue. Hello, Aimee. I don't know your other names."

"These are our work names, only. A whore has to know a person a bit, afore sharing our more personal secrets. Ain't that true for you, Two Blankets? Don't you Indians have a private name?"

"Two Blankets is a name I earned when I married Mister Johnston. Before that, when I was *mistshimus,* I was just Girl-With-No-Name."

"Girl-With-No-Name? *That* was your name?" Aimee asked.

"It was not even a name, only what I called myself. A *mistshimus* is a slave. A *mistshimus* had no right to any property. Not a name, not long hair, not anything."

Delores whistled. "And you thought you had it bad as a Lottery of the Golden Ingots girl, Aimee."

"It was not so bad, at least it seems so now."

"What is a Lottery-of-the-Golden-Ingots-girl?" Two Blankets ran the words together.

Aimee gave Delores Sue a look. "My mother was a whore and my father a pickpocket and a thief. He said he was a businessman. In France, the government came up with a confidence scheme to fool the public. They sold tickets for one franc apiece for a chance to win a golden ingot. That part was real enough, and several won prizes of different sizes. But the real reason for the Lottery was to finance seventeen ships and five thousand prisoners to go to San Francisco. They basically emptied out the prisons and shipped them off."

Aimee's face assumed a sad and faraway look. "My mother and I were shipped out. My father, who wasn't in prison at the time, was not. We were dumped on the docks of San Francisco with nothing but a bag of clothes apiece. I could speak some English, but my mother only spoke French.

"The pimps and panderers met us on the docks. We didn't have a place to go, so went with them. My mother went to a different house than I did, a rough house where each woman only had a curtained place for her own. I was young and fared better. When I finally got to see her, months later, she was already sick from the life she was forced to live. When she died after a few more months, I ran away and made my way up to Portland."

Aimee fell silent.

"I'm sorry. I didn't mean to pry into your business."

"It's all right. What does Two Blankets mean?"

Two Blankets blushed. Though it only showed a little on the surface of her face, she could still feel it.

"You don't have to answer. I do not mean to pry, either."

"No, I was thinking about when I said, 'We Indians do not have a tradition of whoring,' and you were a bit upset. I was *mistshimus*. My mistress had the rights to my sexual encounters. My first month after I became a woman was bartered for two blankets. In a way, I was lying, though it is still true for free Indians. Among *mistshimus,* anything is possible, even casual execution if the master feels like it."

"I feel like my story's downright dull after you two." Delores Sue spoke out.

"Tell it, anyway, Delores Sue."

"I come out on a wagon train on the Oregon Trail. But my parents died along the way. All that was left was my two brothers and me."

"Were they killed by Indians?" Aimee asked.

"No, we never had no trouble with Indians. A little stealing maybe, but that was all. They was mostly helpful. That Indians killing all the wagon train people is a lie, I think. There might be a few, but it ain't the rule, and that is what our wagon master said too before we left Independence, Missouri."

"In France, there were handbills and stories about the vicious Indians killing many people on the wagon trains. That is one of the reasons why many take ship to California, because travel by ship is much safer—or so they say."

"Well, what do we know about advertising men?" Delores Sue adopted a very knowing look.

"They all lie," Aimee and Delores chorused and laughed.

Two Blankets smiled. She didn't really know what they were laughing about. The softness and comfort of the red fox fur in her lap drew her hands to stroke it.

"What is that you got there in your lap, Two Blankets?"

She lay it on top of the table and smoothed it out. "It is what I have been doing these last few days." She felt somehow shy and proud at the same time.

"Oh, my word, that there is *beautiful,*" Delores Sue stroked it with her single finger at first, then with her whole hand. "and almighty soft."

"May I pick it up, Two Blankets?"

Two Blankets was pleased. "Of course, Aimee."

Aimee picked up the fur and held it against her neck. "Oh, I have not felt anything like this since France. I have seen furs, of course. The west is full of furs. But a fur of this beauty, of this quality...this is a rarity." Her eyes, as she looked at Two Blankets, were dreamy. "I am serious, this is quite astounding."

"It is a beginner's fur, or an apprentice's at best in my culture. The furs of Fox Tail were the very best you could ever find."

"That may be, but I am serious. I would pay a week's earnings for a fur like this, something of quality to remind me, and my customers, of how much I, myself, am worth. Would you—how do you say it?—tan me a fur like this? For a fee, of course."

"I could." Two Blankets thought of the inventory in the hide shed. "I don't think there are any more red fox, but there are silver fox, muskrat, beaver, and one or two small cats like lynx or bobcat. We would have to barter with Marshall for the raw skin."

Aimee draped the fox fur across her shoulders and stood up, walked about the Landing. Two Blankets saw the change in her walk. It became, of a sudden, more dramatic and more seductive.

Two Blankets leaned toward Delores Sue. "What is she doing?"

Delores Sue smiled. "I'd say, if it were me, she's doing two things. She's seeing how the fur makes her feel, and she's calculating how much more she can earn wearing a fur like that."

"Image and style?"

"You got it, honey."

Aimee came to some conclusion. She walked back over to the table, still running her hand over the fur. "Two Blankets, I'll give you twenty dollars plus the cost of the fur, if we can find one I like."

"Twenty dollars?" The price shocked her.

Aimee sat down. "I am sorry. I do not mean to insult your skill. It is all I can afford." She drew off the red fox fur and lay it on the table before Two Blankets. She looked saddened, more than if she had never held the fur in the first place. She took her pipe out and began to stuff tobacco into it, spilling some onto the table.

"No, Aimee, I do not mean it that way. Of course, I will tan a fur for you. I was just surprised at your offer."

Aimee looked at Two Blankets, still suspicious.

"It is more than generous. I thank you very much."

The look on Aimee's face lifted into a tentative smile. "Really?"

"Let us do this like the Chinook do. It is a good bargain." She held out her hand. "This is how you *whitemans* do it? You shake hands on the deal?"

Aimee took her hand. "We do. It is a good bargain."

On the following day, Two Blankets cornered Marshall in a moment when he didn't really have anything to do. He was merely musing at the Landing when she approached him.

"Excuse me, husband Marshall. I do not mean to interrupt, but I have something I would bring to your attention."

"What is it now, Two Blankets? The pickles haven't arrived yet."

"It is not that. It regards the hides in the storehouse."

He looked at her with skepticism, then saw she was serious. "The hides?"

"It would be easier if you would come and see for yourself."

"Oh, all right. But this better be important. I got things to do that you know nothing about."

She led the way to the storehouse and entered. Marshall lit an oil lamp. "If you look at these hides you will see that they have been rolled and stored in a dry place, which is good."

"That is what you have to say?"

"No, that is not it. The hides have not been scraped properly. Some are being attacked by beetles already and the rest... I would imagine they have only about six months at best until most are useless."

He pulled one down and forced it open partially. "Goddammit all. I don't believe that. I told them to scrape them clean, before rolling."

"You see. It is partially done, but the remaining meat and fat will ruin the hide in time. A short time, I think."

"I see that one." He pulled down another and another after that. "I don't like to admit it, but you're right."

"There are at least a hundred hides here."

Marshall pulled out the tally sheet. "One hundred twenty-seven."

"I do not know how to add the value of the different hides, it seems to be a great amount."

"Without a calculation, at least seven hundred dollars, probably more. Damn it."

"I cannot do it all myself. The job is too big. But it is fairly simple. Three men could do it in a month I suspect."

"The trouble is of the men I can spare, and I do have some I might have to let go soon, none of 'em is smart enough to boss this crew."

"I know how to do it. Give me Mister Gilly and a couple of others, and I can do it."

"You? You have this skill?"

"I am not a master, but I tanned this red fox." She took the fox fur from its resting place across her shoulders and handed it to Marshall.

He stepped out into the light and examined the fur, rubbed the fur in various areas, turned it over. "This ain't bad work, Two Blankets. If I didn't know you didn't lie, I'd say you was a liar."

"It is not the work of a Fox Tail, but it is good apprentice work, I think."

"Hell, this is good journeyman work. Now, how we going to get the men to work for a woman and an Indian, that is the problem."

"Mister Gilly will work for me, I know that."

"If we make Gilly the supervisor of the crew, that would solve it. You can train him?"

"I will start tomorrow with Mister Gilly, then two days later the rest of the crew. One more thing. Aimee wants me to tan a fur for her. Can I buy one at company discount?"

"You pull this off, you can have one of the smaller ones—just not the bear or the wolf."

"No, she wants something about the same size as the red fox."

"All right then. Start with Gilly tomorrow, and we got a bargain."

"A Chinook bargain?" Two Blankets smiled.

"Don't push it. I ain't ever making a Chinook bargain again."

The next morning brought Gilly to his new project. Two Blankets led him to the old bunkhouse. They stood in the entrance and viewed the stacks of hides.

"That's a lot of hides."

She laughed. "That is your new project. I will teach you what to do, then in a couple of days you will have a crew to help you."

"Me, in charge of a crew, ma'am? I don't know. I never bossed a crew before."

"Well, it is that, or you'll get let go. Help me pull out these hides and let us soak them in the creek."

Together, they pulled two dozen hides out of the storehouse and placed them in the creek weighted by rocks. They only found one that was mostly eaten by beetles. The rest were undamaged, or at least serviceable.

"Tomorrow, we will start working these when they are soft enough to straighten out. For now, sweep, the bar...."

"And the windows. I know."

"Thank you, Mister Gilly."

"Missus Two Blankets?"

"Mister Gilly, what is it?"

"Thank you for having this trust in me."

Two Blankets walked back to the longhouse. She checked the elk skin and decided it was dry enough to begin the de-hairing process.

She lay the hide across a flat beam and began scraping the hair side. It was a tedious process, but it had a rhythm to it once her body got into the feel of it. Before she knew it, the sun had advanced past mid-day, and she washed up and dressed for the Landing. Aimee and Delores Sue were there, and Two Blankets sat with them.

"Aimee, when we are finished eating here, let us go to the storage shed to choose your skin. Mister Johnston has agreed to our bargain."

"Oooh. I am so excited. Can we go now? I'm ready."

"I have been up since before dawn. Let me eat first."

"All right. I'll wait."

Marshall walked past. "Two Blankets. I got you a whole barrel of pickles. It came in yesterday." He rolled the barrel over and popped the lid off. "Nice and juicy. I don't know what you see in these."

Two Blankets looked down at the dill pickles floating in their brine. "Oh, thank you. *Erp.* Please excuse."

She ran out the door.

"What the hell?" Marshall looked at the door.

Aimee looked at the door and smiled. "She's pregnant. Last week, she wanted coffee and pickles. This week, pickles make her puke, and she wants four or five spoonfuls of sugar in her coffee."

"What am I going to do with these?"

"Put them at the end of the bar. Excuse me, Mister Marshall." Aimee followed Two Blankets out the door.

She found Two Blankets on her knees. Aimee went to her and lifted her by the shoulders.

"At least I didn't retch. What am I going to tell my husband, Marshall?"

"Don't worry. Let us go to the storehouse."

At the storehouse, Two Blankets threw the flap up over the door. They lit a lamp and looked through the hides. She pulled out a fur and then another one. "Here is a gray fox. Here a muskrat."

"These are pretty, but I don't think so."

"Let me pull some outside and then you can look." Two Blankets began rapidly pulling out furs. When she had a dozen, they took them outside and examined them.

"Here you can see them better. The gray fox and muskrat from before. A beaver and an opossum." Aimee picked up each and examined it, as best she could since they were stiff and rolled.

"They're all beautiful. But—"

"Here is a bobcat."

"*Ohh la.* This is *thick.*"

"This last is a Canada lynx. I love the tufted ears, and the color is especially nice. It was trapped in the winter, so has thick fur and lighter in color."

"That one. That's the one." She hadn't even picked it up.

"Are you sure?"

"I know it's the one."

Two Blankets pulled it out. "We will do this one, then. You can decide in a few days whether you want the head on."

"No, no." Aimee shivered. "No head or claws, please."

Two Blankets laughed. "No head. No claws."

The next day, once Gilly had finished with his 'farm' chores for Two Blankets and 'dirty' chores for Marshall, he returned to her for instruction. She led him to the hides loosening up in the stream.

"Mister Gilly, the first step, if the hides are not fleshed correctly to begin with, is to soften them enough to work." They lifted a small deer hide. "This one is relaxed enough, where this one—" and she pulled up a thick moose hide "—is not."

Gilly nodded, absorbing the information and nervous he was missing something. "It just needs to be relaxed enough to unroll?"

"Right." She brought the hide to a beam set in the ground before the storehouse and flopped it over. "Now, you scrape, slowly and carefully, every bit of fat or flesh. Don't scrape too hard and not too soft. You will get the feel for it."

She handed him an elk thigh bone. Gilly began scraping. "Like this?"

"A little firmer, but pay attention. It is easy to scrape a hole. You can relax, but don't dream."

"All right."

Two Blankets saw something on the river. A raft—no, *two* rafts—and they were damaged or sinking. "Mister Gilly, I have noticed every few days a flatboat or a raft going downstream with what look like wagon parts, sides and wheels, and teams. I wonder what they are doing?"

Gilly stopped and looked where she indicated. "Normal-like, they're from wagon trains. They get to The Dalles, then have to abandon the wagon and team and take a steamboat down, or they break down the wagon and make a raft. Sometimes they use Indian canoes, sometimes logs. They still have to portage everything past the Cascades."

"That one is in trouble. It is sinking."

Indeed, one of the men was in the water already. Several natives paddled as hard as possible to reach the shallows, but they still had to clear the abrupt bluff that bordered the camp on the east side. There were four of them in addition to the two male *whitemans*. The dugout canoe that formed one hull of the crude raft was a broken skeleton of its once buoyant self. The two *whitemans,* an elder and a boy, Two Blankets could now see, yelled at each other. A woman, with fair almost bleached hair and a burned and pinched face, sat on the high side holding a girl and wailing.

The team of four oxen that rode in the first raft bellowed and shifted. The lead canoe cleared the bluff and made for the shallow water. Two Blankets could see an expression of relief pass over the two Indians' faces as they eyed the shallow water and redoubled their efforts. They yelled an expletive or a cheer to their two fellows.

"Mister Gilly, call the crew, or some of them. Those people need help."

"Yes, ma'am." He ran for the supervisor, yelling and pointing.

Two Blankets ran toward the bank and the first canoe. Others in the camp now became aware, and Harry Everton and Marshall moved in that direction, as well.

On board the second pair of canoes—or canoe-and-a-half as the case was, they cleared the bluff and made for shallow water. The Indians whooped exhilaration and success.

Two Blankets was close enough to the bank to hear the man shout, "Get clear, Abel. The stove is going to go. I can't hold it."

The boy pulled himself forward, and a great behemoth of a cast-iron stove slid slowly at first, then all in a rush toward the water. It tipped and hung on the edge for a moment, then, to Two Blankets, seemed to tumble slowly through the air into the river. Everyone was quiet for seconds which seemed like minutes, or time interminable, then the stove glugged and sank beneath the water. The woman screamed and stood up, further unbalancing the raft. She even took a step toward the spot that was now just white water as the air escaped the stove. The man yelled at her and pushed her back down.

Even the paddling Indians paused and then laughed and paddled on. By now the first raft had reached the shore and men were taking charge of the frightened animals as they led them off via the gangplank to the nearby dock. The man grounded the second raft, and the Landing crew secured it. The man lifted his wife and daughter from the raft. The woman collapsed to the ground, though the girl looked more interested in life, now that hers was no longer threatened.

The man—an older man—Two Blankets could now see, straightened his posture and adjusted his bowler hat. He brushed off the rough jacket of his suit, and without err located Marshall as the person of decision.

He reached out his hand to shake Marshall's. "I am Holton Stafford. This is my wife, Abigail, and my children."

"Marshall Johnston." He took the hand for a cursory shake. "This here is Johnston's Landing, my place."

"We thank the Lord for delivering us to you, Mister Johnston."

"Looks like He nearly failed in the effort, Mister Stafford. I 'spect you should be thanking your Indian paddlers."

"The Lord placed them in our path, and they took the last of our coin, I am afraid. We will have to depend upon Him and your charity to progress farther."

"Well, this ain't no mission and it ain't no charity, neither. Still, I ain't heartless. You can camp here until you get your load settled. I don't know what you're going to do about that canoe. I 'spect them Washoe going to want something for the destruction of it."

"We trust in the Lord. As I said, there is no more coin in our coffers."

Two Blankets saw that the boy had erected a small tent and was searching for the makings of a fire. She caught Gilly's sleeve. "Mister Gilly, help them gather wood and get settled. It is the least we can do."

"Yes, ma'am." He hurried off after the boy.

"All right, all you men. Back to work. Show's over." To Holton Stafford, he said, "Come on up to the Landing for a drink when you get yourself settled."

"Drink is frowned upon by our Lord. But it is not forbidden. Thank you for your help and the help we will need."

"Just come up to the Landing. The big red building, and we'll talk about that." He turned away mumbling. "Our coffers are empty. Why does the Lord deliver charity cases to my doorstep?"

The natives were unloading the canoe-rafts and piling the cargo and wagon parts haphazardly on the beach. The loss of one canoe had hurt them. The building of a canoe was at least a month's labor.

Two Blankets approached the eldest. "Greetings, eldest warrior of the celebrated Washoe."

He grunted and spoke in broken Chinook Jargon. *"Whiteman* wreck canoe. He is stupid and wreck canoe. Now he no pay."

"Whitemans hard to understand. How are you called?"

He looked at her now and sat on the bank. "I Seven Arrow. I named this way because it take me seven arrow to hit what aiming for."

"Ah, but you swim like fish, Seven Arrow."

"Yes, I swim good."

"I am Two Blankets, wife of warrior Marshall Johnston. Am *Nimi'ipuu* first, then Chinook. I am sorry for the loss of your canoe. Know much work to make."

"Ah, we lose. We begin again. He pay for half of trip, rest pay in Portland. But we get no money, no go farther. I think *whiteman* got no more. We go home."

"I think you are right. I want to bargain with you for stove. You get?"

He looked out to the spot near the bluff. "We can swim. Water not deep. We get."

She placed a silver dollar on the ground between them. "This all I have. No more to bargain. A one-offer bargain."

"I have heard of you at The Dalles. From Little Feather. He is Cayuse, but still a brother."

"Seven Arrow, I think we are all brothers now, brothers and sisters. We are all that is left."

He handed her the dollar. "We try. We get stove, then take dollar. We no get, then we get wet." He rose to his fellows, and a short discussion with much pointing ensued. They finished unloading the first raft, then paddled it back to the spot by the bluff. With some yelling and good-natured pushing, three of them jumped in and disappeared. In a moment, one surfaced, then another. The third surfaced with a whoop. They moved the canoe over to his position and dove again with ropes. Soon, they surfaced and began tautening the ropes. When the ropes were taut, they all climbed out and lifted. It was no simple lift. The stove was ornate and heavy, but they accomplished the feat. They slapped each other and paddled back to the shallows. At the bank, they all jumped out and lifted the stove onto the beach. One of the round burner plate covers was missing, but it was otherwise intact.

Seven Arrow shook himself off and rejoined Two Blankets on the bank. They sat, and Two Blankets handed him the dollar.

She bowed. "Bargain complete? Bargain good?"

He nodded. "Bargain good. I will remember Two Blankets."

"I will remember Seven Arrow and his warrior friends. Before you leave, come up to longhouse." She pointed to her home. "I will give tea and food. Would be best if you left after dark, I think."

Seven Arrow nodded. "Yes, *whiteman* not understand when they not have money to finish bargain."

Later that afternoon, Two Blankets brought some *camas* cakes, venison stew, and smoked salmon to the Stafford's ramshackle tent. It looked as if Mrs. Stafford had attempted to make some order where none existed then just collapsed onto a pile of blankets.

"Good afternoon, Missus Stafford. I am Two Blankets, Mr. Johnston's wife. I brought you some food."

Mrs. Abigail Stafford looked up with dazed eyes. Eyes which changed from total nonrecognition to animosity, with a short stop at incredulity. "You are an Indian."

"Yes, I am *Nimi'ipuu* by birth, what you *whitemans* call Nez Perce."

Mrs. Stafford backed into the blankets. "Get away from me. You are the cause of all that has happened to us. Holton. Holton!"

Holton Stafford came running up. "Abigail? What is it? What are you doing here?" The last was directed to Two Blankets.

"You have had a hard time. I brought food."

"You don't know anything about us. You only want to steal from us, like those we hired to bring our raft to Portland. Now, they won't go farther, not without more money. And I ain't got no more."

The Stafford's son entered. "Ah, food. Thank you."

Abel had food scooped out before his parents could object.

The next morning, well before sunrise, Two Blankets brought *camas* cakes and salmon down to Seven Arrow and his friends. They laughed while they ate. She knew she had made new friends among them. Sometimes, small things like new friends were about as good as it went. As they paddled off with a salute, she felt a wave of sorrow pass over her.

Later in the day, she saw that Mr. Gilly had extended the entrance of the storehouse with a partial roof, at least enough to keep the rain off as winter came on. He had his crew, and he was the boss. Two Blankets smiled. Maybe he would turn out better than Marshall suspected. His skins properly fleshed, were now stretched on frames. More hides were soaking in the creek, and Gilly was busy showing his two new apprentices how to flesh the hides.

Two Blankets laughed. *It is a bit funny how self-important he looks, teaching his new charges.*

Gray Wolf watched. *Gilly is your pet, Two Blankets?*

My pet? And not you?

A growl erupted from Gray Wolf's throat. *I am no one's pet.*

The next day, Two Blankets overheard Holton Stafford and Marshall in an argument, or as Two Blankets knew it now, a bargain, a Chinook bargain, that Holton was bound to lose.

Holton stood stiff, his bowler perched precisely upon his head. His best suit, such as it was primly brushed. "So, you are saying, sir, that you won't do the charitable thing and help us?"

"I'm saying that if you want to cut my trees, you got to pay for them. I don't mind your tenting up here. Any man would give you that much charity."

"You are the same here as at The Dalles. No charity of the Lord for those less fortunate."

"You are welcome to go upstream about five miles and cut all the timber you want. You and the boy should be able to cut it, debranch, and trim it to length, and float it down here in a couple of weeks."

"But I would have to leave Abigail and Huldah here alone. Among all these men... and that Indian woman. No true man would do that."

"No true man of Oregon would expect someone else to pay their way. That's not how we do it. That's why we left to come out here. To come out and make our fortune."

"I promised my wife the Willamette, deep topsoil and the beginnings of civilization. Not The Dalles or Johnston's Landing."

"Well, I ain't going to stop you from going to the Willamette. If you want to talk land, come by and see me."

The next day she saw Holton and Marshall walking up the stream toward the land on the bluff. She knew you could grow some crops up there, but it was not the Willamette. The game was rich up on the bluff, but the soil was shallow.

Two Blankets passed by Mr. Gilly on her way to the Landing.

"Afternoon, Missus Two Blankets. I got my crew working hard on them hides." He smiled.

"Afternoon, Mister Gilly. I see that and good job. Don't forget the cleaning at the Landing."

"Oh, I don't never forget that."

She entered the Landing and took her seat at the table. Aimee and Delores Sue were there. "Anything special you want to eat today? Pickles?"

"That's not even funny anymore." Two Blankets got her coffee and five spoonfuls of sugar. "But the coffee is delicious."

"Funny thing going on with Mister Johnston and that Holton feller." Delores Sue looked knowingly between Aimee and Two Blankets.

"All I know is husband Marshall has offered him one hundred sixty acres up on the high ground. Although, I don't know what an *acre* is. But Mister Stafford doesn't have any money."

Delores Sue leaned forward and lowered her voice, though no one was within earshot. "I heard he was going to rent it to him. Holton builds a cabin up there and works the land and pays rent."

Two Blankets let the true confusion spread across her face. "What is *rent?*"

Aimee said, "Rent is where you pay an amount every month, or every year, for the use of an item. If it is set up right, you never can pay to own the land."

"Ah, it is like the tribal share Marshall agreed to when he married me."

Later, Holton Stafford and Marshall Johnston entered, and Marshall poured them each a drink. They drank, and he poured a second one. Two Blankets could see that he had made a strong bargain, at least it seemed that way from the looks on their faces. Marshall was in his agreeable mode, and Mr. Stafford seemed very unhappy.

"Look at it this way, Holton. You go up there on the bluff. Build a cabin and work the land. We'll figure eighty dollars for a half-year. That will give you some time. It don't work out, you can leave, and I'll keep the cabin and improvements. You make a go of it, and you can eventually buy the land."

"It sounds much like share-cropping to me. We left Missouri to get our own land."

"It might sound a little like that, but it ain't. And what if it does. I got the land up there, doing nothing for me or anybody. You got seed, a team, and the labor, but no coin. I ain't going to make you do anything you don't want to do."

"I still don't see why you won't just loan me the money. The Lord speaks for me when I say I will pay it back."

"I ain't no bank to loan out money. Take it or leave it, Stafford."

"Don't seem like I got much choice. I will take you up on your offer."

"I thought you would. Congratulations, partner." He shook hands with Mr. Stafford.

"I think I could use another drink."

"I think you should get to putting that wagon together. And to telling your wife."

Holton Stafford looked Marshall Johnston in the eye and poured another drink, quaffed it, and left the Landing.

Aimee leaned forward and whispered, "Not a very happy man."

Three days later, Two Blankets saw Marshall and the carpenter in a clear space near the Landing.

"I want you to build a frame barn here, just a rough thing, good enough though for a blacksmith. Dirt floor with a floored sleeping and cooking area in back. I want it big enough for one person, but room for expansion."

"All right. But we don't even have a blacksmith. If we build it rough, it will only take a couple of weeks. No windows?"

"Put a couple of windows in the living quarters. We ain't got a blacksmith now, but this business with Holton got me thinking. I might find a smith, a man with the skills but little coin, in The Dalles to rent the shop. I'll be going up there tomorrow."

"I'll get the boys on it right away, and I'll coordinate with the sawyer."

Interesting, the Landing is shifting toward rents. That could be good, to get the people we need. But the people won't be invested here.

You are becoming a wise woman, White Mouse said.

Two Blankets swatted at her ear. *I am a long way from that.*

BIRTH

CHAPTER 4
NOVEMBER, 1857 TO JANUARY, 1858

TO SAY THAT the next month or three months of Two Blankets pregnancy passed swiftly would be a misapprehension, for it did not. She gradually, as the months passed, swelled in belly and slowed in speed. To say that events did not progress in their normal, intermittent way would also be a mistaken belief. Some weeks went by with nothing seemingly new happening, yet things were always happening. Marshall took the steamboat to The Dalles and returned after two days with the news that he had indeed found a blacksmith willing to rent. True, he was a young man—barely nineteen—but he was eager. He had his own anvil and basic tools, though he had lost much when his wagon had overturned crossing the Snake River. He had also lost his father in the same accident, so he could not be competitive at The Dalles. He would come and try his hand at the Landing. These were the types of men Marshall had to recruit, men with potential. Then he and the Landing would see if they had the skills, the promise, and the ambition to fulfill that potential.

The blacksmith arrived two weeks later, with his anvil and two large chests of tools. After one look at the barn and sleeping place, he nodded his acceptance and, with no more word than that, set to work building his furnace. It took Two Blankets two days just to find out his name was Andrew Olafson, but he would only answer to Arms.

Her friendship with Aimee and Delores Sue also progressed, though

Two Blankets was never sure how much was reported to Marshall. She had to assume that they told all, and this made her more careful. The not knowing also served as an impediment to her friendship. But on the surface, at least, they were friendly, and they were the only two women at the Landing. When, after two weeks of hard labor, she delivered the Canadian Lynx pelt to her, Aimee was overwhelmed. She danced about the Landing, seemingly transfixed, and then kissed Two Blankets. Three times she kissed her, once on each cheek, and once upon the lips.

"Two Blankets, I have never had anyone give me anything like this. Never. I happily pay you the twenty dollars. I am totally pleased." There were tears in her eyes that streaked her careful makeup.

"Please, don't cry. You are ruining your makeup."

"I don't care. The life of a whore doesn't have many moments like this."

These were the only two women excepting Abigail Stafford. Two Blankets saw little of her in her infrequent visits to the Landing. Mrs. Stafford's attitudes were built as solid as a pole barn. She was unhappy with her husband and her circumstance, and she let anyone know it who was within earshot.

Two Blankets thought about how to build a cradleboard for her coming baby. Most Chinook cradleboards were carved like a tiny canoe, hollowed out from a log. She knew she didn't have the capability for this. Her carving skills were the weakest among the skills she did have. However, the *Nimi'ipuu* frequently wove their cradleboards. Cattail leaves were something she had in plenty, and she set about preparing them for the weaving.

First, she softened or "mellowed" the dried stalks she had previously collected. It was simply a matter of soaking the stalks in water, wrapping them and setting them aside to absorb the water. After a few hours, they were sufficiently softened to split and begin weaving. Her first effort was pitiful. Two Blankets could only laugh at her attempt, set it aside and begin again.

Over a period of weeks, she became confident in her technique. She had a serviceable cradleboard. It did not resemble, except superficially, the beautiful objects she remembered from her youth, objects as beautiful as the babies strapped within them, happily observing all that went on about them. But though it was not a beautiful example of the art, Two Blankets could tell it would serve. It was balanced. It had a head strap to carry it about or to hang it on a post or tree branch when she was working. A small frame protected the head from the danger of damage, as well as to serve as a shade protector from the sun. She lay the cradleboard at the head of her sleeping furs with the red fox fur within it.

Gilly was the exception that surprised everyone. He paid off his month and his ten dollar advance for the fine. His experience at tanning gave him hitherto unknown confidence, and the two men who worked with him adjusted to him as their supervisor. The other men were more reticent in that acceptance, but they did take him in as a regular member of the crew.

In late November, as the rainy season began to be felt in earnest, several of the men were let go or took a leave with the promise of work again come the next spring. Among these were the carpenter, Henry Haroldson, and his two apprentices, Ezekiel and Zebediah.

He took a look at the Landing as he waited upon the dock for the steamboat, *Jennie Clark.*

"It has been a good run, building this town. A good beginning. Last year when I saw the cases of windows and piles of lumber I would not have thought that it would turn out so fair."

Marshall Johnston shook his hand and gripped his shoulder. There was some genuine feeling in his words. "Henry, you done you and me proud. You really did. I'm hoping you will come back next spring."

"Let me know, Marshall. I liked the work. But, work is work. If we don't have a big project in the city, we'll be back."

———

TOWARD THE END of December, Two Blankets felt as if she could drop a baby or even two any day. She knew she had to pretend that she was only close to eight months since inception, but day after day such pretense became more and more difficult. She thought that Marshall would not be that hard to fool unless his suspicious mind started puzzling it out. She avoided him, and he, fortunately, avoided her.

Each day she brought drinking water in the whiskey bottles she had saved and wash water in sealed jars to the moon cycle hut. There was only a light snow as she hauled sleeping furs as well as spare clothes and such towels and clean cloths as she could find. Wood she brought as well, a large stack of it. Aimee and Delores Sue eyed her suspiciously. They had not been present when she first came back from Warm Springs, but they were quite capable of backing up to a date that was utterly unacceptable to her plans. Now, all she could do was wait and hope that, perhaps, she would be a few days to a week late in her delivery.

The new year came, and the celebrations at the Landing, mostly excessive drinking, came and went. Daily, it seemed that her belly became more swollen, though Two Blankets knew this could not be so. On January eighth, according to her calendar, her cramps began. Marshall was in Portland for two days, fortunately. It would be a blessing to have the father present, but he was not the father.

She walked, or rather waddled, to the moon cycle hut.

Though only early evening, it was already dark, and a light dusting of snow fell. Once there, she quickly started the fire she had already laid. It was freezing outside, as Two Blankets remembered many days colder wearing no clothes other than sandals. She walked back and forth. When the fire was going, she put on a pot of tea and a large clay jar of water on the edge of the fire to warm.

The hours passed. She had minor and a few major cramps, but knew it was not time yet. She drank her tea and sat for a time dwelling upon her spirit animals, White Mouse and Gray Wolf.

White Mouse sat as usual on her shoulder or occasionally upon her head. *Be at peace, Two Blankets. Be at peace.*

Gray Wolf, who almost never entered a dwelling place, lay down next to her, watching and waiting. *You are a healthy bitch. You will whelp a healthy pup, a fine girl pup.* She lay her head upon Two Blankets lap.

Sometime about midnight, the door flap opened, and Aimee entered. She looked tired from a night of pleasing the men, but she looked excited as well.

Delores Sue also came in. "So, this is where you've hidden yourself to birth this child."

"We been checking your longhouse every night for the last three days. Dolores Sue saw the smoke rising. I brought coffee."

"Holy Christo, it's cold."

"There are sleeping furs on the pallet. Sit down and cover yourselves. What are you doing here?"

"Honey, you think we were going to let you have this babe all by yourself? If this was back home, there'd be a passel of women in here. We're all you get." Delores Sue chuckled. "'Course, each of us is good as any two or three normal women." She poured Two Blankets a cup of coffee with five spoons of sugar and a cup for herself.

"Wait. I need to stand and walk." Two Blankets stood and took her cup. "It is better when I walk. Ow, goddamn it. That one hurt."

"How close are the cramps?" asked Delores Sue.

"Not more than four per handspan of sun or so, but getting closer."

"Well there ain't no sun now." Delores Sue held up her hand. "About four per hour, I'd say. You got some time then. Best to walk a bit, then rest a bit. I'd be surprised if you delivered before dawn."

Two Blankets tried to decide, while walking back and forth, occasionally interrupted by an increasingly strong and more frequently occurring cramp, what she perceived as most significant about her labors. She sat on her sleeping furs for a bit, took some coffee, and went outside to pee. She stood, resting with her hands on her knees and walked about again. She decided it was not the pain, though she knew that could come, and not the swollen belly nor the fatigue of carrying another life within her. It wasn't her aching back or sore ankles, though both made their pain evident. It was the tedium, the utter boredom with this experience. She was tired of this, ready for it to be over.

Occasionally she cursed. She cursed her condition, her aloneness, her pregnancy, and the women who were there to help her. Aimee, who had little experience with women, took offense, then just threw up her hands. Delores Sue, who had much experience, paid it little attention.

"Why are you here? You do not give a damn about me or this baby."

"No, I don't really. But there is little else going on here at the Landing to entertain me, so I just thought I'd drop by."

"Oh, I am sorry, Delores Sue. You know I did not mean that."

"I do, honey. I do. Time to get up and walk a bit."

"I take the apology back and give you the curse in return." Two Blankets took several minutes climbing to her feet. She threw off her sleeping fur. "It is too hot in here and—*oweee*—visions of all the creatures, that one hurt." She half squatted, her elbows on her knees, sweat beading her brow. Sweat now gleamed in the firelight across her entire naked body, her brow and throat, her heavy milk-full breasts, down her swollen belly to her thighs.

"I've seen horses do this with much less sweat or pain." She panted, catching her breath. "They just walk about, then drop the colt."

"It's easy for horses and cows. Baby humans is a different story. Try to walk some more."

Ponderously, because she now felt like a buffalo, she straightened and began walking. Slowly, she walked the length of the hut, turned and walked back. Again, she paced, up to the doorway and back past the fire. A cramp hit her, doubled her over, and suddenly as she partially straightened up, she broke her water. It wasn't water, of course, but a thin, blood-tinged fluid that ran down her legs.

"Ah, good, your water's broke. Aimee, give me a wet rag from that pot on the coals."

Aimee fetched a rag from the clay pot and handed it to Delores Sue. She wrung it out and shook it out to cool it. "Spread 'em, honey. Let me clean you up."

Delores Sue's hands were calm and gentle as she wiped the amniotic fluid off Two Blanket's legs. "There you go. It shouldn't be long now."

Two Blankets let her hand lay on Delores Sue's neck a moment. "Thank you, Delores Sue. I was going to do this alone. I was ready to do it alone or thought I was. But I am glad you are here for me, both of you."

Aimee answered easily. "Women's business is women's business."

"Walk some more now. Breathe slow and just walk."

Two Blankets took a deep breath and let it out. Then, she took a slower breath and released that one. She walked, turned, and walked. Walked, turned, and walked. It slowly became a pacing vision quest. Her movement became the rhythm of her step and her breath.

This is the place, the hollow in the tree where you find the birth. White Mouse clung to her hair and chirruped into her ear. *The glowing seed has grown and grown. Soon, soon, it will slip out.*

Two Blankets reached up and petted White Mouse. "I know, sweet girl. I know."

Aimee and Delores Sue just looked at her.

"It is almost as if she were in a trance," Aimee said.

"Well, it ain't a trance that will last longer than the next contraction."

Gray Wolf paced her step for step. *You can do this. You can do this. You are a strong and wild bitch like no one has ever seen before. You can deliver this little girl pup.*

The next contraction stopped her in her tracks and doubled her up again. After a time she straightened her back and sat in a squat. She panted, then calmed her breath and waited. In a few minutes, another contraction hit her body.

"I felt it move. The child is coming. Soon."

The child didn't come immediately, but it did come inexorably. The contractions were more frequent, though no more intense. Her breath seemed natural now, a combination of panting followed by relaxation followed by a contraction and more panting.

Now there was no more time, the birth was everything, all of her. Delores Sue knelt before her, her hands gently catching the head. When the child's shoulders cleared her vulva Delores Sue said, "Now, *push,* Two Blankets. Push that damn child out."

"I will push her out, the little girl pup."

Delores Sue caught the child. "Now how did she know that? It's a baby girl, a perfect girl as far as I can see." She handed the girl, still attached to her birth cord, which pulsed life into her, to Two Blankets.

"Sees-What-No-One-Else-Sees said you would be a girl and Gray Wolf too." Her whisper could hardly be heard.

"He sure could see what no one else seen. You want the cord tied now?"

Two Blankets licked the blood off the babies face. "Not yet. Wait for the afterbirth." She went back to cleaning the baby's face.

Aimee got another rag from the pot. "Let me have that baby. I can't sit here and watch you lick it."

Hesitantly, Two Blankets handed her the child. Aimee quickly wiped the child down and handed her back. The afterbirth slid from between her thighs and Aimee wiped her down there, too.

"Wait," said Two Blankets. "Wait, until it stops pulsing before you cut the cord."

Delores Sue looked at Aimee and shrugged her shoulders. She waited two or three minutes, then tied off the cord near to the baby and called, "Knife."

Aimee found the hunting knife and handed it to Delores Sue. "This is a mighty big knife for such a tiny thing." She cut the cord. "I will dispose of this."

"There is a small pouch I made for it. Among the *Nimi'ipuu*, the afterbirth is considered sacred, and we bury it. It is on the sleeping furs, next to the cradleboard."

Aimee searched while Delores Sue held the cord awkwardly. "Is this it?" She held out a small pouch, delicately beaded.

"Put the cord and afterbirth in it and close the flap. But first, cut a snip off the umbilical and put it in here, please." She took out another small bag.

"Whatever you say, honey." Aimee cut the snip of umbilical and handed the tiny bag back.

Two Blankets looped the thong from the bag with the snippet of cord around her daughter's neck. Two Blankets put the child to her breast. It took some time. A child suckling is not always an automatic response, but it is not hard to learn. As the baby suckled and she lay back on her furs, she turned to her friends, Delores Sue and Aimee.

"It is a big knife for a warrior child. My child. My Mira."

Delores Sue nodded. "Mira. Mira Johnston. I 'spect she ain't going to be no ordinary child."

Gray Wolf sniffed and laid his head against the now deeply sucking Mira. *This one learns faster than some others. This will be no ordinary bitch pup, this Mira of the Red Fox.*

———————

TWO BLANKETS SPENT the next two days alone with her child, though Delores Sue and Aimee visited when they could. Her schedule was almost the same as her baby Mira's was. When Mira woke and cried for food, Two Blankets gave her the breast and nursed. She lay dreamy-eyed, petting her child, stroking her hair. Though most would say *the child looks like you or the child looks like her father,* Two Blankets knew the truth. The child Mira of the Red Fox looked full on like an Indian, as she should. Her only hope lay in Marshall's ego that he could not conceive of anyone else fathering her child, or in his disinterest. Perhaps it would be both.

She lay Mira in her moss bag, a sack that laced up the front, filled with sphagnum moss, that had been kept in the smoke until any insects within it died. She laced it up snugly with Mira's legs straight and her arms crossed on her chest. Then she placed the baby bundle upon her cradleboard padded by the red fox fur turned fur side out. The legs with the claws she crossed across Mira, the skull with the teeth she pulled up and rested upon the headpiece. She laced her into the cradleboard. Mira was still, but her eyes tracked movement close to her constantly.

Once that was done, she quickly carried the baby through the light snow. She propped Mira up so she could see and removed her moccasins and table-cloth cape. No one was about, and the bathing pool was sufficiently secluded from most camp activity. She immersed herself in the January waters of the stream. It wasn't frozen over, but it was cold enough to be a shock. Two Blankets felt it first as a burning shock of cold, but a cold that almost felt like it burned the skin, then as a refreshing coldness. Steam rose from her body, as if she had just come from the sweat lodge.

She knew that would not last and rinsed her hair quickly, then climbed out of the pool, drew on her red and white cape and grabbed her moccasins. Mira seemed to watch the proceedings.

"I don't think you want a bath yet, sweet Mira of the Red Fox." She picked up the cradleboard and headed for her longhouse. It was chill within, but Two Blankets was glad she had asked Delores Sue to add a little wood to the fire and bank it. Hanging the cradleboard from a peg, she stirred the few coals back into life and added wood.

Two Blankets wrapped herself in her elk-skin, glad that it fit better now that she was no longer pregnant. She brushed out her hair and laced up her moccasins.

"Do I look good enough to visit the Landing, Mira? Your father should be there."

The words "your father" made her choke up. Mira's father would certainly not be there, but she could not say that, should not even think it. It would be such a kindness if Standing Bear could be there for this moment, even though he might have another wife.

She put the cradleboard on her back and walked up to the Landing. It was mid-afternoon, and the weather was foul, and quite possibly because Marshall had still not arrived, several of the crew were there. Delores Sue and Aimee welcomed her, and there was much "to do" about the baby, Mira of the Red Fox, as she was passed from hand to hand.

The whistle of the *Mary* and the hunger cries of Mira almost coincided. Aimee laughed, then Delores Sue. Several of the men chuckled.

Harry Everton laughed. "When that baby is hungry, she don't wait. She wants to be fed now."

The baby was passed, cradleboard and all, back to Two Blankets, who parted her dress and gave her the breast. Soon, Mira, almost totally hidden by the cradleboard, was happily suckling. The crew dispersed looking for anything to busy themselves. Harry went back to his drink and his plans.

Marshall opened the door and stomped his boots. "It's as cold as charity out there, not that I've ever seen any." He strode over to the bar, and Harry passed him the drink he had already poured.

"Good trip?"

"A successful one. What's happened here since I been gone? I see everyone is scurrying like grasshoppers looking for any grain they might've missed."

"Well, there has been a new addition to our company." Harry Everton motioned to Two Blankets.

Marshall looked, started, then walked over. Two Blankets detached Mira from her breast and handed the cradleboard to Marshall. "It is a baby girl, husband Marshall."

Marshall looked into the dark eyes. "Did you name her? When I wasn't here?"

"Her name is Mira."

"I was thinking of Elizabeth, if it was a girl, after my ma."

"Mira Elizabeth Johnston, then."

Mira began to cry, and Two Blankets took her back to her breast.

"You can't do that here. Your titties is all exposed."

"That is silly, husband Marshall. I am covered by my dress and by the cradleboard."

"It don't matter. Your titty is out. Everyone knows it. It's disgusting and wrong. You will have to do that elsewhere."

Two Blankets looked about, into the small crowd, who showed no support for Marshall's behavior, but also none for her own. All they seemed to allow was an interest in how this conflict would play out, and it could only play out one way.

"I feel it is *you* who is wrong, husband Marshall. The rutted thought patterns that you got from your ignorant parents, your mother and father, and that they got from their ignorant parents. That is what is disgusting and wrong, not this innocent baby."

The slap, when it came, rocked her almost off her chair. "Get out. Get out of here. You have no more modesty than a whore."

"I have more respect for these whores than I do for you." Two Blankets held her hand to the reddened mark on her face. "Do not think of sharing my furs, unless you want to leave them with your guts hanging out."

Two Blankets levered herself up off the chair.

Marshall turned to his men. "You see. You see how she disrespects her husband, her man."

No one responded.

Two Blankets stood straight and walked slowly to the Landing door. "For those who were not upset and expressed your congratulations and happy thoughts, I thank you." She opened the door and walked through, leaving it swinging agape.

MIRA:
YEAR ONE

CHAPTER 5
1858

THE FIRST DAY passed with Two Blankets in a fury. She tried to be calm when feeding Mira, but the rest of the time she spent in talking to herself. "How can he kick me out as if I had nothing to do with the success of the Landing? Oh, all right, he is a man, a *whiteman* in a *whiteman's* world. I should have known that. But I was happy before, and now I am sad."

Then she cried. Her anger could no longer keep it at bay. Mira was propped against the disused bar watching. Her tears were angry, to begin with, then sad and forlorn, then they became the sobs of the totally lost. She cried for almost a half hour before she ran out of tears. Several times, she tried to break out in tears once more, but there were no more.

Are you quite finished? Gray Wolf did not look concerned or sorry at all. *I wouldn't want to interrupt.*

"Damn, you. Can I not even have a half day to be happy?"

I misunderstood. I thought you were feeling sorry for yourself. Let me know when you are finished being happy. She lay down and looked up at Two Blankets, waiting.

"I am not happy. I am mad."

You are a wolf, in part. A lone wolf bitch without a pack. And you have a cub.

"Marshall has a pack. He is *Tyee* of the Landing."

You can submit, be docile, and be first wife of the Tyee.

"I don't want that. The first wife of the *Tyee* is *not* docile."

You have chosen, then, not he. He has not changed. You cannot go back to the Chinook and be mistshimus. *You must be a lone wolf or find your own pack. I, Gray Wolf, will be of Two Blanket's pack.*

"You *are* pack, dear one."

You, Mira, and I are pack. We will run where the snow has no tracks. There will be many times we will go hungry, but when we make a kill, the blood will run from our jaws hot and sweet.

White Mouse tucked her head beneath Two Blankets hair where it touched her shoulders. *And what of me? What of White Mouse? Am I not pack?*

Does the vision of mouse blood seeping from your jaws make the saliva run from your body, little one?

Mouse blood? No. I do not eat meat, but I still care as much as you about Two Blankets and Mira.

"White Mouse is pack, too."

I am happy no other wolf can hear this. A prey as pack. Impossible. Gray Wolf turned away and lay down near the fire.

Two days later, in the early hours, Mr. Gilly slipped in to record the number of eggs collected. Two Blankets watched him as he wrote his total. There was something there, a little more confidence, maybe, but definitely, something that showed itself in an undefined manner.

"Mister Gilly." Two Blankets sat up from her nursing of Mira on her furs.

"Missus Johnston. I'm sorry. I didn't mean to disturb you."

"Do not worry, Mister Gilly. My knife is sheathed for you."

Mr. Gilly paled. "Now, I am nervous, a bit. I mean, I didn't never think you would gut me. There's talk, but I never did nothing against you."

"Your project with the hides is done. Would you like to learn the next steps in tanning?"

"I think I would. We would have to get Mister Johnston's approval."

"Perhaps you could rent the storage shed as a tanning shed, just like the blacksmith did."

"Maybe. I will have to think about how to ask Mister Johnston."

"Think about it. We have a lot of hides."

"I will." Gilly exited the longhouse.

Later on in the afternoon, there was a scratching at the door flap and an immediate entrance by Delores Sue with a stew pot and Aimee with coffee and a plate of bread. Two Blankets rose up to a sitting position on her sleeping furs.

Delores Sue set the stew aside and searched for bowls. "Don't mind us, honey. We're just planning a little meal."

Aimee set out her bread and coffee and found spoons for the stew. "Do you have sugar for the coffee?"

"I have a honeycomb."

"Now, let me see that baby. It's been two days, and they grow uncommon fast." Delores Sue picked up the cradleboard. Mira followed her with her dark eyes, once she got close. "She don't seem to mind this, what did you call it?"

"A cradleboard."

"A cradleboard. She don't seem to mind it at all. I only seen white babies before, mostly whore's children. They are always left lying loose and later crawling everywhere. You could take this cradleboard everywhere with you."

"Yes, that is the idea. The baby goes everywhere and sees everything. Let's hang her up by the bar and eat."

Delores Sue stroked the small wisp of dark hair. "I don't want to let her go."

Two Blankets hung her on a peg near the bar. "I am happy you came by. I was afraid I would not see you again."

Aimee poured the coffee. "But for Missus Stafford, we're the women of the camp. Child business is women's business."

Two Blankets started to spoon in honey. Delores Sue laid her hand across Two Blankets'. "Careful, honey. Last time you had coffee, you was pregnant. You might not like it tasting like syrup anymore."

Two Blankets stirred the one spoonful and tasted it. "This is fine just like this. Are you sure I used to drink it with five spoonfuls of sugar?"

"Oh, you did. Anyway, speaking of child business, my grandma used to say, "Woman provides the furrow, then man plants the seed. After that, he is pretty much done with the project. Up to the woman from then on."

Aimee nodded. "Like I said, children is women's business. They'll come along after about ten years and interfere then with what the boys should do, who the girls can see, but until that time, it's all ours."

"That is much different from the way the tribe does it. It is true that women care for the children mostly, but everyone takes an interest, from the oldest man to the young girls. I will have to get used to this new way."

"In your case, I'd say it may be a blessing. Some men are way more trouble than they're worth. Mind you, I never said that about any *particular* man." Aimee looked at Two Blankets in a serious and warning way.

"No, you never said it. But I will remember it always. Thank you."

Delores Sue picked up the stew pot and the empty coffee pot. "Well, Aimee, we better get ourselves back to the Landing."

"Yes, I suppose you're right." She wrapped her lynx fur about her shoulders.

"I am glad you like the fur, Aimee. It looks wonderful on you, and so warm."

"I'm always cold here in the winter." She stroked the fur. "But this helps."

"I'd say, wait a couple more days, then feed baby Mira and bring her to the Landing. Long as you don't nurse her there, you'll be fine," Delores Sue said.

Two Blankets began to sputter a protest.

"I know. I know. Every woman in this country— 'cepting maybe women like Missus Stafford—been through this. It's perfect natural, it is. But men gotta make a fuss about it. Believe me, Two Blankets, you can't win this one. You just can't."

"I will follow your advice, Delores Sue. I won't make it an issue."

"Enough said. Aimee, let's get on up to the Landing and see who we can start our enchantment on for this evening."

Aimee laughed. "Darling, you're so handsome, and you still have some of your teeth."

Two Blankets waited until the following day when Mr. Gilly was finished with his feeding and collecting chores. She fed Mira and watched her eyes as she focused for a few moments at a time upon her face. From the time she was born, she seemed to respond to Two Blanket's voice. This sustained her, and Two Blankets talked to her continually.

She unstrapped her from the cradleboard and moss bag. New moss and a quick washing down and Mira was ready for travel. She rewrapped the baby in the moss bag, then lay her on her red fox fur and strapped her in. Mira was already drowsing.

Two Blankets opened the Warm Springs box and took out the placenta bag. She tucked it into her dress and put the tumpline across her forehead. With the cradleboard comfortable on her back, she picked up her knife and strapped it on.

Exiting the longhouse, she scanned the Landing and the sky. Because of the weather, the camp was mostly vacant, though she could hear the rhythmical clanging of the blacksmith. There was only an inch of snow, and a few flakes swirled down from a gray sky. Two Blankets thought it would snow heavier as the day went on. The *Nch'i-wána* flowed by, its surface as gray as the sky, but shiny like a polished, darkened stone.

She turned toward the Landing and just before she reached the stream bent her path into the woods along the new road Marshall built. The road had torn into the forest along its side, and Two Blankets hoped she would be able to identify the place. The place was a small opening into the undergrowth leading to a clearing in the forest where she had spent time alone when Virgil and Henry had roamed the empty camp.

Before that, was the night I spent here with Standing Bear.

Tears moistened her eyes. She walked up the road until she thought she was near. The roughness of the cut the sawyer had made alongside the road, as well as the brush and branches—lopped off and left behind—nearly obscured the rabbit trail that led to the side. She pushed aside the dead branches and slipped within. It was only a short distance now to the place she sought.

When she entered the small glade she fell to her knees.

I had not expected it to be like this. It is just a clearing.

But the memory of her time spent here with Standing Bear—the last time when nothing was expected, when they had only sought the pleasures of each other's bodies, the pleasures of *wootlat* and *skutch*—washed her like a spring flood.

I will always have the memory. And I will have you, Mira.

She found a likely spot near a red cedar and leaned the cradleboard against the great tree.

She removed the packet and held it close to Mira. "This is the afterbirth from your entrance into the world. I am going to bury it here, so we will always be able to find it."

She dug with the knife, first clearing away the leaves and moss. The ground was not frozen, soft enough to dig easily. When she had a hole about two feet deep—"Two U.S. government feet, "Two Blankets whispered with a smile—she held the packet in front of her mouth and kissed it. She had applied a beading representing a towering bear standing over a gray wolf. It wasn't an exceptional beading job, as her beading was not much better than Standing Bear's, but she would never be able to tell him that.

Especially now, I will never be able to tell him. Too many things I will never share with the warrior I love.

She placed the bag into the hole and covered it up, then placed rocks over the spot. She did not want a wolf or other predator digging it back up.

"I do not know any ritual that goes with this burial. I have never seen one. I can only say goodbye."

She cleaned the knife and sheathed it, then picked up Mira's cradleboard and swung it onto her back, adjusting the tumpline across her forehead. Backing out of the clearing, she brushed off her footprints until she reached the edge of the road. Brush and branches were here in plenty, and she tossed discarded branches across the rabbit trail.

"Anyone who did not know it was there would never see it."

With a sense of completion, of something important finished and done with, she walked back down the road. The snow was coming down thickly now, she could only see a few feet in front of her, and it was two or three inches deep, covering her moccasins with each step.

But snow held no fear for her. She knew where she was, and she would be at the longhouse and the warmth of a fire in a few more minutes.

EVENTS FLOWED ONWARD, for the next year, and often significant events took several years to reach culmination. Though to Two Blankets, her life proceeded day by day as always, some days, and even months seemed to merge together. She had set herself to oppose Marshall, but covertly. She had her child, she kept reminding herself. That was the critical part, the element that must be protected no matter what other accommodations she must make. She found that he paid her little attention as long as she did not nurse in public and as long as she did not challenge him. She had learned that lesson and did not need to learn it again.

One event that took her by surprise was the transformation of Mr. Gilly. One morning during the summer of 1858, according to her calendar, if one could add another year to the one at the top of the calendar, he entered to make his marks on the egg tally sheet.

"Good morning to you, Missus Two Blankets Johnston."

Two Blankets saw that he was dressed in a new suit of clothes, not fancy like Mr. Shales, but definitely new. "Mister Gilly."

"Would you mind coming outside for a moment? I would like to discuss something with you."

"Certainly." She picked up Mira's cradleboard, the coffee pot, two cups, and went outside to the big table. Leaning the cradleboard against a bench, she poured coffee for Mr. Gilly and herself.

"Coffee, Mister Gilly?"

"Yes, ma'am. Thank you, ma'am."

"Your outfit is very becoming—if that is the right word."

Mr. Gilly blushed. "It ain't quite. It is more a word used to describe a woman, but I take it as a compliment coming from you. Remember when you said you might be willing to teach me to tan hides? I don't know if you remember offering, or if you really meant it...."

Two Blankets stirred a spoonful of honey into her coffee and swallowed a bit. She smiled. "*Whitemans* are always in such a hurry to bargain or do business. Yes, of course, I remember, and I *did* mean it. Though I am only a journeyman at best. You need to know that."

"You are better than anyone else here, and that is the truth. Marshall says I can rent the storehouse for six dollars a month if I want to tan. He will give me a share in the hides that are there, and I can trade for others on my own."

She took another swallow. "Know that my husband Marshall is an expert trader. I have only seen the Chinook get the better of him."

"Oh, I well know that, but he has been fair to me, especially considering I come in with Small Willie. I know I won't get the better of him in trade, but it is a chance for me to make a better place."

Two Blankets held up her hand. "I was just giving warning. Yes, I would be glad to teach you what I know. It will be fun in a way, as long as I don't have to do it myself."

"I can't pay you much, but—"

"No pay. But perhaps we can trade, or exchange as a *potlatch* between friends, yes?"

Mr. Gilly stood up and held out his hand. "A deal then?"

She shook his hand in *whiteman's* fashion. "A bargain, Mister Gilly."

He went off to the remainder of his chores whistling.

———

THE STAFFORDS VANISHED sometime during the late spring. This event did not seem to bother Marshall or even take him by surprise. They had apparently taken their wagons some several miles downriver to a natural slope toward the *Nch'i-wána,* winched them down, chopped down trees, built rafts, and departed.

"The Lord delivered them penniless unto my hands, and penniless they departed," was Marshall's only comment one evening when she sat in her regular place. "Meantime, I got a little labor from them and a small cabin."

Marshall had some fortune finding another tenant to farm the plains, and they arrived in early summer with wagon, wife, and three children. Two Blankets only glimpsed them in passing. She did hear their names, though—Zeke and Mary Kinley, and their children: Polly, James, and Michael. Their wagon spent a night in the Landing yard and then headed up the road to the high ground. The two boys drove a herd of some twenty cattle and two goats behind.

In the fall of the same year, the Landing had an unusual visitor. It was not as if a visitor were unusual. Traders from the paddle-wheelers frequently stopped for a day or two, to drink at the Landing and make what trade they could. The blacksmith occasionally got business from The Dalles. But this visitor did seem to be different.

As she watched the *Mary* at the dock, she saw him walking down the gangplank, followed by a heavily laden horse and a pack mule. Though she had seen many get off and on the paddle-wheelers during her time here, this one seemed different. He was tall, almost extremely tall—what Standing Bear would call over "six U.S. Government feet." His clothing was unusual, as well. He still wore a suit of crisply creased wool, black pants, jacket and vest, topped by a bowler, but a bowler somewhat different from what was common. The cut of his suit seemed different, too, though she could not identify the difference. His shirt was immaculately white. In short, though his clothing was not immediately different from those around him, it was just different enough.

She had just finished her midday feeding of Mira and judged it safe to go up to the Landing. But first, she would dress up a little herself. Though she didn't have many options, she made the most of them and left her longhouse feeling good about herself.

Delores Sue and Aimee were there in their usual places and gestured her to join them. Several of the crew were finishing up their midday meal. Marshall was there as well, with his typical whiskey in hand when the visitor entered.

Aimee adjusted her Canada Lynx fur, though it was warm in the room. "Ah, a handsome man, though he is a bit dark for my taste."

Indeed, the man's features *were* dark, more of a tone of stained wood. His hair was as black as Two Blankets', his eyebrows bold.

Two Blankets leaned forward. "His cheekbones are quite high, don't you think? Does he have Native blood?"

"I think—" Aimee thought a bit, gnawing on a knuckle, then caught herself. "I think he's a Creole."

The man introduced himself to a suspicious Marshall, then stepped over to the three women. He removed his hat, spilling his dark locks. Clean shaven, his features were sharp, as if carved from his face. He bowed deeply.

"Good day, ladies. It is a happy occasion when I meet three women as beautiful as you. I am Jean Michel Bayonne." He lifted each woman's hand in turn, beginning with Delores Sue and ending with Two Blankets, and lightly brushed the fingertips with his lips, his black eyes never leaving the gaze of the woman he viewed. Somehow he managed to make a simple greeting into a quiet invitation.

"I'm Delores Sue, Mister Bayonne." She blushed under the thickness of her makeup.

"I am very pleased to greet you, Miss Delores Sue."

"Aimee, *Monsieur* Jean Michel. I believe we are from the same country."

"I am always happy to meet a fellow woman from France. Even at this great distance, Paris dances in our blood."

"Missus Two Blankets Johnston. I am happy to meet you."

"Ah, *you* are the esteemed Two Blankets. You are both warm and beautiful. *mon cherie.*"

Marshall said, "They're just whores, Jean, no need to fawn over them. Have a drink on the house."

"I do not mean to be contrary, *Monsieur* Johnston. They are all women. A beautiful woman is a flower wherever you find her."

"Like I said, 'round here women equals whores. Whores equals women. All the same."

"This Landing is your place, *Monsieur.* We must agree to disagree."

Marshall turned back to the bar. "Let's have a drink, and we'll talk trade."

Monsieur Jean Michel Bayonne turned to Two Blankets. "This is your *bébé?*" Mira looked levelly into his face, without blinking and without fear. "She is a brave child."

"Yes. She is Mira, and she is a female warrior."

"I can see that. *Mademoiselle* Mira, I am very pleased to meet you." He bowed deeply and paid her the same compliment, with the same amount of seriousness, as he had to the other three women. "Perhaps I will see you tomorrow morning, *Madame* Two Blankets, if you want to trade."

Delores Sue fanned herself with a handkerchief. "My, oh my, I would call that man sex with a capital "S.""

Marshall confronted *Monsieur* Bayonne. "You look like you got some Indian in you. And maybe some nigra, as well. That true, Mister Bayonne?"

"I am a free Creole of color, if you will. We have always been free men and women. If you are speaking of my ancestors, they were French and West African."

"So, you *are* a nigra?"

"I am a free man. My people have always been free."

"Well, I don't know. We got territorial laws here in Oregon that don't allow no nigras, but let's have a drink, anyways."

The next day, *Monsieur* Bayonne walked his horse and mule toward Two Blankets' longhouse. Behind him, she could see Delores Sue and Aimee. Hurrying, she brought out her coffee pot and several cups. She thought, then brought out *camas* cakes as well.

"I will see how he likes native food."

He bowed and brushed his lips across her fingertips. "Good day, *Madame* Two Blankets Johnston."

"Good morning. Please, call me Two Blankets. Will you have some coffee and *camas* cake?"

"You are generous, thank you. I suspect you are like the Chinook. You do not rush to bargain."

"I *am* Chinook. We say to rush to bargain is like the salmon rushing upstream. We consider it uncivilized."

He sat, and Delores Sue and Aimee sat also. "Perhaps, it is also like the hunting of the buffalo. There is a time that is right for that, as well, as the Nez Perce believe?"

Two Blankets ducked her head, then straightened and looked him in the eyes. "You have caught me out. It is true. I am *Nimi'ipuu.* But I was Chinook after and for longer. I am Chinook, as well." She poured the coffee.

He took the coffee with grace, though it was only a tin cup. She noticed that his hands were clean and his nails trimmed neatly. "Believe me, *Madame* Two Blankets, I had no wish to catch you out, as you say. I have made a casual study of the various native tribes. You have the look of the Nez Perce as my people would say. The *Nimi'ipuu,* as you more correctly speak of them."

Delores Sue set her cup down. "Can we look at what you have brought, *Monsieur* Bayonne?"

He eyed Two Blankets who nodded. "Ah, some are like the salmon." He went to the mule, loosened the diamond hitch, and drew out several packets from beneath the canvas. "I brought a few things. I have a wagon in Oregon City, but it is not worth it to bring the whole wagon to The Dalles, not with sternwheeler freight charges." He lay the packets on the table and unrolled them. There were needles and sewing supplies, beads and other decorations, lace, and small fabric pieces. Delores Sue and Aimee immediately began 'ooo'ing and ah'ing' over this piece and that one. *Monsieur* Bayonne took a healthy bite of a *camas* cake. "This is quite good. There is a bit of sweetness to it. I have seen the work needed to prepare it while I was with the *Nimi'ipuu*."

"Thank you, sir. Let us see what you have to bargain."

The three women searched through and commented on virtually everything. It was a joy to examine his goods. Aimee finally bought a glass bead necklace and a small inlaid pocketknife. Delores Sue purchased a set of ribbons for her hair, and Two Blankets searched through his bead collection and bought a handful. Finally, they settled, and he rolled up his canvas packets and stowed them on his mule.

"I thank you, ladies. Until the next time we meet." He swept them a bow and headed down toward the dock.

VISIT BY BAYONNE

CHAPTER 6
1859

TWO BLANKETS MARKED the beginning of 1859 by visiting the burying place of her placenta. Typically, among the *Nimi'ip-uu* or the Chinook, the placenta was not something to be marked ceremonially, although it was treated as sacred. Two Blankets used this day as a marker of Standing Bear, as well as Mira's birthday.

She rose before the dawn, dressed in her best native garb, and took Mira with her to the burial place. She knew where it was now and found it easily, a quarter mile up the creek. The day was cold, with a wind blowing as it so often did at this time of year, though no snow was on the ground, or threatened.

She entered the small clearing and hung Mira, in her cradleboard, where she could see. Mira's eyes tracked everything, watched all. Her hands were free now, and she played with the small dreamcatcher hanging over her head.

Two Blankets knelt on a piece of canvas she had brought with her and lay a piece of salmon and a *camas* cake in front of the small pile of stones that served as a shrine of sorts.

"I come here dear Standing Bear, Bone Rattler, Stinging Nettle, and to you especially, Moon Song, in remembrance of what you have done for me. I bring Mira, my daughter, with me so she may also. Let my modest offering pass on to you."

She bowed low over the shrine and held the bow for a time, then got up and, placing the cradleboard across her back, backed out of the grove, hiding her recent visit with a brushing away of all footprints. In another half hour, she had returned to the Landing.

She set down the cradleboard and unlaced it. Mira crawled into her lap and nursed a bit. Two Blankets knew she wasn't really hungry, but it was still a bonding experience. Mira looked up at Two Blankets and murmured. "Mama. Mama."

It warmed her, though she knew in *Nimi'ipuu,* the word for mother was not "mama." That word was "pike." *Mama* was Mira's first word, and she said it when she meant mother. Two Blankets stroked Mira's straight black hair and relaxed into her furs.

In another month, on February 14th, per the newest calendar she had been able to convince Marshall to give her, there was an extraordinary event in the evening. She'd learned of the event when she visited the Landing.

Upon entering, there was an air of excitement, something that could be felt even if one did not know exactly what it was.

She sat down with Delores Sue and Aimee, propping Mira in another chair.

"Mama. Mama. *Mama.*"

"You see, she knows you. Mama. Yes, that is mama. Your mama." Delores Sue spoke in a babyish tongue.

"*Máma* means wife's brother's child in *Nimi'ipuu.* I don't speak English to her, but it was just her first word."

"Well, she must speak English, then. You *are* her mama."

Two Blankets just shrugged. There was no arguing with Delores Sue when she was in this mood. She looked about and saw there were many men in the Landing. Most were drinking and talking loudly.

"What is happening here? I don't ever remember seeing it like this."

"You don't know?" Aimee gestured to the men. "You don't know why everyone is incredibly excited?"

"No, I honestly do not."

"Today is February 14."

"I *do* know that, from my calendar."

"Today, Oregon becomes a state. A free state in the United States."

"A state. That is like a tribe in a group of tribes? Or a clan in a tribe?"

Delores Sue waved her hands. "Don't worry about that part, Two Blankets. It is too complicated for this woman to understand."

Harry Everton walked over. "Good day, ladies. It *is* important. Being recognized as a state means we got more power to determine our own affairs. We ain't a territory anymore, and we'll have Senators and Congressmen in the government in Washington."

"That doesn't sound so complicated. It is like the *Oglála* became a member of the Seven Council Fires or the Great Sioux Nation as you know it."

Delores Sue and Aimee looked at Two Blankets like she was speaking a foreign language.

Harry Everton thought a moment. "Your analogy isn't exact, but it is appropriate. Very much like that."

"Of course, the *Oglála* have been Sioux for many hundreds of summers. In that sense it is different."

Harry laughed. "You are full of surprises Two Blankets. Full of surprises, but you are right again."

"Well, I never," said Delores Sue. "How you learn all that, Two Blankets?"

"When I was young, I listened to the storytellers of the *Nimi'ipuu.*"

"Well, I never listened too much at school, and my folks didn't talk much 'bout nothing. I knew you was Nimypoo or Nez Perce. How you learn about the Sioux?"

"The *Nimi'ipuu* traded with the western Sioux."

Aimee took a sip of her drink. "It is important to know as much as you can about your past."

Two Blankets mused. "Perhaps, we Indians are the old people, and our time is passing. The *whitemans* are children, but they are many and their time is coming."

"You come back tonight, and you 'll see something special."

Though Two Blankets asked several times, all she could get was "fireworks" and "come back tonight."

When she returned to the space in front of the Landing, everyone seemed to be there. The ground in the small clearing was filled with strange devices like tubes. Everyone, even those who did not usually drink, had a bottle or a glass, and Two Blankets accepted a tin cup filled with a strong smelling liquid.

Marshall, who was drunker than usual, held his bottle to the sky. "Today is a special day. Everyone will remember it, the day Oregon became a free state in these here United States." He took a big gulp. "Raise your glass—or bottle, or tin cup—to the new state of Oregon."

The glasses, bottles, and tin cups lifted to the sky and came down as one. Some drank theirs off in one gulp. Two Blankets took a sip and choked down the burn of the cheap whiskey. The words, "To Oregon," rang out on the evening air.

Marshall lit the first fireworks within reach then ran about lighting them with a pattern in mind. Suddenly the air was filled with fire. The red, white, and blue fire turned the night into day, a day that sparkled in every set of eyes.

"To Oregon," rang out again.

"As fireworks go, it ain't much. but for the Landing, it ain't too bad."

Two Blankets stood enthralled. "Truly, I have never seen anything like it in my life. So do the children impress their elders."

———————

THE ROUTINES OF life, of harvest, preparation for storage, and cooking for a woman basically alone, began to shape the life of Two Blankets. There was some early herb gathering in the spring, the collection of the stalks in the late spring and early summer, cattail heads in the fall. Salmon to spear in the spring run during April and May, and again in the larger fall run.

She had skins to tan and the intermittent instruction of Mr. Gilly. Always, she had the daily cleaning and cooking chores for herself and Mira. Marshall did not intrude on these plans. He had absented himself at the Landing. This was a blessing in most regards, though occasionally she did miss even his company. Then, she would think about what it meant, shake her head, and wonder why she had even had the thought in the first place.

Always there was the daily growth of her child. Though not evident when examined day by day, over a period of weeks or months her progress to becoming a person was self-evident. Her language skills expanded slowly at first, then more rapidly. Her physical skills transitioned quickly from arm waving to crawling, to dragging herself up on any object within reach to stand, to walking. She nursed only occasionally now, mostly when she seemed to want the closeness rather than out of need. Two Blankets allowed it. Nursing gave her the same sense of closeness that it did to Mira.

One day, in late spring of 1859, while the mornings were still crisp, frost was still the rule, and the days warmed rapidly, Two Blankets sat in the Landing with her friends Aimee and Delores Sue. They still dressed nicely and put on some makeup before they came down the stairs. They enjoyed playing and making a fuss over Mira.

Two Blankets had made Mira an outfit of the buckskin she had tanned. It consisted of a wraparound skirt and a jacket of sorts with a rabbit skin collar. She had beaded the jacket with an image on one side of Celilo Falls and on the other a salmon, using some of the beads she had bought from *Monsieur* Bayonne. Mira seemed to love it, spinning to make the skirt flare out.

Today, she had brought Mira without the cradleboard, and she was busy walking from the table to the bar and back to the table. Then, she would laugh, pleased with her achievement. She would repeat the journey, to all intents as serious as the grave upon her goal, return, and then laugh.

Two Blankets, Aimee and Delores Sue all laughed when Mira did, then made serious faces when Mira traveled her loop to the bar and back.

Otherwise, the Landing was empty for the time being. Mira was just returning when the door opened, and *Monsieur* Jean Michel stepped through. Mira reached the table, and all laughed. Then they noticed *Monsieur* Jean Michel and covered their faces and giggles with a hand, or for Two Blankets, just by ducking her head.

"Good afternoon, *Monsieur* Bayonne. Believe me, we were not laughing at you."

Delores Sue giggled. "No, we were not. Hello *Monsieur* Jean Michel. We are pleased to see you here."

"It always delights me to stop at the Landing, to see the lovely000 ladies." *Monsieur* Jean Michel Bayonne doffed his bowler and bowed.

Mira completed her return and burst out with her laugh, followed by simultaneous giggles from the three women. Bayonne looked up, paused a moment, then laughed himself. His was a hearty laugh, without sarcasm, just a chuckle that originated from deep within him.

"I can see one beautiful lady who takes what she is doing as more important than the appearance of *Monsieur* Bayonne."

Mira walked to stand slightly behind Two Blankets.

Monsieur Bayonne knelt before Mira, then bowed as deeply as before. "*Mademoiselle* Mira, I am *Monsieur* Jean Michel Bayonne. I am very happy to meet you again."

"The man is so tall," Mira said to Two Blankets.

"Yes, he is. If you wish you may offer him your hand in greeting, like this." She offered her hand, and *Monsieur* Bayonne brushed it with his lips.

"Very pleased," she said.

Mira held out her hand. "I want, too."

Monsieur Jean Michel lifted her tiny hand gently to his lips and kissed it. "Very pleased to greet you, *Mademoiselle* Mira."

Mira looked to her mother then to Jean Michel. "Very peased." She smiled a tiny smile for Jean Michel.

Aimee got up and fetched a cup for *Monsieur* Bayonne and poured coffee for him. "Now, we got all the introductions done. You are looking particularly fine today."

Monsieur Bayonne gave Mira's hand a squeeze suitable for a person as small as she was and sat down. "You are too kind *Mademoiselle* Aimee. I enjoyed our last little visit, and I have been looking forward to this one ever since."

Aimee blushed in what she thought a pretty way. "Oh, *Monsieur* Bayonne, you are so genteel, such a gentleman."

He greeted Delores Sue in the same way and then sat down to chat a bit about various innocuous frontier elements. They talked about Oregon's statehood and the fireworks display. After a half hour of this *Monsieur* Bayonne bowed out for a few minutes and returned with several canvas wraps which he unrolled upon the table. Many exclamations ensued especially by Aimee, who, it seemed to Two Blankets, was overdoing it.

Perhaps this is just the way of a whiteman woman among the men of their kind,
though she is not so extravagant among the men of the camp.

Gray Wolf sniffed. *She smells like a bitch in heat.*

Two Blankets swatted at Gray Wolf's head, though her hand went right
through. *You, sometimes, can be quite crude.*

The three of them examined each piece he brought out. Delores Sue finally bought a pair of fine linen handkerchiefs with elaborate embroidery.
Aimee bought a carved ivory hairpiece which she finagled Monsieur Bayonne into placing into her black locks. Two Blankets bought more beads,
two needles for beading, and one for sewing.

Then, *Monsieur* brought out something small and soft. It was a tiny bonnet. It was white, with just a bit of lace.

"I hope I have not erred in bringing this for Mira. If I have, I apologize.
No offense or supposition is intended. It is just a gift for her."

Two Blankets placed it upon Mira's head and tied it beneath her chin. She
shook her head and the lace ruffled in the breeze. Two Blankets held up the
small mirror *Monsieur* Bayonne provided. Mira looked at herself, touched
the cloth and the lace and looked to her mother.

"It is from *Monsieur* Bayonne. If you like it, you must thank him."

"It is not necessary to thank me."

"It is. Mira, do you like it?"

Mira buried her head beneath her mother's arm. "Yes."

"Then you must thank, *Monsieur* Bayonne. You know how to do it."

Mira stood straight and stepped forward. "Thank you."

"You are very welcome, *Mademoiselle* Mira."

"Thank you, *Monsieur* Bayonne," said Two Blankets.

"Please, call me Jean Michel."

The door to the Landing opened, and Marshall and Harry Everton entered. Three or four other men followed.

"Excuse me please, ladies." *Monsieur* Bayonne stood to greet the men.
"Mister Johnston. Mister Everton. Gentlemen." He bowed over his bowler.

"Well, if it ain't the Indian trader. Or the nigra one. I can't figure ought
which yet."

"Mister Johnston, I am a free Creole of color. Perhaps this is the time to add a new category to your categories of humans."

"I don't see no reason to do that, but I will trade with anyone, whatever color they are, and I'll drink with anyone I trade with." With that non-apology, he grabbed up a bottle and poured himself and *Monsieur* Bayonne a drink. He passed the bottle. "Pour for the rest, Harry."

Monsieur Bayonne lifted his glass. "To the State of Oregon."

"To Oregon." The others concurred and lifted and drank.

"I see you been selling gimcracks to my women."

"As you say, I trade with anyone worthwhile."

"They're all whores. Trade with them if you want. You want more than trade, you gotta pay."

Two Blankets got up to leave. She whispered a "good-bye" to Delores Sue and Aimee and gathered Mira into her.

"Marshall, I am only here for trade, I assure you."

Marshall Johnston turned to the other men. "Maybe you just ain't into women." He laughed. "Let's see what you got to trade."

Two Blankets scooted out the door while the men were still at the bar.

————————

MAY CAME AND the fishing and spearing of salmon. Though previously most salmon fishing had been done at Celilo Falls, since the tribe had been restricted to the reservation, Two Blankets had speared salmon. She couldn't catch twenty or thirty in a day, like a fisherman at the falls, but she could still spear three or four. She enjoyed it, something about the challenge of the wait until precisely the right moment, then the plunge of the spear and success and a salmon, or an empty spear and another wait.

Mira enjoyed the fishing, as well, though she had to spend it in her cradleboard. Two Blankets could not watch her and the salmon at once. But she did notice Mira watching, her hands tightly clasped, until a salmon was wriggling on the end of the spear. Then, she threw her arms out and said, *"Názog. Názog."*

Somehow it did not seem like a backbreaking routine when it was punctuated with Mira's cries of, *"Názog. Názog."*

During the early summer, she harvested cattail fronds. In the more swampy areas near the entrance of the stream to the great *Nch'i-wána* was a cluster from which she would collect the stalks, and later in the fall, the tops for the fluff.

With Mira on her cradleboard, so she didn't fall into the water, Two Blankets waded in the shallow water, taking some stalks from each plant and piling them onto the bank. This was the second day of harvesting, and sweat rolled down her forehead. Her hair was tied back into a tail, and she wore her worst skirt and the old red and white tablecloth cape tied in front as a cover-up.

The whistle from the approaching paddle-wheeler sounded from down river. She straightened and watched it pull around the bluff and head toward the dock. The boat was new to the Landing this year, the *Carrie Ladd,* white and bright and shiny, another new sternwheeler captained by Mr. John Ainsworth. As she watched, *Monsieur* Bayonne came down the gangplank, looking as crisp as ever. Two Blankets ducked down.

"Why am I hiding from *Monsieur* Bayonne? I am a working woman and a married one besides." Nevertheless, she still stooped and watched. She checked her *tatoosh*. Nothing showing. Below, nothing but leg below the knee. Her clothing would have to do if she were seen.

He looked about the Landing, then spotting her, he led his animals over toward her.

"Now, I am truly caught." She straightened up with an armload of stalks as if that were her intention all along.

"Good afternoon, *Madame* Johnston." He bowed as was his wont. "May I help carry some of those?"

She gave over the stalks, bent to take another armload, then swung Mira's cradleboard onto her other hip. They walked up to her longhouse side by side. Once there, they dropped their bundles and returned for another load. *Monsieur* Bayonne fetched his grazing animals. He loaded a pile on top of the mule and strolled with him alongside Two Blankets.

Monsieur Bayonne brushed off his suit. Two Blankets attempted to assist, but he was still covered with dust and little pieces of cattail.

"You will require a more serious brushing, I am afraid."

Monsieur Bayonne took off his coat and was brushing off the sleeves. "Yes, but, it is not the first time I have seen dirt."

Marshall walked up. "I see you're over here sniffing around my wife again, Mister Bayonne."

"Excuse me, sir, I was just carrying the stalks for her. No disrespect intended to you or to her."

"Every time I see you, you're near her snuffling with that French nose. I'm just warning you. I don't know what you were used to back there in New Orleans. I've heard you don't mind sharing much. We don't stand for none of that out here in the west."

"We Creoles are Roman Catholic. There is much respect for family and married women there."

"Just see that you keep that in mind."

———————

EACH YEAR—AND this year was no exception—Two Blankets gathered herself and her supplies to dig the *camas* bulb. They weren't as plentiful on the plains above the creek as they had been up the *Nch'i-wána* and above Celilo Falls where she gathered them with Stinging Nettle, but still, there were enough. She strapped Mira in her cradleboard, gathered together several grain sacks, her digging sticks, and food for lunch and dinner.

It was early in the morning when she set out hiking up the streamside road. The day would be warm, she knew, but in the early dawn it was still cool, and she pulled her rabbit fur cloak about her. She wondered how she had used to feel comfortable in no clothing, and now she felt the cool of the river and the wind.

Mira kept up a constant comment on the landscape, whether exterior or interior, Two Blankets could not be sure. Mira's vocabulary was a mixture of principally *Nimi'ipuu*, but also some Chinook Jargon and English. The rest were words Two Blankets could not understand, so she presumed that they were either gibberish or Mira's own private language.

She crossed the bridge about half-way up the stream and noted it was built in a way to last. That was one thing about Marshall, he built solid. His work and the work of those under him was not shabby. The stream talked to itself as it passed on its way to the *Nch'i-wána* and the sea.

Two Blankets reached the top, and her view of the surroundings expanded. Off to her left lay the majority of Marshall's claim. She could see, over near the forest, perhaps a quarter of a mile away, two cabins. One, which was the Stafford's previously, was smaller but now seemed much improved. A herd of cattle grazed near it, and a large garden grew near the cabin.

Farther away, a cabin stood half-finished with a man and two boys cutting a tree in the forest. A woman planted a fall garden behind the cabin.

Two Blankets crossed the stream and headed for her *camas* bulb patch. She leaned the cradleboard in the shade of a lone oak tree where she could keep an eye on it. It was doubtful that she would encounter a predator in the daylight, but there were still bears, cougars, wolves, coyotes and others up here. Most were afraid of people, but they were not always wary.

Dropping her sacks, she gave Mira a drink of water and took one herself. Under typical circumstances, she would be harvesting in another six weeks if Stinging Nettle or Bone Rattler were here. Several others of the native women would do as well. The *Blue Camas* bulbs which she sought looked almost exactly the same as the *White Death Camas*. Fortunately, the *Death Camas* flowered two or three weeks later, in June, and its cream-colored flowers were easily identifiable.

She dug with her stick and pulled out a bulb, then took a couple of steps before digging and pulling another. If she only harvested one in four, they would reseed for next year. The harvesting became a routine. It would take a long time, given that each bulb was only about an inch, to gather enough for a whole year. In the past, she had always had someone to share the work and to converse and tell stories while working.

"Now I only have you, Mira. And you, suddenly, have nothing to say." Two Blankets looked over to the oak where Mira lay in her cradleboard.

She had moved farther than she had thought in her harvesting. A coyote was nosing about, though not really in threatening distance. Two Blankets got up and threw a *camas* root at it. The coyote dodged the missile and pulled back.

"Take your jokes elsewhere, Sly Coyote."

The wind blows from Brother Coyote toward Mira. You notice, she was silent. She is already showing herself to be a hunter.

Two Blankets thought about it. "You are right Gray Wolf. A short span of time ago, she was babbling away. Then, she was silent as a mouse, like White Mouse, and observant."

She opened her bag and took out the always present *camas* cakes, some dried salmon, and water.

"*Camas. Camas. Camas* and *názog.*"

She handed the child a broken piece of *camas* cake. "Is that *camas*? Or is that *názog*?"

Mira viewed Two Blankets with suspicion. "You silly. It *camas*."

She peeled off a piece of salmon. "And what is this?"

"Silly. It *názog.*" She reached out her hand for a piece.

Thus, it went, all that day and the next. The next and next for the following two weeks or so. Then, a day to haul the bags back to her longhouse and the next step in the cycle of living. She sorted and cleaned the roots. After that, they had to be cooked in a pit for two days. Some were dried to make flour for *camas* cakes, a staple in the native diet, others, kept in root form, to be re-hydrated later to be eaten as much as years later.

In the late fall of that year, Two Blankets harvested cattail heads. In this, Delores Sue joined her one day.

"What in the world you doing out here wading in the wet?"

Two Blankets turned to Delores Sue with a smile. "I am harvesting cattail fluff. I use it for moon cycle pads and to stuff pillows and such."

She demonstrated by cutting the flower head off, then stripping the fluff in one big spiral.

"That looks like fun, for a while, at least. Can I help?"

"Let me fetch you a knife. You'll need to take off your shoes and stockings, and hitch up your skirt." Two Blankets got another knife and jogged back to the streamside. "For now, just cut the heads off."

For the next two hours, they cut the heads and chatted. Aimee walked up, took one look and went back to the Landing.

When they had a significant amount, Two Blankets called a halt.

"I think that is enough. Help me put these in the sack." Together they stuffed the cattail heads into a large flour sack. "That is good. You can put your shoes and stockings back on." She flicked a handful of water at Delores Sue with a mischievous laugh. Delores Sue jumped into a puddle, splashing them both.

When they reached her longhouse, after a short delay for water play, Two Blankets spread out the cattail heads.

"Now, you just grab the stalk with one hand and unwind the fuzz with the other."

Soon, they had a whole pile of fluff centered on the table, fluff in their hair and on their dresses. "If you want some of this for moon cycle pads just let me know. I am going to the stream to bathe as soon as I bag this."

"I will have a bath drawn in my room. Bring your baby, and you can have a hot bath as well."

———

IN THE LATE fall of 1859, *Monsieur* Bayonne paid another visit to the Landing, his last of the year. Traffic at the Landing had slowed down considerably in the fall. There seemed to be fewer people on the river bringing their wagons down. River traffic, in general, was up as represented by the building of two more lower Columbia sternwheelers, the *Carrie Ladd* and the *Mountain Buck,* as well as *Venture* and *Hasseloe* on the middle Columbia serving The Dalles and the *Colonel Wright* above Celilo Falls. Now there was a portage railroad of sorts on both sides of the river and competition between sternwheelers and railroads.

Two Blankets had noticed the slowdown of the wagon train traffic for the last three or four years. The increase in trade going upriver surprised her. Where was it all going? Some was obviously supplies for The Dalles and beyond upstream. Zeke Kinley had driven his thirty cattle down and boarded a steamer scow bound for sale at The Dalles.

She was out in front of her longhouse grinding *camas* bulbs into flour for *camas* cakes when she saw the *Carrie Ladd* making landing and *Monsieur* Bayonne disembarking. Momentarily she stopped what she was doing.

"Why do I feel so disoriented whenever he is here? It is not that I expect anything from him, or could expect anything. I am married and cannot do anything. He has done nothing but be polite to me, as polite as he is to Delores Sue or Aimee. I don't understand him, and I certainly don't understand myself."

She felt a stomach cramp—not a large one, but one strong enough to make her sit down for a moment.

"What is this? Am I starting to get sick?" The cramp left her, and she straightened up.

He waved at her as he walked his horse and mule toward the Landing. She felt her face heat up and looked down, pretending not to see him. Then, she grabbed Mira's cradleboard and ran inside. Another cramp hit her once she got inside.

"This is ridiculous. I am embarrassed, and I have cramps besides."

There is no question about that, Gray Wolf observed. *But you will be ridiculous, anyway.*

"*Háma kine. Háma kine.*" Mira clapped her hands.

"Man here, Mira? That is what you are saying?"

"*He. Taz háma. Taz háma kine.*" She clapped her hands again.

"Yes, Mira, the good man is here." What a strange thought to have.

"The man is here. The *good* man is here."

"Shush. That is something I don't need." A third wave of cramps passed over her. "And this is also something I don't need."

Mira looked at her mother and stopped commenting.

Two Blankets dressed quickly in her best, buckskin beaded skirt, jacket, and moccasins. She brushed out her hair.

She suddenly thought. I haven't had these cramps for over two years. She picked up a moon cycle pad and tied it between her legs.

"I don't know why I am doing this, but I know what the cramps mean."

She grabbed up Mira in her cradleboard and walked up to the Landing. She walked in, and *Monsieur* Bayonne stood to greet her.

"*Madame* Two Blankets Johnston." He bent to kiss her fingertips as before, and she quickly shook his hand instead.

His eyes flicked to hers, then to her hand and he shook it.

"Of course, perhaps I am too familiar."

"*Monsieur* Bayonne, I am pleased you understand."

"I had not thought that I might cause you problems. I will be careful in the future."

Mira reached out her hand. *Monsieur* Bayonne bent and kissed it. "I am happy to greet you again, *Mademoiselle* Mira."

Mira smiled happily. *"Taz háma. Taz háma."*

Monsieur Bayonne looked questioningly at Two Blankets.

"Just the babbling of a child. What do you have for us, *Monsieur* Bayonne?"

He proceeded to show them various small items, hair combs, necklaces and bracelets, beads and handkerchiefs. He had small scissors for nail trimming and some coloring for make-ups. It was actually quite surprising what a range of items he carried on that horse and mule.

"I have had much practice in packing that mule for men and women. Often, I must bring the order back the next time when I have to pack in such a way. Other places, like Salem up the Willamette, I can take the wagon."

"We are always pleased to see you." Aimee danced through the room waving a new scarf. "We have few opportunities to get goods such as you so kindly bring us."

"I am pleased that my goods make you happy, *Mademoiselle* Aimee."

"Oh, mon cher, you make me very happy, indeed, Jean Michel."

"I have also brought you something special, ladies." He brought out a large paper-wrapped bundle and untied it. "When I saw this, I thought of you, *Mademoiselle* Delores Sue." The paper unfolded like leaves enclosing a flower, the flower within, a pale blue satin dress. There were small ruffles across the bodice with a silvery fabric beneath, and the skirts were cut in a series of flounces. The dress was cut to be worn off the shoulder and without a hoop.

"Oh, my gawd, that is the most beautiful dress I have ever *seen. Monsieur* Bayonne. But can I afford it?"

"It is not that expensive. We will talk about that. For you, my beautiful Aimee, I have this." He handed the package to Aimee. "I hope you like it. I could only pick one."

Aimee opened the package like it was her birthday. Her eyes got large, and she held the dress up against her. This dress was also cut off the shoulder with a low bodice, but the color was a dark crimson satin with black lace trim. The skirt was also flounced. Aimee swirled around letting the dress flow out and around her.

"Oh, mon cher, c'est magnifique."

Monsieur Bayonne smiled. "No, *Mademoiselle* Aimee. *Tu es magnifique."*

Aimee suddenly sat in his lap and gave *Monsieur* Bayonne a very long kiss. "Thank you, Jean Michel. We will make a purchase, I am sure."

If *Monsieur* Bayonne looked a bit discomfited, Two Blankets was the only one to notice. He eased Aimee from his lap and passed her two packages. Neither was as bulky as the packages Delores Sue and Aimee had opened.

"You must know that I could never buy a dress like the ones Delores Sue and Aimee have. They would not be appropriate."

"Just open it and see what you think."

She opened the first and held it up against her body. The neckline was high. It had long sleeves and a long full skirt. Made of dark blue wool, it was still detailed with delicate buttons and pretty ribbon work.

"Monsieur Bayonne, I don't know what to say, or what I have to trade in return."

Aimee said, "It is pretty plain."

Delores Sue held the fabric in her hand. "It might be a might plain by our tastes, Aimee, but the fabric is fine, and the work around the button-holes is beautiful."

Two Blankets held it against her. "I do not think it is plain at all. It is practical, and I like that very much." She indicated the other package. "May I?"

Monsieur Bayonne nodded. "Of course, *Madame* Two Blankets."

She opened the second package. Within was a pretty but simple cotton dress in a flowery print. Again the bodice was high, and the skirt was ankle length. In a *whiteman's* fashion sense it would have been called a sensible but pretty summer dress suitable for a dinner at home or a Sunday at church.

"This is actually exactly what I need. We will have to bargain, and the only things I have to barter are the furs I have tanned, like the red fox on Mira's cradleboard, or the Canadian lynx I tanned for Aimee. But I don't have anything as nice as either of those."

"If you like the dresses, I am sure we can come to an agreement, *Madame* Two Blankets. as I will with *Mademoiselle* Delores Sue and *Mademoiselle* Aimee. We will bargain until all are happy."

Marshall Johnston entered the Landing about this time. Or perhaps *during* this time, Two Blankets was not sure.

"You sniffing around my whores again, Bayonne? I thought I warned you about that."

"Merely doing a little business and waiting for you to arrive. If I might conclude it, I would be glad to join you."

"Just understand, you want a whore, you gotta pay, and my wife don't do that business. At least she don't since she married me. I don't want her dressing like she's selling quim."

Two Blankets got up and swung Mira's cradleboard onto her back. "If you will excuse me, *Monsieur* Bayonne, ladies."

"Mister Johnston, I will return in a few minutes. These are the dresses I brought for your wife if you choose to approve?" He held out the dresses to Marshall's inspection.

"No, them's all right."

"I will come down to your longhouse, and you can show me the furs you have to trade." He picked up the dresses he brought for Two Blankets and followed her out. When they reached the large table outside Two Blankets' longhouse, he laid the dresses down.

"I will get the furs." She slipped inside and within minutes was back out with an armload of skins and furs.

"This is what I have. I am not certain how much they are worth compared to the dresses."

Monsieur Bayonne examined the skins and furs, turning each one over and feeling for weak points or stiffness that showed incomplete tanning.

"These are quite well done, as good as any I have seen. Certainly as good as any furs or skins tanned by a white man."

"They are brain tanned. It is a difficult process, but the only way to get skins this soft."

"I would trade these two dresses for this one large buckskin, or these three rabbit pelts and this one mink. I can make money on either in Portland."

"Take the rabbit pelts and mink then. I can get more of those, and I would rather tan small."

"May I ask you a question? A personal one?"

Two Blankets thought about this for a minute or two. "Ask your question, *Monsieur* Bayonne. I cannot promise I will answer."

"Why do you allow Mister Johnston to treat you so badly?"

"That is hard to answer and show proper respect to my husband. Among the Chinook, a woman can leave her husband if he does not respect her. Then, she goes back to her previous status. I was a *mistshimus,* a slave to the Chinook. If I left Marshall and went to Warm Springs reservation as a Chinook, I would have to go back to being a *mistshimus.* Mira, also, would be *mistshimus.* Here, we are under *whiteman's* rules. We are both free. It is not freedom like you have, and not the freedom of a *whiteman,* but it is freedom of a sort. Now that I have told you this, I would appreciate it if you would keep it between us. I am trusting you in this."

"Thank you for your trust, *Madame* Two Blankets. It is not misplaced."

"Thank you, sir—and now I must—" she doubled over "—ask your forgiveness. It is—"

Monsieur Bayonne had looked confused, then thoughtful, then his face cleared. "Women's business?"

"Yes. Women's business."

"Of course. We have a bargain on the dresses, and I will see you the next time I am here to trade, *Madame* Johnston." He turned and walked back to the Landing.

She immediately jumped up and moved the remaining furs to the inside.

Food and baby clothes she gathered up, Mira in her cradleboard and a glowing branch from the fire. Once at the moon cycle hut, she lit the fire and sat down with Mira.

"Oh, Mira, Mira. Why am I so confused? And now I have my blood time again to further confuse things." She knew that her monthlies frequently disturbed her thoughts.

She built up the fire and then took a burning brand to light the fire within the inner sweat lodge. A call from Mira brought her attention to her child. Once unstrapped from the cradleboard and cleaned up she busied herself exploring this new realm.

"Mira, just be careful of the fire and don't go outside."

"Careful of fire. Don't go outside," Mira repeated.

Two Blankets put out food on a wooden trencher for Mira and ate a little herself. Another cramp hit her, and she began stripping for the sweat lodge. She piled her clothing neatly by the entrance.

"Mira, remember what I said?"

"Yes, *Pike.* Be careful of fire. Don't go outside." She was busy exploring.

"I'll be out in a while." Two Blankets pushed the door flap aside and entered the sweat lodge. She crossed her legs, settled into a comfortable spot and tried to relax.

I don't understand why I am confused by this man. It is true that he has always been polite to me, but so has Harry Everton, and Big Ed... and Mr. Gilly, for that matter.

Gray Wolf squeezed in.

"Hello, Gray Wolf. Are you sure you want to be here?" Two Blankets smiled and scratched her ruff. "I know you don't like closed in spaces or the heat."

Now you are being silly. I am a vision quest animal. I don't take up space or feel the heat.

Yes, Two Blankets is silly. Silly, silly. White Mouse slid down to her shoulder. *You don't understand why you are confused?*

"No, I don't."

The door flap opened, and Mira crawled in completely naked. She stood and looked about, filled with wonder. She looked at Two Blankets, then sat opposite her in an almost perfect imitation of Two Blankets, legs crossed, back straight but relaxed, hands on her tiny but chubby thighs, and her head up. Her eyes rested upon Two Blankets.

"Do you like the sweat lodge, little one?"

"Ilekíuzitske taz háma."

"Yes, it is good to sweat."

"Háma taz."

"Háma taz? Man good?"

Mira sighed and screwed up her face for a moment, then the calm look occupied her again. "Yes, *Pike.* Jean Michel is good man. Is nice. And polite. Not like *cultus whiteman,* Marshall." Her utterance was delivered in perfect if abbreviated English.

"Where? When did you learn such good English? I only speak *Nimi'ipuu* with you."

"Nimi'ipuu is our language—private. Everyone speak English. I learn."

"And Marshall is your father."

"He is *cultus.* I not tell him, but he is *cultus."*

"I can't argue that. But we must be careful what we say. Understand?"

"Only *Nimi'ipuu* when *whitemans* can hear."

The child, Mira, is wise. You are confused because Bayonne is good. And he is good for no reason.

"So, I am confused because *Monsieur* Bayonne is good and kind and polite to me for no reason at all. He is just that way, and I am attracted to him for that?"

Mira smiled. "Yes."

Gray Wolf rolled onto her back. *Yes.*

From the little White Mouse, dangling from a forelock. *You have it right.*

RETALIATION

CHAPTER 7
APRIL 3 AND 4, 1860

WHEN SHE AWAKENED, she felt a diminishing dream, and the heart of the dream was the burial ground. Two Blankets gathered up Mira and exited her longhouse. Her goal was the burial ground. She wasn't sure why she needed to go there. She warned the child to be still and headed off at a brisk walk. Her course followed the road for a short distance up the creek, then along an overgrown path into the wood, a wood that began with rough brush along the new road but quickly degenerated into a moss-draped tunnel. She remembered the times when she had come here with the whole clan. She had been a *mistshimus* then but still allowed to participate in the ritual.

As she got closer and could see the grove and its burial canoes. Two Blankets looked for a spot where she could meditate upon the ramifications of her dream. She found an enclosed clearing, not much larger than she was, protected on all sides from discovery. Setting Mira down, she adopted her sweat lodge pose and sat quietly, listening to the sounds of the forest. She noticed that Mira sat likewise, whether it was in imitation of her own pose or a natural stance, she could not be sure. In either case, two silent individuals sat with legs crossed, listening and sensing.

She heard the river, always flowing in the background, the stream gurgling nearer, the crows and other birds cawing and chirping. Her own feeling of her body relaxed into the environment, the overall sense of the place.

With each exhalation, she released a built-up tension. With each inhalation, she brought into herself a greater appreciation of her expanding sensorium.

Near her, the Grove of the Dead began— a sacred place for the clan, where the dead had been raised for thousands of years. Though Two Blankets did not know precisely what a thousand years was, she could still feel the almost timelessness of it, the periods of deaths and lives overlapping from the most recent, near the edge, where their canoes were still painted brightly and the wood they were made from intact, to farther in where the paint was gone and the canoes rotten. Farther inward still, the canoes had often collapsed to the ground and the bones within were scattered and rotting into the dirt.

All this she could feel. There was a sense of spirit animals as well, though less defined. It was not that she could see or feel a wolf here or a bear, but she could sense an amalgam of spirits. The bones and the spirits were, if not at peace per se, at least not restless.

There were words, or perhaps a trace of them coming through the forest. She followed the mumble of voices and heard the occasional footstep as well. Opening her eyes, she shushed Mira, though she showed no attempt to speak out. The footsteps came closer, and now she could hear Marshall's voice and the occasional response from Ike, the sawyer.

Marshall spoke, giving directives. "We need to clear a flat area to expand the Landing. Sawn lumber is a merchantable product. I want you to start cutting in here."

Ike didn't respond immediately. "But sir, that there is a burial ground. I understand what you are saying, but people are superstitious. Hell, I'm superstitious. There's dead in there going back a thousand years."

"That's why I want you to start here. Cut the grove first, then cut toward the river. That way it'll be done where no one can see it."

"All due respect, sir. You been good to me and my boys, but I ain't going to cut in there. I'll cut up to here, but I ain't cutting in no cemetery."

"Give me that ax."

Ike handed him the ax.

"This is what I think of this cemetery." He began chopping a six-inch-thick tree that ran up some forty or fifty feet into the canopy. "Them's Indians in there." *Chop. Chop.* "They ain't people." *Chop. Chop.* "I ain't going to have my plans stopped by some old bones."

Two Blankets looked at Mira. Fearful of a noise, she pulled her in and held her close. The chopping sound continued, and she couldn't keep her eyes away.

Why? What on the source of all life and death did Marshall think he was doing?

The tree started to crack, then toppled into the grove. On the way down it knocked branches loose, which fell before it toward the ground. For a moment, it seemed to hang on a giant cedar, then it dropped with a crash directly toward a recently placed canoe, almost breaking it at the midpoint. Collapsed canoe, bones, and debris fell upon the ground.

"Jaysus! Marshall, are you crazy?"

"You make a decision, Ike. You either cut where I say or pack your bags. I want that grove cut down, and we'll bury the bones. It'll be like they was never there."

"I been working here for nigh on four years and good work I will say, sir, and you going to threaten me with a firing? After four years? I'll tell you here and now, I ain't going to cut that grove. I'll cut up to it, but I won't cut there."

"You think about it, Ike. You just think about it. You disgust me, you and all your superstitious nonsense." Marshall threw down the ax and stalked away.

Ike picked up the ax and looked back at the tree and the destruction. "I don't like this one little bit. Not a bit." He followed Marshall out of the forest.

Two Blankets released Mira.

What are we going to do? Oh, what are we going to do?

She traipsed back to the longhouse contemplating this problem.

White Mouse spoke to the air. *She is thinking about doing something perilous again, something very perilous, I'm afraid.*

She is, little White Mouse. We will have to wait and guide her because we can't stop her.

When Two Blankets got back to the longhouse, she began her preparations. She carefully gathered in five chickens and killed them. Then she drained their blood into a jar. She searched and found a sealed jar of skunk scent. From the muskrats that she or the clan had tanned, there was a jar of musk oil. There was a large jar of fat and grease from various animals as well. Then she lay down for a well-deserved rest.

About midnight she set out to do what she could. Looking about, she saw that the moon was rising and was mostly full. She set out first for the portable steam-powered sawmill. When she got there, she carefully painted it with some of the chicken blood with an old paintbrush. Then a bit of the grease and fat, and finally, very carefully, half of the skunk scent. In some areas of the Burial Grove, she painted the chicken blood. From the downed canoe, she found a skeleton that was still mostly connected by sinew and hung it into a nearby tree. The warrior's chest armor she hung around his ribcage and the head she balanced above it. She looked at it critically. She dipped the brush into the jar of blood and painted the skeleton in warpaint.

"I apologize, warrior, for any disrespect I have done to you. I am trying to stop the destruction, I really am."

She backed out of the area, being careful not to leave any footprints, and walked back to the longhouse. Checking within, she saw that Mira was still asleep. Now she had to be careful and not get caught. Sneaking over to the cabin where Ike and Frank Milson slept, she painted a design on the door that looked like a warpaint design. She dipped the paintbrush into the jar of grease and fat and coated the door and the handle as well. Last she painted it with a bit of skunk oil. Sliding into the dark, she crossed to the longhouse. She coated grease on the door and painted a warpaint design on it as well. She doused it with the last of the skunk scent.

She smiled. It smelled like hell and stank to the treetops. "This will do."

At the Landing, she repeated the same process, painting it with musk oil instead of skunk scent. She felt she had done enough and taken enough chances. It would never do to be caught in any of this. There would be suspicion surrounding her, in any case. She made her way back to the longhouse. The brush stank of skunk and she sealed it in the jar with the grease. The rest of the jars sealed up, she hid them away.

"Pike, what that smell? It stink."

"Go back to sleep, Mira. I will take care of it." But how? She had a couple quarts of vinegar and tried rinsing her hands in it. It seemed to help. She went back outside and stripped off her dress. She looked at it. It was fortunate she had chosen this dress—the first Marshall had bought her. It would probably have to be burned. She doused it with vinegar and stuffed them into a waterproof basket and sealed it up as best she could. Then she wiped herself down with the vinegar and rinsed it off. It would have to do.

She left the lid off the vinegar and crept back into her sleeping furs.

"Now, you smell like pickles. But it is better."

"Let us go to sleep, Mira." She put her arms around Mira had hugged her close. Sleep gradually came to her.

In the morning she awakened to the sound of men shouting. Two Blankets put on her buckskins and stepped outside. The shouting was coming from the bunkhouse and Ike's hut. She walked down until she was close enough to hear their talk, though not clearly. She was far enough away to avoid attention.

"What the hell is going on?" Several men were outside the longhouse and more emerged half-dressed.

"Looks like blood painted on the door. Indians?"

"Indians?" The man looked suspiciously around, and Two Blankets ducked behind the midden pile. "Indians or their spirit critters."

"You don't know nothing about Indians or spirit critters. It stanks like a skunk sprayed it."

"It *is* skunk, you fool. I got it on my hands, along with this grease."

"I leaned against it. Now I stink like a skunk."

"How would you know? You *always* stink."

At Ike's hut, the talk was more subdued. He and his apprentice were visibly upset. "Going up to the Landing. Try not to touch anything. I don't like this. Could be Indians heard about Marshall's plans here."

Ike walked to the Landing. It was apparent to Two Blankets that he was troubled, at least. When he got there, he stopped and examined the door, then carefully opened it. He disappeared within. In a few minutes, the door opened again, and he and Marshall exited, careful not to touch anything.

Marshall eyed the damage critically. "Gawd dammit. Who would do something like this? It's sticky, too." He ran his finger along the door jamb. "like old grease or fat. What's the smell?"

"Over at the bunkhouse and my hut, it is skunk. This smells more like musk. You can get it from gators and crocs back east. Musk turtle, too, I hear. Out here, I'd say, most likely muskrat."

"Muskrat is local, then." Marshall was getting over just being angry. He was starting to think. "Why would anyone collect that?"

"Yeah, likely local. then. They use it in perfume, I hear. Come look at the bunkhouse."

"What do you think the painting means?"

"I don't know. Looks like warpaint."

When he reached the hut, they examined it, checked the grease and paint. "It sure does stink."

At the longhouse, everyone started talking at once. "Everyone shut up. Anyone see anything during the night? Hear anything?"

No one had heard or seen anything.

"All right. Harry, get some men cleaning up the Landing first and make sure they clean it good. Then the hut and bunkhouse."

Harry nodded to his orders and charged Gilly and two others with the Landing clean-up. Another three men he detailed to Ike's hut.

Marshall looked to Harry, Ike, and Big Ed. "Any ideas?"

"It's definitely blood," Big Ed said. "Looks Injun to me."

Harry examined the blood paint. "Looks Indian to me, too. Ain't seen this particular design before, but every warpaint design is different. They got different designs when it's not warpaint too, and they are angry."

Marshall suddenly turned and started jogging toward the creek and the forest. "Jaysus, let's check the sawmill."

Two Blankets backpedaled to the longhouse and stepped in. She put on her moccasins and called Mira to her and stepped back out.

"Husband Marshall, what is happening?"

"Seems like someone is not very happy with us. You hear anything during the night? See anything?"

Two Blankets thought for a moment. She did not like to lie to Marshall.

It wasn't that she had any objections to telling him an untruth. He just had an instinct for ferreting out a lie. "I did not see or hear anything unusual, husband Marshall."

He didn't bother with an answer, just continued on his path. She followed at a curious distance. At the sawmill, Ike was already checking the machine.

"Any damage Ike?"

"I don't see any. Just the same paint, grease, and skunk odor."

"All right. Get yourself some breakfast, then come on back and clean up the sawmill."

"I will. Frank and I will do it right after we eat."

"Somebody just don't like us at all."

SECOND
NIGHT

CHAPTER 8
APRIL 5, 1860

TWO BLANKETS HID the chickens in a basket and took them and Mira to the moon cycle hut. She didn't like using the hut for surreptitious purposes for it was a sacred place, but it was the only place where even Marshall was unlikely to interrupt. Others of the crew would not, probably even if the hut was on fire.

Mira sat and looked on interestedly as Two Blankets tied the legs together and hung up the first chicken. She cut the first leg in a circle about where the feathers started and again at the base of the leg. Then she peeled the skin upward toward the foot. She repeated the process with the second leg. Cutting the skin between the legs at the bottom of the abdomen, she pulled it toward the back. Some more delicate cutting was necessary along the back and around the wings, but soon she had the entire skin pulled up to the neck. For her purposes, she did not need the neck, and she cut the skin off there with the neck. Likewise, she didn't want the wings beyond the first sections, and she cut them off at that point. Finally, she separated the legs at the first joint, and she had a reasonably clean and skinned carcass. She used the knife to slit carefully upward from the anus until she could pull out the intestines.

She set the chicken to one side and sat back on her heels. "That's one down. Four to go, Mira."

Mira clapped her hands. *"Pike* is good at that."

She skinned the next four chickens, then butchered off as much meat as she could manage. "It is a waste of meat, but we don't want any chicken bones to give us away."

The meat she cut up into small pieces and put them into a waterproof basket. The carcasses and skins with feathers attached she put into another one. She peeked out, and seeing no one in the immediate vicinity, she turned to Mira, who ran to join her. Hoisting the baskets onto one hip, she left the hut. If anyone saw her leave, she didn't see them. She walked as natural as possible toward her longhouse. No one seemed to take any notice. When she reached the other side the midden pile, she dug a small hole in the side of the eight-foot height. She looked around again.

"Good. No one is looking, or I can't see anyone, at least." She dumped the basket of chicken carcasses and the skins into the hole and quickly covered it up.

Mira looked at her, a question on her face, but none reached her mouth. Carrying on, Two Blankets walked to the longhouse. The smell of skunk was diminished, though now there was a hint of vinegar. She set the basket of chicken meat down and cut chunks of four or five pounds of bacon into it. She mixed in the leftover grease and fat and stirred the parts together.

Mira came over and looked down into the basket. "I know, Mira, it doesn't look like we'd want to eat it, but the bears might like it. Ah, what about salmon?" From another basket, she took out a piece for Mira and a piece for herself. There were always pieces that were not so good to eat in the basket, and Two Blankets found many.

"What will I do if Marshall has my longhouse watched tonight? Only one way out, and the whole plan will be spoiled." She thought about it, eyed the doorway, then looked at the back of the longhouse.

"Mira, wait here a moment. *Pike* will be right back."

She exited the hut and walked along on the side away from the Landing. When she reached the back, she saw she was at least partially concealed. This longhouse had never been in good condition. The better part, which had been standing when Marshall had repaired it, was in the back. The front was all new, or newer at least, and tightly constructed. Marshall was like that. He did build to last. But perhaps this rear part had escaped his attentions when he had first moved here.

She examined the boards. They were heavy, two inches thick, but only pegged into posts driven into the ground. She tugged. The first did not move, but the second came loose easily. There was room for her to slip in between the wide boards. She put it back in place and returned to the front and the flap door.

"I need to sleep, Mira. You come and take a little sleep with *Pike?*"

"I sleep with *Pike.*" Mira joined her on the sleeping furs in the back of the longhouse.

Two Blankets slept but lightly and dreamed of bears, mountain lions, coyotes, foxes, and lynxes. When she awoke, she knew there were other animals as well, but all she could remember were pairs of eyes in the dark. Mira was playing quietly nearby. It raised a choking feeling in her throat when she saw her. It was so difficult living and working alone, but Mira made any trial worthwhile.

They ate a meal of smoked venison and *camas* and washed it down with a pot of tea. "I am going to have to go out tonight, Mira. I want you to stay in the sleeping furs. Do you understand?"

"Hide still in furs. *Pike* play grouse with broken wing? Lead enemy away?"

"Yes, exactly. Can you do it?" Two Blankets didn't even remember telling Mira of the baby grouse and the mother pretending to have a broken wing.

"I can do it."

"If anyone opens the door flap, just stay still like the baby grouse."

"I will."

"If they say anything, just say I am asleep. I don't think that will happen."

"We play it together." Mira looked perfectly serious.

Two Blankets checked the door flap. It was darkening outside, and she knew moon rise would not be for several hours. Several men were positioned in various areas of the landing including nigh on in front of her longhouse. They had torches, which would actually limit their night vision. She dropped the door flap and came back to the sleeping furs.

"I will need to sleep a couple more hours. Can you sleep, too?"

"Yes, *Pike,* I sleep."

She woke in a few more hours and checked the door flap. One of the men sat out front on a stump, his head half slumped. Then he would straighten his back and shake his head. He had a fire going in the pit, and Two Blankets knew he wouldn't be able to see much beyond the firelight. She closed the flap and crept back to the furs.

Mira opened her eyes.

"Baby grouse," Two Blankets said.

"Baby grouse go to sleep now and stay quiet."

Two Blankets maneuvered the basket out through the loosened board. She brought along another smaller basket so she would not have to lug such a large load everywhere and then squeezed through herself. She reached back through and pulled a dark fur over her shoulders. She filled the smaller basket and moved off into the forest.

It was difficult moving through the forest, trying to leave as small a trace as possible. Any competent tracker from the clan would have been able to follow her. Most of these men were city or farm men, and she didn't think they possessed the skills necessary. Even if they could follow her, what would they find?

As she approached the mill—perhaps the most dangerous area because of Marshall's paranoia and Ike's intelligence—she was heartened to see another man sitting on a downed log and staring into the dark next to his flickering torch. The mill was pulled into a small clearing, but was close to the forest on the inland side. She sneaked along in a wide arc then closed back in when she had reached the far side. The man was tired and spent most of his time watching the clearing in front of him. She waited and saw that he did occasionally look toward the forest.

She spread bits and pieces of the meat mix along a fifty pace length of the wood, some deeper in and some right on the verge of the clearing. Then she closed back on the mill and settled in to wait. The moon was up, but its light was as much shadow here in the forest. When his head dipped, she tossed a few chunks of chicken and bacon onto the ground under the mill at his feet. He started and lifted his torch peering around. His head shook, and he sat back down on the log. She ducked under her fur cape and waited. When the moon had moved another handspan, his head dropped again. She scattered the rest of her meat mix on the ground between them and slipped back into the forest.

I hope this works. Otherwise, when daylight comes, there will just be bait all over the place.

Back at the longhouse, she filled her basket again. Sneaking along the edge of the forest between her longhouse and the Landing, she spread her bait, concentrating primarily on the areas to the rear of the storehouse, the bunkhouse, and Ike's hut. It took her several trips back to refill her basket until she finally reached the Landing. She wanted desperately to do the Landing, but that was also Marshall's territory.

Will he be awake, peering through the darkened windows, or will he be asleep?

As much as she wanted to deliver her load of meat scraps right up to the door of his office, she opted for safety. In shadow, and covered by her fur, she tossed scraps toward the building. When she was out of the shadows, she carefully backed away, wiping away her footprints as she went. As she was backing away, she looked behind her. There were two pairs of eyes watching her from deep within the verge. That was when she heard the first shot. A minute later she heard a second. She dashed to the forest edge and then she was safe. She huddled down beneath her furs, breathing heavily.

A couple of men came running out of the bunkhouse, and Ike emerged from his hut. He stood there a moment, then went back inside. Just as she was about to move, he emerged again with his boots on. He took the men from the front of the bunkhouse and headed toward the sawmill. When they were sufficiently along the path, she advanced toward the back of her own longhouse. She paused beside the midden pile, then waded the stream and hurried to the almost black shadows at the rear of her own longhouse. The man from the front came walking back toward her. She ducked down beneath the furs with her baskets in the darkest shadows.

The man kept coming. He was only twenty feet away, and her fur hidden shape was clearly within the circle of his torchlight, but he was only looking into the forest. As quietly as possible she slipped away around the corner.

Then she hurried with her baskets to the front of her longhouse and slid within. She held up her hand for Mira to stay where she was, set her baskets to the side and went back out the door.

As long as I come out where I am expected, and he has been watching, this is my best move. It is what they would expect.

Wrapping herself in her cloak, she walked to the rear and her "guard."

"What is happening? I was asleep, and then I thought I heard a shot."

"I don't know, Missus Johnston. But here comes Ike and another two men."

"I'm telling you, Ike. I was just sitting there, just like I was told to. I turned around toward the forest, and there was a dozen eyes looking at me. Different colors, but all mean like. Then I looked down and right at my boots was the biggest raccoon I ever saw. I shot at it, and it ran. I loaded and shot at the eyes in the forest. Then all the eyes was gone."

"Might as well set a first-grader to guard that mill. You're probably the worst guard I ever seen."

"I know I ain't no guard. But I was awake. My head would duck down and hit my chest, but I never went to sleep."

NOTHING MEANS NOTHING

CHAPTER 9
APRIL 6, 1860

TWO BLANKETS KNEW she couldn't make a foray this night. There would be too many watching for interference in Marshall's plans. What could she do to advance her plan to interfere? As she headed back into her longhouse, she felt the beginning of a cramp.

"Why, when I am on the verge of something, I do not know what, I get my monthly?"

She picked up Mira from within, a brand from the fire, and headed for the moon cycle hut. Halfway there, another cramp doubled her over her belly.

"Oh, damn, damn, damn."

"Pike, you feel bad?"

"I'm all right, honey."

"Fine, don't tell me. We go to the moon cycle hut."

There it was, right in front of them. She felt the queasiness passing over her and dropped the brand onto the fire. The previously-laid fire blazed up immediately. It crackled and popped. She sat down. *What can I do?* The immediate response came back from somewhere. *Try doing nothing, nothing at all.*

Now that the central fire was going well, she picked up a brand from it, carried it into the sweat lodge and lit that fire as well. Nothing at all. What does *that* mean?

Gray Wolf nuzzled her hand. *It means precisely what it says. Nothing is nothing. Do nothing means do nothing.*

She pulled off her clothes and noticed Mira folding her clothes neatly into a pile next to the door flap. Then, Mira entered the sweat lodge, and Two Blankets followed.

"Nothing means nothing."

She sat back and crossed her legs. She lay her hands open on her knees and relaxed her back.

"Nothing means nothing."

Her breathing was tight, and she relaxed her inhalations and exhalations. She breathed in slowly and deeply through the nose and exhaled through her mouth.

Two Blankets looked down. Mira was laying in her lap. She got up, and taking the tired little body with her, exited the sweat lodge.

"Are you hungry, little one?"

"Yes, can we have venison?"

Two Blankets put a pot of water on the fire and filled it with dried venison. They allowed it to cook a bit and ate together.

"*Pike,* you are trying too hard."

"Trying too hard to do what, dear?"

"To talk with the spirit animals. That is what you want to do, isn't it?"

Two Blankets was surprised and amazed. That was what she was trying to do. But how did Mira know? Well, how did Sees-What-No-One-Else-Sees see what he saw? Or know what he knew? He just did, that's all. He didn't try, he just knew.

"You are a smart girl, Mira. Very smart." She pointed her spoon at her as a gesture.

"I know. I am smart."

"Let us rest a bit, then after dark, we will try again." She lay down on the sleeping furs and let sleep take her.

The Gray Wolf's green eyes looked down upon her. *Wake now and join us. Is she awake? Is she, now?* White Mouse said.

Gray Wolf stood waiting patiently. Two Blankets got up and, following

Gray Wolf, walked to the sweat lodge. She looked back and saw Mira laying in her own embrace.

She entered the sweat lodge and sat down.

We go now, White Mouse and I, to speak with the vision quest animals. Do you wish to travel with us?

Two Blankets nodded. *Yes.*

Then you must merge with me.

How?

How is the wrong question? Do nothing. Do you understand?

Do nothing. Yes, I think I do understand.

Two Blankets collapsed into a seated position. She was calm and peaceful. She didn't know what was climbing through her mind but didn't worry about it.

Gray Wolf stared directly into her eyes. *Do nothing.*

I will do nothing.

Two Blankets felt herself flowing toward and into Gray Wolf.

Hang on. Gray Wolf turned and ran out of the sweat lodge. Two Blankets clung to her ruff. White Mouse ran alongside at the same speed. They ran on toward the burial grove. Gray Wolf's green eyes seemed to glow huge in the dark.

This is fun. White Mouse said, from the top of Gray Wolf's head, hanging on to her ear.

They ran right through a member of the crew guarding the fire in front of Two Blanket's longhouse. The man spun about with their passing. They ran through the fire as well, sending sparks flying.

At the grove, they saw a segment of the vision quest animals' population she had never seen before. A giant bear rubbed against a tree. Lynxes, coyotes, several wolves, all the way down to creatures the size of White Mouse. It was the physical world, but it wasn't. They were together on this. Some kind of communication was taking place while her spirit was there.

Welcome to the community of spirit animals.

Thank you. She directed her thoughts to Gray Wolf. *I don't know what to do.*

Do nothing. Remember that.

Do nothing. She repeated.

Gray Wolf let out a howl that pierced the air. When Two Blankets looked again the clearing was crowded with spirit animals. Gray Wolf howled, and the animals flowed back into the verge of the forest. Although she was nominally a person, and a plain one at that, she was not afraid.

A conference took place among the animals. This she was not privy to, not to the actual content of it. Time passed or did not. She was not sure which.

All she could think of was Gray Wolf's injunction, to do nothing. Do nothing. This she paid attention to and this only. There was a confusion of activity all about her, a few dozen eyes, hungry and angry, eyes that could seemingly drill into her and extract whatever was there.

They are confused, said White Mouse. *They are roused and upset but do not know what to do.*

Do nothing. Follow us but do nothing. She looked to Gray Wolf for confirmation. She looked deep and saw herself reflected back from her green eyes.

Yes. The eyes seemed to say to her.

Come, ride me and do nothing.

She looked deep into her green eyes and followed them inward until she was looking out. Her vision on this night was much improved in detail, especially if she looked straight ahead. To the sides, her vision was not binocular as usual for a human but still improved through the yellow, blue, and gray color range. She noted offhandedly that she couldn't see anything red—not a hint of it. Reds were seen as shades of dark gray to black.

They ran, and such a run it was. There was an exhilaration in movement, in running, that Two Blankets had never felt before.

Whee. I like this.

A snort of disgust built in her nose. She stifled it.

To her right ran White Mouse. She glanced out the right eye then looked hard. White Mouse was there, but she was as large as Gray Wolf.

White Mouse is big, huge even. I have never seen her so large.

She is as big as she wants or needs to be.

Gray Wolf expanded in size until the whole Landing was visible below her, then shrank back to her natural stature.

I like this better. There is the sawmill ahead of us.

They halted on the verge of the forest. Two Blankets looked through Gray Wolf's eyes. It did not look the way she was used to seeing. The whole shape was there, and in a clarity and detail, she would not normally see at night. There was one of the two men watching over the sawmill, but she could only see him in tones of blue, yellow and gray. He smelled horrible, and not in a way that made her hungry. She assumed this was Gray Wolf's sensation. His torch glowed, but in tones of yellow, bright and dark.

We need for all to see us at once.

Yesss. We should wait. I will howl to the others. She howled, and the spirit creatures lay down, impatient but understanding.

They waited while the last of the spirit animals joined them, in this case, a huge bison, old and scarred.

Now? asked Gray Wolf.

Yes, now. But slowly, very slowly.

Gray wolf howled again, and all the other spirit animals got up and advanced at a slow walking pace toward the sawmill and the two men.

"Did you see that, Miller?" One man lifted his gun.

"What the hell you talking about, Fredrick? I don't see no—holy crap I just saw something."

Fredrick whirled about, pointing his rifle at Miller. "Where? What did you see?"

"Hey, stop pointing that thing at me. Behind you, I thought I saw a wolf. Biggest one I ever seen, too."

Fredrick whirled back and faced, eye to eye—or eyes to eyes—the green eyes of Gray Wolf.

Gray Wolf smiled her wolfish, hungry smile and growled. Fredrick's gun fired, echoing through the dark and now scary forest. Miller's rifle followed in quick succession. Fredrick looked back to Miller, who was reloading, and moved closer.

"Stop just standing there and reload, damn you."

Fredrick started to reload his own rifle. His hands were shaking, and he had to dump the powder cartridge in twice, the first lost somewhere on the ground. The creatures began to circle the mill moving anti-clockwise. The two men's eyes followed the movement.

"You see them, too?" Fredrick gave up on his gun and pulled his knife, making stabbing motions whenever a creature pushed in too close.

"Of course, I did. I ain't shooting at nothing at all."

Both heard the footsteps running in their direction at the same time.

Miller shouted, "Who goes there? Identify yourself."

Marshall's voice rang out. "Hold up, dammit. What are you shooting at?"

"I was shooting at the eyes, sir, and the creatures that stand behind them. There's dozens of them." Miller pointed his gun directly over Marshall's shoulder toward the forest. "Fredrick saw them first. Then I saw them, too. We both shot at them."

Marshall turned in the direction indicated. "This way?"

Gray Wolf stood directly in front of him, her large green eyes looking right at Marshall. *This one does not see me, or any of us.*

No, he does not believe at all.

"You have any sense of this at all, Everton?"

Harry Everton stalked toward the forest verge, bent down and examined the soil, stood up and sniffed. He squinted and whirled about always looking to the side.

"What the hell are you doing, Harry? Having a fit?"

Gray Wolf sidled up to him, blinked her membrane down so her low light vision would be increased. This also had the effect of reflecting light back through her retina and created the phenomenon known as 'eyeshine.'

"I thought I could catch something, don't know exactly what. But I could see something like eyes in the dark." He shook his head. "Don't know though, but I 'spect there is something there."

"Well, these two ain't going to be good for nothing tonight, 'cept maybe shooting each other. Ike, you and your apprentice check the mill over, and then you two guard it for the rest of the night." Marshall turned toward the Landing and started off.

"Begging your pardon sir, but I can already see them."

Marshall whirled back. "You, too, Ike? Where?"

Gray Wolf was leading the group past Marshall, Fredrick, and Miller.

"I see them. They're walking right past you."

"You see them' too, Milson? I take it you ain't afraid?"

"No, I ain't afraid of no man or thing. I don't see nothing much, sir. Some movement out the corner of my eye when I ain't looking directly, so to speak."

"Orders stand. You two watch here."

Several gunshots resounded from the direction of the Landing. Marshall and Harry Everton ran in that direction. When they reached the clearing, they could see the remaining crew in a semi-circle near the entrance of the bunkhouse. Several were to the rear loading, while those in front swung their weapons from side to side as if they could see something that Marshall could not. They could undoubtedly see every one of the spirit animals. One man lay in front of the others, holding his foot.

"Stop shooting," Marshall ordered. The crew brought their guns up. "I said, stop. Harry, check that man. See if he's going to live."

Two Blankets looked through green eyes at each man in turn. Some seemed to recognize the wolf's gaze and shrank back, some did not and looked right through her.

"Now, what are you men shooting at? Eyes, I presume?"

"Yes, sir." There were several nods, and several men just looked confused now, confused and embarrassed.

He stepped up among them and pressed down a couple of guns that were still raised.

Two Blankets noticed Mr. Gilly standing near the back, looking straight at her, almost as if he recognized her in Gray Wolf's spirit body.

"You! Gilly! You see anything?"

Gilly met Marshall's eyes. "Yes, sir, I do. Right behind you. I see a huge gray wolf with green eyes."

Gray Wolf smiled her hungry smile and looked at Gilly. Then he nodded.

"She looks very hungry if I do say so."

"Well, as my grandma used to say, 'We's all up now, might as well have a drink.' Let's go on up to the Landing and have one. What do you say, men? A drink on the house?"

There was some uplift in the men's spirits, but Two Blankets could see it came more from the offer of a free drink than any disbelief in what they had just seen.

Gray Wolf howled again, and some of the men jumped. The spirit animals accompanied the crew toward the Landing, and some of the men moved to the center of the group. As they passed through the door, looking back and fingering their triggers nervously, the spirit animals drifted away toward the Sacred Grove.

Gray Wolf and White Mouse walked back to the moon cycle hut and through the door flap. Two Blankets, looking through Gray Wolf's eyes, saw her body atop the sleeping furs with Mira in her arms.

Mira opened her eyes and smiled at them.

Now we must put your spirit-self back into your body. Ease out of me and allow your spirit body to flow back into yourself.

Two Blankets allowed her spirit body to disconnect gradually, first from behind Gray Wolf's eyes. Her vision snapped back and disconcerted her.

Close your eyes. It is the same as before. Do nothing is the key. Do nothing.

Do nothing. Two Blankets closed her eyes to the shock of the vision change. Her legs slid from Gray Wolf's body and slipped into the top of the head of her sleeping body. With the sense of a "whoosh," she slid almost all the way into her own body. Only the top of her head was still out and attached by a bright cord to Gray Wolf. Gray Wolf licked the cord with her tongue and gently nosed Two Blankets into herself. She exhaled sharply then fell into a deep sleep.

Mira reached a small hand out to Gray Wolf and petted her on the ruff of her neck, then put her arms around Two Blankets' throat and rested her head back on her mother's breast.

"Thank you, Gray Wolf."

Gray Wolf settled down and lay her head on Two Blankets lap. *We have really started something now, White Mouse.*

White Mouse shrank in size until she could perch on Two Blanket's shoulder. She chittered. *Yes, we did.*

Thank you for shrinking back down. It was disconcerting to have you so big.

The day following, Two Blankets woke late and stretched. There was activity outside, and she had to find out what it was. Disengaging Mira's arm, she pulled the sleeping fur over her shoulders and poked her head out the door flap. Marshall was there instructing his workmen.

"All right. I hear what you men are saying about the Injun graveyard. I ain't saying you are right, mind you, but I ain't one to make a fight where one ain't needed. This is what we are going to do. Ike, take the sawmill and start cutting along the river, all the way to the bluff. Keep on cutting until you get close to the graveyard and stop there."

"I ain't fired?"

"No, I ain't going to fire you, but you really pissed me off. You don't want to do that again."

"No, sir. We'll get right on it." Ike signaled his apprentice, and they started up toward the grove and the sawmill.

"The rest of you, what the hell you standing around here for? Let's get to work." Marshall glanced over at the moon cycle hut and screwed up his brows into a questioning look.

Well, she thought, *at least this is one he can't blame me for.*

MONSIEUR BAYONNE

CHAPTER 10
SUMMER AND FALL, 1860

THE REMAINDER OF the spring followed much as such things did, one event chasing another through the year. Circumstances remained somewhat calm at the Landing, and trade slowed down, at least trade toward Portland. Trade toward The Dalles improved, though not enough to make up the difference. There just weren't as many pioneers traveling downriver. They had developed and built a new road from The Dalles toward Mt. Hood and the Willamette. All of this did not bother Two Blankets in the least in her seasonal routines.

One day in mid-spring, she decided to go over to the Landing. She hadn't been there but a couple of times since the events surrounding the sawmill. She bathed and dressed carefully in the cotton print dress she had obtained from *Monsieur* Bayonne. Mira insisted on wearing her bonnet, though it was now almost too small for her.

"Jean Michel gave me this. I wear for him."

"It is unlikely we will see *Monsieur* Bayonne today."

"He will be there. I wear for him."

Two Blankets smiled and wrapped Mira in her skirt of buckskin and her jacket. "This jacket is almost too small. I will have to make you another."

Mira was putting on her moccasins and jumped up when she had finished. "I ready."

They entered the Landing and saw her friends Aimee and Delores Sue.

Delores Sue waved her over. Aimee just rolled her eyes. Mira climbed up into Delores Sue's lap, who began talking baby talk with her. Mira played along and baby talked right back.

There was a sense of anticipation in the room.

Aimee glanced toward the door. "We are waiting for Jean Michel. Of course, we been waiting all week. I so need a distraction from this boredom." She fanned herself with her hand.

"Coffee?" Delores Sue offered, pouring from the unending pot.

"Thank you, Delores Sue."

Two Blankets drank her coffee and sighed.

The whistle from the steamboat sounded across the clearing. Aimee walked languorously to the window.

"Is it the *Carrie Ladd, Mademoiselle* Aimee?"

Aimee pulled the curtain aside and peeked out. "Oh, I don't know, perhaps it is." She strolled back to her seat and relaxed into it, like a cat.

The door opened finally to admit *Monsieur* Bayonne. Mira looked up smiling. *"Pike,* it is *taz háma."*

"Ah, it is my favorite group of beautiful ladies." He greeted each in turn, ending with Aimee and then Mira. "The dress looks very nice on you, Missus Johnston."

Two Blankets flushed. *Why, oh why does this happen to me?*

She raised her head. "Thank you, *Monsieur* Bayonne."

"We have been so bored here without any company from outside." Aimee fluttered her eyelashes like a butterfly. "Won't you join us and give us news?"

"Of course." He sat down. "I am to be joined by my brother. I don't think I have told you that."

"Your brother?" Aimee laughed. "No, you have not told us you had a brother. Is he as handsome as you?"

"If you can call a free Creole of color handsome, then perhaps he is." Jean Michel Bayonne smiled his most gracious smile at Aimee.

"Oh, sir. Do *not* smile at me like that. What will people think?"

Two Blankets drank her coffee. "Is he coming down the Oregon Trail?"

"Oh, no. I did not, either. He is coming by boat, from New Orleans, then across the Panama by railroad. It costs a little more but cuts forty days from the trek by wagon."

"I thought everyone came by wagon, *Monsieur* Bayonne. I did not know of this railroad."

"Yes. It was built by a New York company at great expense, a million dollars I have heard, headed by William Aspinall. It was finished in 1855. He took a ship from New Orleans to the Panama and thence by railroad across Panama. Then by boat up to Portland."

"Oh, that is exciting. Will he be in trade with you?" Aimee said.

"That is the plan. So, Aimee, perhaps the next time I come by here, you will have two Bayonne brothers to shower with your beauty."

"Ah, *Monsieur* Bayonne, you are too kind." Aimee dipped her head in a mock blush.

Two Blankets looked to Delores Sue who raised her hand to her forehead and yawned at Aimee's obvious pretense. She and Delores Sue both giggled.

They could hear the conversations and boot steps outside before the door opened. *Monsieur* Bayonne excused himself and moved to the bar, perhaps to avoid another "don't sniff around my whores" conversation with Marshall. Two Blankets noticed that his greeting to Marshall was expansive and polite as always. Aimee sat back down and made a moue of disappointment.

Mira climbed down off Delores Sue's lap and began wandering about the Landing. Two Blankets watched her protectively. Then the little girl ran to *Monsieur* Bayonne and hugged him about the boot. He petted her atop her bonnet. She smiled and ran to Two Blankets. She repeated the process with a laugh and returned to her mother.

The men's voices rose. Two Blankets heard *Monsieur* Bayonne's voice assume a commanding tone. "Perhaps, I should take my trade elsewhere. Is that what you would like, Mister Johnston?"

"Now, don't go on like that. Just 'cause I call you a nigra and an Injun ain't no reason for you to take offense. It is true, ain't it?"

Mira ran to hug Bayonne's leg. *"Monsieur* Bayonne is *taz háma, Pike."*

"It is true that I am a Creole of color and a free man. I have always been a free man."

Marshall turned to Two Blankets. "Get that damn kid out of here. This is men's business, adult business."

Monsieur Bayonne bent to Mira. "Mira. You are a sweet child. Please go back to your mother."

Mira looked up into *Monsieur* Bayonne's eyes. "Yes, sir. I just want say, you *taz háma*." She released him and ran back to Two Blankets.

Bayonne rose from his crouch. His lips mimed the words *"taz háma?"*

"Mebbe I should just say you are a sniffer of quim? Of course, that would apply to all men." Marshall lifted his glass.

"If I were to call you an ignorant fool, would that insult you?"

"Now, you're talking about a fight here. You don't want to do that."

"I will take my trade elsewhere for this trip. Good day gentlemen, ladies." He dropped a coin on the bar for the drink and walked out.

"Touchy feller, I have to say." Marshall lifted his glass.

"Damn Marshall, why did you have to go and run him off? I really wanted to buy some needles," Big Ed said.

Ike said, "I needed some other small goods myself. We don't see many traders here."

"Sweet Jaysus. If you're going to complain, then get back to work." His comment was to the men, but his look was upon Two Blankets.

"Please excuse me, ladies." Two Blankets pushed her chair back.

As she was walking out, she overheard Aimee's last comment, "Now that she spoiled everything, she leaves."

Now she had lost a friend and *Monsieur* Bayonne both. Although Aimee was never a friend, she was, at least, someone who should understand.

Why is Aimee against me? What have I done to her? Tears formed in her eyes. *Because she wants* Monsieur *Bayonne for herself, is that why? I do not stand in her way.*

Mira tugged her skirt. *"Pike,* are you sad?"

Two Blankets rubbed her eyes and picked Mira up. "Oh, dear one, *Pike* is just confused. It is nothing. Are you happy?"

Mira gazed into her face a long while. *"Monsieur* Bayonne is *taz háma*. I like him."

"Yes, darling, *Monsieur* Jean Michel Bayonne is *taz háma.* I like him, too."

———————

TWO BLANKETS HAD much of the summer to contemplate *Monsieur* Jean Michel Bayonne, and if truth be told, she did not spend much of her time considering him. She did visit the Landing several more times and found that Aimee's animosity toward her had not diminished. If anything, it had hardened. Eventually, with apologies, she stopped visiting. It was a lonely time in one sense, and not so in another.

For she had Mira and together they went about what was, to Two Blankets, routine, but to Mira, was a continual world of wonder... and learning.

Occasionally, Delores Sue would come and visit her, and these days were special to her. On one such, as they were having tea, and Delores Sue was telling a story about her background, Two Blankets finally blurted out what had been bothering her.

"Why is Aimee so angry with me, Delores Sue? I have always tried to treat her with the politeness she deserves as a woman and a working woman at that."

"You really don't understand, do you?"

"No. I would like to, but I do not."

"Sometimes you amaze me with what you have gone through. The stories of you being kidnapped and being a *mistshimus* and all that. You have been so brave and smart. Then something—or someone I should say—like Aimee comes along and tips your wagon right over, and you don't understand it."

"No, and I would like to. Perhaps there is something I could do."

"I don't think so, honey." Delores Sue picked up the ball of leather and tossed it for Mira to chase. "Aimee hates you because she thinks you have come between her and her love, Jean Michel."

"But I never have. I was only polite and nice to him. Just as he has been to us. To you and Aimee and me."

Mira came running back laughing, and Delores Sue threw the ball again. "She's like a cat that's got the heat. Logicality ain't got nothing to do with it.

He don't respond to her, and he does to you. That's all Aimee can see. Truth to tell, girl, she's getting on my nerves, too. Now, you got any more of this raspberry tea? Did I tell you about the time I had to take care of three men, and all of them wanted to be first?"

Two Blankets poured the tea and mused. *What to do? What to do?*

Gray Wolf sidled up to her. *I'd say do nothing. There is nothing to do with a bitch in heat unless you want to kill her.*

"Do nothing, and no, I don't want to fight."

Delores looked up from her story, laughing. "What's that, Two Blankets?"

"Ah, nothing. Sometimes there is nothing you can do."

"Ain't that the truth, honey." She chuckled.

————————

WHEN *MONSIEUR* BAYONNE next came to the Landing some three months later, in the late summer, Two Blankets was outside working. She heard the whistle of the steamboat and felt something within her melt for a moment. Then she stiffened her spine and resolved to remain where she was.

Every time I hear the steamboat whistle I feel like this, disturbed I think.

The *Carrie Ladd* pulled up to the dock, and *Monsieur* Bayonne led his horse and mule off and toward the Landing.

I must stay here and do nothing, even if what I want to do is go to the Landing.

As the steamboat pulled away with another authoritative whistle, Mira ran up. *"Pike,* it is *taz háma, Monsieur* Bayonne."

Two Blankets looked down and watched him surreptitiously. "I know, little one."

"But it is Jean Michel. Aren't we going up to the Landing?"

"No, I think not."

"But I want to." Tears were forming in her eyes.

Two Blankets knelt and opened her arms. She did not command Mira, but the invitation was there. Mira collapsed into her embrace. "He is nice to me. No one else is."

"What about Delores Sue? Isn't she nice?"

"Yes, she is. But not Aimee."

"No, not Aimee." This comment set her to thinking. *What can I do about Aimee?*

I say nothing. Anything you do will make the situation worse.

"Yes, Gray Wolf, so you said."

Mira reached down and put one arm around Gray Wolf's neck. *"Pike?"*

"Yes, Mira."

"Does Gray Wolf talk to you?"

"Yes, darling, she does. Does she talk to you?"

"Only, sometimes. Mostly she just looks at me, and I know things, and she makes me feel better."

"I don't think we will go up to the Landing today. I do like *Monsieur* Bayonne, but I remember what happened the last time. Do you remember, the last time?"

"Yes, I remember. Mister Johnston got mad at him, and he left. I do not know why."

Two Blankets held Mira tightly and rocked her to and fro. "It is something I cannot explain right now, but someday I fear you will understand too well."

"Pike, you are squeezing too tight. If you do not want to go to the Landing, do you want to go fishing?"

Two Blankets was surprised at how quickly Mira could change her mind. "Shall we?"

"Yes, let us go get a *názog.* A really big one."

———

IN OCTOBER OF 1860, Two Blankets was headed from the storehouse when *Carrie Ladd* announced her presence again and puffed around the bluff. Two Blankets stopped what she was doing and watched. She was coming into the Landing. When she pulled in, Two Blankets saw *Monsieur* Bayonne disembarking with another man. The second man resembled *Monsieur* Bayonne from this distance. Perhaps it could be his brother. He led a horse and mule as well.

Two Blankets considered. Marshall was gone to Oregon City and Salem for a few days and there would not be any arguments there.

"Aimee is—well, she's just Aimee. I will go up there."

She hurried back to her longhouse and pulled the dark-blue wool dress out from the trunk she kept it in. She didn't have any petticoats and only this one suit of underclothes. They would have to do. She dressed quickly and brushed her hair.

"Would you like to go to the Landing and see *Monsieur* Bayonne, Mira?"

Mira looked up from the blocks of wood she was stacking. "Oh, yes. I will be very still. Very polite."

"Just take care, Mira." Two Blankets wondered about the tension she felt in her belly. They hurried out of the longhouse and up to the Landing.

As they entered, they saw *Monsieur* Bayonne greeting Delores Sue and Aimee, and she held back to allow him to complete his introduction of the man who was, in fact, his brother.

"Allow me to introduce you, Missus Johnston, to my brother, Gerard."

Gerard took her hand as *Monsieur* Bayonne had before and looked her straight in the eyes. "Ah, the beautiful Missus Johnston. Your reputation precedes you. I am pleased to finally meet you." He bowed deeply and kissed the tips of her fingers.

Gerard was a shorter and stockier version of his brother. Also, he was a bit darker in complexion.

"I am pleased to meet you as well, *Monsieur* Gerard. You will be trading like your brother?"

"Yes. I have a horse and mule, and we are building a wagon for me, too."

"Do you live in the wagon as well as trade from it?" Aimee asked.

"Yes, we have no house other than the wagons."

"Ah, that is so sad." Aimee's mock pout was evident to Two Blankets. What was this woman after? "I thought you would at least have a house to go home to."

"Alas no, my pretty lady. Only the wagons."

"But surely you are only doing that for a short time, while you are trading?"

"One can only hope, *Mademoiselle*. Our family back home is well off, like those of many free Creoles of color. Our family has been in the Cane River area for a hundred years. But Jean Michel and I are the youngest of eight children. So we are here, and we depend on your trade for our livelihood."

"Ah, I think I understand. When you two have proved yourselves as skillful traders, you will go back home to a secure future."

Gerard looked at Jean Michel, and both laughed. "No, *Mademoiselle.* I am here because of my brother. He has done fairly well as a trader here, thanks to you, in part. When my brother left, the family disowned him."

"Not that there was much to disown." Jean Michel laughed.

"So, when I joined him, I joined him in his disgrace."

"We live like gypsies in our wagons," Jean Michel said.

"It seems rather foolish," Aimee said.

Two Blankets said, "I think it is courageous."

"Perhaps it is a little of both, foolish and courageous." Jean Michel's smile lit the gathering.

Mira yawned, and Two Blankets picked her up. "I will take Mira back to sleep this afternoon. Perhaps I may see you for trading early tomorrow morning before the steamboat comes in."

Both *Monsiers* Bayonne got up to say goodbye. Two Blankets whispered to Jean Michel, "Perhaps I am too forward, but I do not wish my husband, Marshall, to see us trading, at least not here at the Landing."

"I understand. I will be careful and come at around ten o'clock."

Two Blankets did not know what ten o'clock was, but she agreed.

The next morning she dressed again in her blue dress and made some raspberry tea for her guests. After the greetings, she served the tea to the Bayonne brothers.

"That dress looks very good on you, but when I sold it to you, I never thought you wouldn't have petticoats."

"Or, I am somewhat embarrassed to say, much of anything at all regarding underclothing."

"I am sorry to put you in such a position, to have to talk about such things with a man," he said.

"Oh, I don't care about that. There are many things the *whitemans* have that you can't do or talk about. I am only embarrassed to admit that my husband has not provided for me." She looked down, ashamed, then realized it was not her fault and looked back up proud and strong. "I was *mistshimus* when I was sold to Marshall as his wife."

"What is a *mistshimus*, if I may ask?"

"A slave. Perhaps you don't have those in your culture?"

Monsieur Jean Michel looked to Gerard. "Slaves? Oh, yes, there are many slaves where we come from."

"As a *mistshimus*, we were not even allowed any property, not clothing, long hair, or even a name. When I became Marshall's wife, that was a great improvement for me. I earned a name, and he bought me a dress. I didn't know about the underclothing part. I have my own money. What have you for me?"

"I would say you need a chemise, drawers, and a simple petticoat—not a flounced petticoat, just a simple one. These will protect your dress from the dirt that you may get on your body. I think we can accommodate you." He motioned to his brother who dug into his mule's pack. "Two sets for three dollars a set. Let us say five dollars."

Two Blankets took the crisp linen garments and examined the stitching. "How do they get the stitching so even, I wonder?"

"These are made on a sewing machine, not by hand."

She got out her twenty dollar double eagle that she had received from Aimee, and *Monsieur* Jean Michel gave her back three five dollar half-eagle gold coins.

Two Blankets looked at the coins. "So, these three coins are worth the fifteen dollars?"

"Yes, you can see the five and a D, here. That's five dollars."

"Ah, thank you."

"You will forgive me, but you don't look like a Chinook to me."

"I was taken from the *Nimi'ipuu*, the Nez Perce, as the *whitemans* say."

"Ah, did you know that Nez Perce means pierced nose in French?"

"But the *Nimi'ipuu* do not pierce their noses. The Chinook do."

"Well, that shows what the French trappers knew." He laughed. "When they called your people that."

"Monsieur Jean Michel, you say you are a free Creole of color?"

"Yes, my people are French. In fact, one of my female ancestors was a Baleine Bride, a prostitute sent to the colony by the King of France in 1721. That makes me, I suppose, somewhat like Aimee. The Indian part is from the Natchitoches tribe. The nigra part was brought from West Africa. Though they were originally slaves, they had earned their freedom a long time ago."

"But Marshall calls you an Indian and a nigra. I know what an Indian is, of course, but what is a nigra?"

"You have never met a black man?"

"No, I have never seen one. Are there truly people who are black?"

"Some are light-skinned, as light as you. They are of mixed blood, mostly from their white owners taking their pleasure from their slaves. Some are so dark they are almost the color of night."

"That must be something to see, an almost blue-black man. What a wonder the spirits of this world produce. There many of these men, and women I suppose?"

"Not as many as the buffalo, but as many as the *Nimi'ipuu* and all the *Sioux* together, ten times as many. The white man's ships were busy."

"They are all *mistshimus?*"

"Almost all. There are free men among them. But most are slaves, mistshimus, as you say."

Gerard nodded and said, "That is why there may be war in the United States. If Lincoln is elected, I believe the southern slave states will secede and then there will be war."

"When is this election of your chief?"

"In November, this year. Lincoln is a moderate on slavery. He doesn't like it, but he says he won't abolish it either. But the southern states don't believe him. They believe he will continue the inclusion of free states, like Oregon, into the Union."

"Well, it is too big for me, *Monsieur* Jean Michel and *Monsieur* Gerard. I only know I was a *mistshimus,* and no one should have to go through that."

Monsieur Jean Michel nodded. "We are sorry to bring that memory to mind, *Mademoiselle,* truly we are. It was callous of us."

"I am sorry, too," *Monsieur* Gerard said.

"It is not something you did. I did ask, gentlemen."

CIVIL WAR

CHAPTER 11
1861

MARSHALL THREW DOWN his newspaper on the bar. "I *knew* it. Look at this."

Harry Everton picked up the *Portland Weekly Oregonian* and read the headline. *"South Carolina Secedes."*

"Here it is, too, in the *Salem Journal.* Those fools. Lincoln gets elected and just because he's a Republican, they secede. Lincoln ain't even that anti-slavery."

"Well, he's never been an abolitionist, but he certainly wasn't no friend of the Dredd Scott decision."

"Goddammit, goddammit. What do you think Oregon will do?"

"We're a free state, Marshall. That'll stay the same. If it comes to war between the North and the South, I'd guess we'd support the North."

"You're goddamn right we will." Marshall slammed the bottle he was drinking from back down on the bar.

———

A FEW WEEKS later, in late March of 1861, discussions were hot again. Marshall poked the paper with his finger. *"Lincoln Inauguration"* read the headline. "You see here. Lincoln is now president of these here United States and the southern states just can't accept it."

Argument erupted along the bar among Marshall's employees.

"It says here that despite Lincoln's appeasement efforts for southern beliefs, they hate him." He read from the newspaper, "This is the part I want. President Lincoln says, *I have no purpose, directly or indirectly to interfere with the institution of slavery in the United States where it exists. I believe I have no lawful right to do so, and I have no inclination to do so.'* You see, he ain't going to change anything for the South."

"What about extending slave states into the west?" one of the men asked.

"To where? The Arizona Territory? The Washington Territory?"

"There's many in the Arizona who would go with the Confederacy."

"Well, we ain't going to have no nigra slaves here in Oregon. Or in Washington, either, for that matter. Lincoln has said as much, and I believe it."

"What about Governor John Whiteaker? He's a damn pro-slavery secessionist and governor of Oregon."

"He don't speak for the whole state," Marshall said. "Now, let's have another drink and talk about something more promising, like how lovely Aimee and Delores Sue look tonight." He stroked Aimee along the cheek.

TOWARD THE END of April, Marshall got another set of newspapers off the steamboat, *Carrie Ladd.* As he walked back up to the Landing, examining his mail, he stopped suddenly. "Holy Christ. I knew it was coming, and now we're in for it."

Harry Everton joined him. "What is it, Marshall?"

"Just take a look at this." He handed his newspaper over to Harry and searched out another one. He shook it out. "Yep. It's here, too. The Civil War started on April 12, 1861. The South fired on Fort Sumter."

Two Blankets, who had been observing, walked up to Marshall. "Husband Marshall, how do you find out so soon? It has been less than eighteen days since April 12. It used to take one hundred twenty days or more for wagons on the Oregon Trail."

"You don't know about the Pony Express, do you?"

"No, I don't. What is this Pony Express?"

"It started last year. There's a series of some one hundred and sixty or so stations all the way from Independence to Sacramento, set about ten to twenty-five miles apart. A rider rides top speed from one to another, then switches horses and keeps going. They ride about seventy-five miles a day and then pass their mail on to the next rider. They can cross the country in ten days or so."

"It is that important to get news so quickly?"

Marshall just stood there looking incredulously at Two Blankets. "Of course it is. I keep forgetting how ignorant you are."

"Well, why? Why is it so important to get the news right away? This whole Pony Express must have cost a lot of money to set up to run so quickly. What makes it so important?"

"Well, suppose it took twenty days, then I wouldn't know for another ten days about the war starting."

"I understand that part. What I wonder is what difference it would make?"

"The difference is I wouldn't know about it. Can't you see that?" He looked at her totally exasperated. "Forget it, Two Blankets. It is too difficult to explain to someone like you."

———————

THE FIRST MONTHS of the Civil War—a war that in a year would consume the Republic—were strange. There were nightly arguments and discussions at the Landing. Most among the small group of workmen, including Marshall Johnston himself, were confident that this war would not last, in fact, could not last. Most felt it would not last but a few months at most.

"The first battle of the Civil War, the First Battle of Bull Run, it says in this here newspaper," said Marshall, reading from the *Portland Oregonian*, "was attended by dozens of members of Congress and a couple hundred Washington socialites all dressed up for a Sunday outing and packing picnic lunches." He shuffled his newspapers. "Ah, here in *The Boston Herald* there's a poem by H. R. Tracy that describes it. Ahem." He cleared his throat.

"The Civilians at Bull Run

Have you heard of the story, so lacking in glory,

About the civilians who went to the fight?

With every thing handy, from sandwich to brandy,

To fill their broad stomachs, and make them all tight.

There were bulls from our State street, and cattle from Wall street,

And members of Congress to see the great fun;

Newspaper reporters, (some regular snorters,)

On a beautiful Sunday went to Bull Run

"The poem goes on. Ah ha, here is the end.

Did they come down there balmy, to stampede the army?

It would seem so, for how like a Jehu they drive!

O'er the dead and the wounded their vehicles bounded,

They caring for naught but to get home alive.

For the sharp desolation that struck through the nation,

We hold to account the civilians and — rum;

When our soldiers next go to battle the foe,

May our portly civilians be kept here at home.

"It says here that when the Confederates won the first battle, all were in shock. The carriages of the onlookers rushed from the scene rolling over some of the wounded. One congressman, Congressman Alfred Ely, was captured by the Confederates."

All of the men in the Landing took a sorrowful drink.

———

FOR SEVERAL MONTHS it continued thusly. Each event in the beginnings of the war received heated discussion. Most at the Landing felt that the Civil War could not last long. It would not last long, would it?

At the beginning of the war, when Fort Sumter was attacked on April 12, the whole of the U. S. Army totaled only 16,000 men. Lincoln called for 75,000 volunteers. To begin with, there were more than the Union could train or equip, but within a year that soon became untrue as the length of the conflict and the realities of death and maiming became evident.

An afternoon in November, Marshall came into the Landing, sadness on his face carrying his newspapers. *Monsieur* Jean Michel Bayonne was there on this particular afternoon. "Your *Monsieur* Johnston looks disturbed today."

"Yes, he does, *Monsieur* Bayonne, and I do not know the reason."

"Monsieur Johnston, what disturbs you?"

"Senator Edward Baker has been killed in battle."

"Senator Baker, from Oregon?"

"Yes, he was the only Senator to volunteer in the army. A good friend of President Lincoln, too. He just went to Washington D.C. as a Senator, but asked for a command in the army."

"Ah, and he was involved in a recent battle?"

"Yes," Marshall looked for details in the newspaper, "it was a raid on a Confederate camp at Red Bluff. It was supposed to be unguarded. Apparently, it wasn't. Baker was hit by a volley of bullets to the head and heart."

"This is a sad thing when a brave man dies," said Bayonne.

"It says here according to George Wilkes, a journalist from the *Spirit of the Times,* in August of this year, that Baker said, *'I am certain I shall not live through this war, and if my troops should show any want of resolution, I shall fall in the first battle. I cannot afford, after my career in Mexico, and as a Senator of the United States, to turn my face from the enemy.'* Damn. Why is it always the strong and right that are taken?"

"Have a drink, my friend."

Marshall took the drink gratefully and drank it down. He tipped the bottle to the glass and poured another one.

"Husband Marshall, why is it that I see paddle-wheelers going upriver with soldiers and their equipment aboard?"

"President Lincoln has called back all the U.S. troops to the east for the duration of the war."

"Won't that leave the settlements here unprotected?"

"Here in Oregon—and I am sure in California and the Washington territory—they're calling up the militia. They'll keep order with the damn Indians."

"Tell me, my friend," said *Monsieur* Jean Michel Bayonne, "why is it that you don't like nigras or Indians?"

"It ain't like I don't like them. They're all right in their place, and I ain't prejudiced or nothing. I just don't want to live near them. That's why I came to Oregon and not California, for instance. The legislature of the territory put it into the constitution of Oregon all the way back to 1844 that this should be an anti-slavery territory. That proves I ain't no pro-slavery secessionist. But at the same time, they put it into the constitution that no Negroes could live here. Peter Burnett done that. Any slaveholder that came to Oregon had to free their slaves within three years or leave the territory. Once free, the slave had to leave within two years. This here is a white state. Period. I like it that way. We got no nigras here. Don't make me prejudiced. I just want to live with people like me."

"Interesting. A person like me, who has never been a slave, what are you to do about me?" Two Blankets noted a tension in *Monsieur* Bayonne's voice.

Marshall turned to *Monsieur* Bayonne thought about the question for a moment. "Well, that does present the problem, don't it? You say you are a free Creole of color?"

"That is true. Since before the United States was formed, we have been free."

"I ain't no scholar. I would guess we would just have to create a third category for your brother and you."

Monsieur Bayonne tipped his glass to Marshall. "I would say you have a clever mind to come up with that one, Marshall."

"As long as you don't get cozy with my wife, that is."

"Of course. I never have been anything but polite."

"Let's just say, I'll trade with you as long as you ain't *too* polite." Marshall touched glasses with *Monsieur* Bayonne and drank it down. But his eyes never left the trader.

"As you say, Marshall Johnston."

WAR & GOLD

CHAPTER 12
1862

I N THE EARLY spring of 1862, the men at the Landing were discussing the war as usual. Two Blankets had, by this time, established a routine of visiting her friends during the evenings with Mira. The little girl was very good at playing quietly in a corner and listening to all that went on. Delores Sue had become quite a good friend, it appeared, but Two Blankets was still not sure about Aimee.

Actually, I am pretty sure that Aimee, for whatever reason, is no friend of mine. It is a sad thing that of the only two women here, there is only one I can count on as a friend. But mayhap I am mistaken and seeing this situation all wrong.

Mr. Gilly was speaking, and for once he was making his point. "There comes a time when a man has to make up his mind and stand up for what he believes in."

Marshall Johnston tipped his drink toward Gilly. "That's the spirit, Gilly. That's the spirit."

"What are we, out here in Oregon and California, doing for the war effort?"

"You mean besides taxes? We sent our soldiers."

"But, Mister Johnston, I mean, what are we contributing *personally*? What sacrifice are we making?"

"President Lincoln ain't called for no sacrifice or troop levy from California and Oregon. I, for one, ain't going to sacrifice my life before it's called for, I can tell you that much." Marshall drank his glass down and refilled it, making sure to refill Gilly's glass as well. The other men, for the most part, seconded that proposal, but some supported Gilly.

"My family is from New York, at least the part that didn't move to Missouri, and two of my brothers there have volunteered. They get a uniform, a new rifle, and one hundred dollars signing bonus—as well as a salary," Big Ed declared.

"I heard you only get part of the bonus when you sign up," Marshall said. "You only get the rest if you survive your three years."

Gilly slammed his glass down on the bar. "The money ain't the point. I got a brother in Pennsylvania who signed up. He didn't do it for the uniform, though he says in a letter I got, the ladies seem to like it."

"You got a letter?" Marshall said in good humor. "I didn't know you could read." His last comment was sarcastic.

"I got a letter, and I got someone to read it to me. What I'm saying, Mister Johnston, is that it ain't the uniform and it ain't the pay or the bonus. A man signs up because it's right. Supporting the Union is... it's *patriotic* is what it is."

"Are you going to do the patriotic thing, then Gilly? You going all the way back there to enlist?"

"Well, I ain't no coward." He looked around at the other men. "You men know me. I wasn't worth nothing when I first come here, but you all gave me another chance." He turned to Marshall Johnston. "I'm going back and sign up. I am."

"Well, you are a braver man than I am, Gilly. Of course, the war will probably be over afore you get a chance to sign up."

"Gilly," said Big Ed, "I'll ride with you."

"Huzzah. Huzzah," shouted the men surrounding the bar. Drinks were proffered, and backs slapped.

The next day Gilly and Big Ed waited near the dock.

Two Blankets approached them and gave Big Ed a hug. "Thank you for being the man you are, and good luck."

"You are a good woman, Two Blankets."

She turned to Mr. Gilly as he waited in the background for the steamboat.

"Oh, Mister Gilly. Please come back to us. I will always remember what you have done for me."

"I have done for *you*? You remember how I came to you. In what shame. I was just Gilly. You gave me a new life, Two Blankets. You were the only one to call me *Mister* Gilly. You gave me a second chance to be a man. You don't know what that means to me."

She hugged him close to her. "You have got to come back, Mister Gilly." She held him at arm's length. "You hear me."

By this time, both had tears running down their faces. The boat whistled, and the men got on board to join their compatriots.

———

AS THE MONTHS wore on into 1862, the opinions began to vary, then cement into a surety that there would be no clear early winner.

Like many cultures where a war of significant proportions is taking place, but far away, life at the Landing assumed a routine. There were the discussions of the Landing "generals," as Two Blankets came to think of them, under the leadership of General Marshall Johnston.

The one exception was *Monsieur* Bayonne, when he was in residence on one of his infrequent trading visits in 1862.

"I am telling you, *Monsieur* Johnston, the will of the Confederates is strong, even if their cause is wrong."

"Oh, I don't know about that. When them cowards see the strength gathered against them and the impossibility of winning, they'll sue for peace."

"You have to grow up among them to understand. The average southerner is stubborn to the point of this impossibility you speak of, and the more impossible, the better."

Whether the Union was winning or not was questionable. If they were, it was slow, and the Confederates had their share of victories. The casualties were atrocious. As the war wound into 1862, it became apparent to all that Bayonne was correct. In September, at the battle of Antietam, total casualties amounted to almost 23,000 in one day.

———

THE OTHER EVENT of note that took place in 1862, as far as the Landing was concerned, was the discovery of gold in the Boise region. Marshall came into the Landing with his usual sheaf of newspapers. The gleam of acquisition was in his eyes.

"Look at this gentlemen, and give me a drink. I ain't been this excited since the day I made the bargain with the old *Tyee.*"

Two Blankets leaned forward from her seat at the table. "What has excited you so, husband Marshall?"

Behind her back, Aimee mimed her sentence.

"They have found gold in the Boise basin, not more than two or three weeks' travel time from here by horse. It says here that, on August 2, a party led by a George Grimes discovered gold in the Boise region. This could be bigger than the California gold rush."

The men poured over the paper. Marshall sat back at a table and started making some notes or calculations. His face had that scheming look that Two Blankets had come to know so well. She could almost predict when he would make his decision.

"I've got to get myself up there right away. Harry, you're going to have to run things here while I'm gone. If I leave tomorrow, I should be able to be in the area in two weeks, if I push my horse a little. It's a good thing I got that horse from Small Willie. I'll get a mule at The Dalles and whatever supplies we ain't got here."

"Husband Marshall, must you go so soon?"

"I don't know what *you've* got to say about it, Two Blankets."

"I apologize. I am not arguing with you. I am simply trying to understand. Will not the gold still be there in four weeks as in two?"

"No. The first ones there will make the most. It's already been almost a month since the discovery. I may already be too late. The locals will grab up the good claims. Two Blankets, here's a list of supplies I'll need. If I know anything, they will be incredibly expensive in Idaho City. Harry, send a man up to Kinley's place. He's got how many cattle now, a hundred?"

"More like hundred and twenty, I'd say."

"Get him down here. Tell him I'll pay The Dalles prices right here, if he can have them ready to go right away, within a day or so. Samuel, can you and Kenny drive them up to Idaho city? I'll leave you cash for the transport up to The Dalles and across the river and your expenses."

Samuel thought for a minute. "I'm going to need a third boy at least."

"You can take Frank Milson if Ike will let him go. If you need a couple more, you can hire in The Dalles. I'll make it worth your while, I promise."

Samuel turned to Kenny, "You heard the man?"

"Yes, sir."

"Well, why you still standing here? Get on up to Kinley's. Don't say nothing about gold, neither."

"Yes, sir." Kenny ran out of the door.

Two Blankets looked from one man to another. This was like the formation of a war party, only less organized.

"What the hell you still doing here, Two Blankets? I need them supplies."

"Yes, husband Marshall." She began to hurry out of the Landing. She looked at the paper and stopped suddenly. She couldn't read it. She did not want to ask him.

Delores Sue joined her. "I'll help, honey. Let's go." Gathering up Mira, they left the building.

They walked to the longhouse and began bringing out supplies to the table. "Let's see," Delores Sue said, "twenty pounds bacon," and Two Blankets ran to get the meat. "Two sacks of fifty pounds flour and five pounds of soda. Do you have any venison?"

"I have a haunch here."

"Good. Let's see.... Ten pounds coffee, a saucepan, coffee pot, metal plate, a spoon, and a fork."

"I have all that. Here are two sleeping furs, as well."

"That's good. It will be cold before he gets back. That's about it for this list. Oh, wait. Whiskey, twenty bottles. Hah. That should last about a week."

"I don't see how he's going to haul all that."

Delores Sue looked over the pile of supplies. "Well, I'd say that was going to be his problem. I got to go back up to the Landing and make myself pretty for tonight."

"You have been so helpful. I don't know how to thank you."

The next day Marshall had his horse loaded and still had a pile of supplies. "I'll get a mule or two in The Dalles. These supplies are going to be worth a fortune in Idaho City, or I ain't no trader at all."

When the whistle sounded and the paddle-wheeler puffed around the bluff, Marshall was still stalking about the Landing giving orders, a bottle of whiskey in one hand and a cigar clamped between his teeth.

Two Blankets walked down with Mira toward the dock with Delores Sue. Two Blankets covered her eyes from the bright sun. "That isn't the *Carrie Ladd,* is it?"

"No, hadn't you heard? The *Carrie Ladd* went down just this June, near Cape Horn, up by the Cascades. The *Mountain Buck* took off the passengers, and she was raised. I don't know if she's being repaired or not. That there is the *Mountain Buck.*"

There was a crowd at the dock. Marshall just looked at Two Blankets. "You watch out for that Bayonne feller, you hear me, Two Blankets?"

"You have nothing to fear from *Monsieur* Bayonne, husband Marshall."

"Well, just remember what I said." Then the whistle sounded, and Marshall got on board. The sternwheel turned, and the boat backed out into the current. She whistled again, the sternwheel reversed directions, and she churned upstream.

It is strange. I thought I would feel something, but I feel nothing at all. If anything, I feel at peace.

Two days later, when the *Mountain Buck* stopped at the Landing dock, a curious wagon rolled off its bow pulled by two mules and with a horse trailing behind. This wasn't like the prairie wagons or even the Conestoga wagons. For one thing, it was built a lot lighter, and for another, it was boxed in on top. It was painted purple—purple with yellow wheels and trim. The sides and front were a purple canvas that could be rolled up.

Monsieur Bayonne waved to the group, who all stood open-mouthed. They waved back. After the greetings in the Landing, Bayonne sat and replied to questions. "Well, you know about the gold discovery at Boise? I am headed up there. It is not so far, maybe three weeks by wagon. I suspect there will be much profit to it. If I do all right, then my brother will come up as well."

Aimee fluttered about. "That's your wagon outside? The purple one? It's passing strange."

"Yes, my dear Aimee, would you like to look at my home?" He held out his hand. "I will show you."

Monsieur Bayonne walked to the back and dropped the tailgate. Pulling the canvas aside to expose the interior, he lifted Aimee up to the tailgate, then motioned inside.

Aimee looked within then turned out. "I've seen enough. This is too tiny for even one person. It makes me feel—how do you say it—*claustrophobic*. How can you live like this?"

He lifted Aimee to the ground. Spotting Two Blankets, he offered, "Do you want to see, *Madam* Two Blankets?"

"Oh, yes, please." He placed his hands about her waist and gracefully lifted her to the tailgate.

"*Monsieur* Bayonne, it is perfect. It is like a small *Nimi'ipuu* summer hut. There is a bed, and a tiny stove for heat and cooking. Not much room to turn around with all these supplies, but I expect many of these will be sold as soon as you get to Idaho City." She edged in toward the front of the wagon and turned around. "It really is quite lovely."

He lifted her down from the tailgate. "Thank you, *Madam*. Anyone else?"

Delores Sue stepped forward. "I would like to take a look, *Monsieur* Jean Michel, please."

He lifted her up. "Whee. That was fun. I'll tell you, Aimee, I've lived in some cribs as small as this and our rooms at the Landing ain't much bigger. This is a fine wagon, *Monsieur* Bayonne." He set her down on the ground.

Aimee turned to go up to the Landing. "Well. It *is* fine for a temporary home when you're working. I agree with that. But it is no decent house for a real man."

Bayonne, Delores Sue, and Two Blankets watched her go.

"What's got her in an uproar?" Delores Sue asked.

BAYONNE'S LAST VISIT

CHAPTER 13
FALL, 1862

THE FOLLOWING THREE months passed in a flurry of work for Two Blankets and then a slow return to the routine she was used to. After Kinley's cattle were driven to The Dalles, and beyond to the Boise area, the Landing was suddenly lonely. With Gilly and Big Ed gone to the war and no news of them, and with Samuel, Kenny, and Frank Milson on the cattle drive, the Landing was an empty place. The season gradually progressed into fall.

Two Blankets continued her visits to the Landing, though few were there of an evening. What company there was improved her mood. Delores Sue was always polite to her and particularly kind to Mira. This was the basis for a slow-growing, but meaningful friendship. Aimee, possessed of an unending jealousy, which persisted no matter what Two Blankets did, was a different problem. Two Blankets had tried politeness, confrontation, and indifference, all to no avail. She continued with courtesy, more out of habit than anything else. It didn't seem to help, but polite was her normal mode, and she stuck with that.

One afternoon, when the paddle-wheeler steamed around the upriver bluff, its whistle blew, signaling a visit to the Landing. On the foredeck was a wagon that could not be mistaken for anyone's other than *Monsieur* Bayonne's. Two Blankets looked up from her recent tanning project to see him get off the boat.

Her heart was aflutter. *Why in the world do I feel like this? The man is only polite to me, no more.* Yet, she was already on the move toward her hut and fresh clothes. She dressed in her new chemise, drawers, and petticoat, then pulled on her blue wool dress. She brushed her hair and looked into the shard of a mirror she had.

"Mayhap *Monsieur* Bayonne has a small mirror I could afford."

Mira saw her dressing and started trying to dress in her best buckskin wrap. Two Blankets smiled and went to help.

"You want help, Mira?"

"*Taz háma* is here, *Pike.* Yes, help me."

Two Blankets tied the wraparound and then started to help Mira into her moccasins.

"I can do these by myself, *Pike.* You do not even have yours on." She pulled on her moccasins and attempted to pull on her bonnet.

"Oh, Mira, it's too small. It won't fit on your head."

"*Taz háma* gave it to me."

"You can tie it around your neck, like a scarf."

"Yes, *Pike,* tie it."

Two Blankets tied it on, and they left for the Landing.

"Good afternoon, *Madam* Two Blankets." *Monsieur* Bayonne greeted her in his usual affable manner. He lifted her hand and Two Blankets at first shrank back. Then she saw Aimee's triumphant look, and she let him kiss her fingertips. "And *Mademoiselle* Mira, as well." He gave Mira as much attention as he had Two Blankets.

"I do not understand why you make such a fuss over an Indian and her child," Aimee said. "It is disgusting."

"Do you find my attentions to you disgusting, *Mademoiselle* Aimee? Do I not greet you properly?"

"Well, no. But I'm a white woman."

"But I am in part at least a 'disgusting Indian,' as you say."

"You steal words from my mouth. I did not mean it that way." She turned away to the other men in the bar.

Two Blankets said, "I'm sorry to cause such distress, but do you have news?"

"Ah, my mission to Idaho City was a success. I had offers of gold nuggets for the clothes upon my back. Even my hat." He laughed. "I believe your husband, Marshall, was also successful. One thing about him, he is a competent trader, very competent. He knows well how to read a man."

Delores Sue questioned, "Is it so bustling there, then?"

"Oh, Idaho City, which used to be a building or two with twenty inhabitants, if that, is now a major town with two thousand living there. It will likely be a city by next year. And the prices! Oh, my, there are places where a good meal costs twenty-five dollars or more, a two dollar bottle of whiskey sells for ten dollars if you can find one."

"You said your brother was joining you?" Delores Sue asked.

"Yes, he joined about two weeks after I got there in his own wagon. He is even more effusive than I, if you can imagine." Delores Sue laughed, and after a moment Two Blankets did also. "He made even more money than I did. He had no shame in his pricing. He even sold women's bloomers to men who needed clothes, something I could not do. At five times the normal prices." Now, there was no wait for the laughter. "Given the conditions, the men looked quite well in fine linens and ruffles."

"Mira, say goodbye to *Monsieur* Bayonne. Perhaps we may see you tomorrow. As you can see, Mira does need a new bonnet."

"Yes, *Pike.*" Mira held out her hand. Bayonne took it in all seriousness. *"Monsieur* Bayonne, *taz háma,* thank you. We see you tomorrow?" Her tone was grave, and no one laughed.

"Yes, *Mademoiselle* Mira. You certainly will." He bent over her extended hand and gently kissed her fingertips. He then lifted and kissed Two Blankets' fingers as well.

"Enjoy your evening, then. I will see you tomorrow."

"Indeed, *Madam* Two Blankets."

Two Blankets rose from her chair and left the Landing. Mira hugged Bayonne about the boots, then ran to catch up with her mother. No one saw the angry look Aimee gave her as she left.

As she crossed the grounds, Two Blankets let out a huge breath. The day was fresh and new, with the sun shining through the fall sky. The sky looked a thin blue, clear but promising cold weather to come. She flipped open the flap on the hut door and entered the longhouse.

Sitting back on her sleeping furs, she pondered the day's events. Her spirits were indeed lifted whenever she saw *Monsieur* Bayonne, but it was more like when she saw Fox Tail than when she met with Standing Bear.

Is that it? Is Monsieur Bayonne a Two Spirits like Fox Tail? Is that why he is so polite to me and all women but doesn't seem interested in us? Is that why Aimee has no appeal for him? She takes it as a personal insult, yet he will never take passion in her or any woman?

These questions plagued her as she went to sleep that night. When she woke the next morning, the fog still covered the treetops. Below the fog, all was gray. Two Blankets looked up toward the Landing and saw *Monsieur* Bayonne stretching off his night's sleep. He noticed her and gave a wave which she returned. Then she saw him duck back into the Landing.

Is he coming here? Oh, what shall I do? I know I don't want to seem too anxious. But I don't want to give insult either. Well, maybe he won't come here. But he did say he would bring a bonnet by for Mira.

Two Blankets looked down at herself. She shucked out of her work dress and slipped into a fresh pair of drawers, her petticoat, her blue wool dress, and moccasins. She brushed off the hairs on the dress and combed out her own hair.

Oh, my goodness. What am I doing? I am acting like a little girl.

She heard a scratching on the tent flap and responded, "Come in."

Monsieur Bayonne ducked under the flap. "Should I be in here?"

"I think for a short time it will be all right. Hello, *Monsieur* Bayonne. I am glad to see you."

"Ah, and I am glad to see you as well, *Madam* Two Blankets. Truly, I am." He looked and saw Mira still asleep. "I did bring a bonnet for *Mademoiselle* Mira. The other one is about a year too small."

Two Blankets approached near the entrance and took the proffered bonnet. "This is beautiful. The embroidery is lovely. How much would it be?"

"Let us call it a gift, my friend. We have known each other for long enough. You may call me Jean Michel, if you want."

"I don't know if I could—or *should, Monsieur* Bayonne." She looked up at him, and tears rushed to her eyes. "You have been surpassing kind to us, and I don't know why."

Monsieur Bayonne took another step closer and, taking his handkerchief from his jacket pocket, gently brushed the dampness from her eyes. "Do not cry, dear *Madam* Two Blankets. I do not know how you continue to bear up under the abuse you suffer."

"I know, or I suspect, you cannot continue to comfort me, *Monsieur*—"

He put his fingertips on her lips.

"—Jean Michel, but could you just hold me for a little while?"

"You are a silly girl," he said as his strong arms came up around her. Slowly he rocked from side to side. Her head rested on his chest. "Why would you say you suspected I could not do this?"

"Oh, and now I am ashamed if I am wrong." She pulled back to look him in the eyes. "I cannot be sure, but I had a feeling you might be a Two Spirits. Oh, if I am wrong, please forgive me."

"A Two Spirits? Do you mean a man and a woman in one body?"

"Please don't be angry. But that is what I thought."

"You understand that if I admitted that, among white society, it would be worth my life."

"Yes, I do. So please do not answer me. Not that I would ever tell anyone. I know how the *whitemans* are on this issue. My good friend among the Chinook, Fox Tail, was a Two Spirits and honored for it."

"It is a weighty question. If I admitted to being a Two Spirits, you could accept my friendship, and ask for no more?"

"Oh, Jean Michel, I would accept it in any way offered. I would never ask for more. It would just help to understand, but that is not necessary either."

"Well—ahem—it is true. I *am* a Two Spirits, as you call it. Please know why I could not say before. It would literally be worth my life if it got out."

"Thank you." She sighed. "No one shall ever know from me." His arms tightened around her, and she held to him.

They both heard the boot on the gravel outside the flap at the same time and stepped apart. The flap was ripped up and half off the hut.

"I *knew* I would catch you out with her. I just knew it." Marshall's red face poked in, his eyes working to see in the dim light.

"Husband Marshall, you have returned. How—I did not hear the paddle wheeler come in. How did you get here?"

"Ha! I come down on a flatboat. I didn't wait for the steamer. *That's* how I caught you."

"Now, *Monsieur* Johnston, the Madam has done nothing wrong. Not in deed and not in word either, I assure you."

"I know that cunny's been after you for a year. And I seen you sniffing around her. Being all nice and polite and all. A man only acts like that for one thing, when he's after what she's got between her legs."

"I have done nothing. *Monsieur* Bayonne has done nothing. Let him go."

"I should kill him, that's what I should do." His eyes turned hard and calculating.

Others had now joined him in front of the longhouse.

"But if he comes out all nice like, I won't kill him."

"I will come. Just leave *Madam* Two Blankets out of this. She has done nothing wrong. If this is to be, then it should be between men."

"Don't trust him, Jean Michel. Don't trust that man."

Jean Michel looked her sweetly in the eyes. "On my word, I will not, *Madam* Two Blankets." He smiled and bowed low, kissing her fingertips. Then he straightened and strode toward the entrance.

Bayonne exited the hut. Marshall backed up. "Grab him, boys. This nigra's been fucking my whore of a wife." Two men stepped up and took his arms. "Is that roof tar around? Put it on the fire to warm up a bit. We're going to have some fun with this son of a bitch before we send him on his way."

Two men kicked up the fire and rolled the barrel of tar over to it.

"It's too cold right now, Marshall."

"Oh, it'll warm up presently, and then we're going to send him packing as black as he really is. You two, harness up his team and take it down to the dock."

"So, Marshall, this is how you keep your word?"

"Oh, I ain't going to kill you. That's all I promised. But I tell you what, you'll sure remember Marshall Johnston and Johnston's Landing after this little experience."

"Marshall, just let him go. He won't come back." Two Blankets stood by the entrance of the longhouse.

"You, shut the fuck up. I'll deal with you later."

"You said you would let her go, *Monsieur* Johnston."

"You live here on this river long enough, you learn people lie about what they're going to do. To you and to others." Bayonne struggled against the men holding him. "Tie his arms and tie his feet about a foot apart."

The men complied. The pair with the wagon drove it down to the dock and then came running back up to join their compatriots. Their eyes were eager. Delores Sue and Aimee stepped out onto the porch of the Landing their skirts rustling. Aimee was shading her eyes, pointing, and, Two Blankets thought, smiling.

"Now, blindfold him. Don't want to get any of this tar in his pretty eyes." Two men tied a bandanna over his eyes. "Now, here's the task. You get to the wagon, and that'll be the end of this. As long as you don't come back."

Marshall pulled the tarring stick from the barrel. It was just a long spar with a tar saturated cloth tied to the end. "Better fix that location in your mind, Bayonne." He poked him in the back with the tarring stick. "Well, what are you boys waiting for? Grab a stick and have some fun." He poked Bayonne again.

Bayonne began walking in short steps toward the wagon. A man pushed him with another tar-soaked spar and laughed. A third poked him with a stick from the other side. Bayonne tripped and fell, then he kicked out, and the man landed on his own stick. Bayonne got up and kicked out again but his reach was shortened, and he only caught the man in the ribs.

Marshall dipped his cloth again and slammed his stick into Bayonne's back. Bayonne took several steps forward before he caught his balance. He still had a good hundred feet to go. Rather than run, he stopped and brought his arms up to his face. Suddenly, his hands were free. A fourth man took a swipe at his face, and the tar ran down his chest. Now he had his blindfold off. The men circled him, taunting. He looked at them through his one clear eye, then bent down slowly and untied a foot. A man jabbed at him with his stick, but he was too close, and when he fell back onto the ground, he was almost as covered with tar as Bayonne, and Bayonne had his stick.

Swinging it back and forth, he backed toward his wagon. One man on his right swung at him high and hard. He went to one knee and poked the man hard in the diaphragm. The man gasped and bent over to meet the stick in Bayonne's hand as it came up hard. Marshall advanced upon him, then looked around. His followers were only following, not leading anymore. Two were down and sticky. A third backed up Marshall but wasn't making any leading moves.

Marshall threw his spar down. "All right men, that's enough." His view encompassed the group. "Ike, you got your rifle."

"I thought we might need it."

"Hold him right there until the boat comes. No, don't shoot the nigra. I don't want any law here digging their noses into things. Remember the problems we had with Small Willie. Clean kill and it was like we was on trial. I got me a wife to discipline."

"Don't worry. I'll hold him."

Marshall marched back up to the longhouse. "Get yourselves cleaned up and get back to work. Lotta good you lot were. This here's between me and Two Blankets."

She backed away into the longhouse. Mira was there sitting up on the sleeping furs. "Whatever happens, just stay there, Mira. This is between Marshall and me."

"Did *taz háma* leave?"

"He had to leave. It will be all right." She looked for her knife. It was laying on the bar. She didn't know if she could take Marshall. He was bigger than she was, a lot bigger if she wanted to be truthful. She knew he was crafty. On the other hand, he was a coward at heart. She had that going for her at least.

Be oh, so careful, Two Blankets. He is dangerous.

"I know sweet White Mouse. I will."

You must stalk him. You will not get many chances. Gray Wolf growled deep in her throat.

"Now bitch, we got some things to get straight." Marshall peeked in through the door flap.

"You *bastard!* Bayonne never did anything with me. If I wanted to fuck a man, I've had lots of opportunities with this crew. You didn't know that, did you?"

"You're a lying bitch. Aimee told me all about what you and that Bayonne feller been up to while I been gone. I went there first thing I got back. She said Bayonne was out all night with you. You deny that?"

"I do. I don't blame her for what she has to do to live, but she's lying. Now, get away from me and get out of here." She circled to the left toward the bar and grabbed her knife. Crouching she held the blade low.

Marshall advanced on her, his hands held wide, his eyes wary and watching the knife. "Now, come on Two Blankets. You give me what I want, maybe I'll only slap you around a bit. That's pretty damn generous of me, you got to admit."

"I admit nothing because there is nothing to admit."

Marshall lunged and she whirled, slicing his arm. He stood there for a moment looking at the blood welling up. It wasn't a deep cut, but the color of it stunned him. She lunged with the knife and caught him by surprise with a gash on the shoulder. He slapped at her knife hand, and it dropped to the floor. He hit her across the temple with his fist, and she fell. He kicked her. She rolled over, and he kicked her a second time in the ribs.

He hauled his booted foot back again to kick her a third time. Mira ran toward him and grabbed him about the boot. "You leave *Pike* alone. Leave her alone."

Johnston shook his boot. "Let go you little bitch. Let go my boot." He snapped his foot out. She flew off and landed on the sleeping furs.

"You *dare* hurt my child?" Two Blankets picked up the knife and got to her feet. There was insanity now behind her eyes. She stalked toward him.

"I'm all right, *Pike*. I'm all right."

"You just stay right there. I will take care of this bastard."

"Now, you don't want to do that, Two Blankets. You remember the last time you took that knife to me."

She was in a crouch, shifting from side to side. Where had she learned to do that? "You hurt my child, you bastard."

She lunged toward his face. He slapped at the knife, but she wasn't there anymore. She had dropped down to his boot. He shook the boot trying to rid himself of her, but she wouldn't let go. He stumbled and went down. Suddenly, she raised up with both hands on the handle and plunged down with it, upon his exposed leg just above the boot. He managed to push her off with his other boot, as he crab-crawled out the tent flap. He yelled in pain as he pulled the blade out and dropped it to the ground.

Two Blankets remembered what Gray Wolf had once said—*Knock him down and hamstring him. Then stand on his chest and howl.*

She got to her feet, favoring her kicked ribs, and walked to the entrance. Reaching down to pick up the knife, she glanced down at the blood running down over her hand. Marshall was still backing away on his bottom.

Two Blankets held the knife to the sky and shook it. Everyone in the camp was looking at her. Then she howled a wolf bitch's cry, the howl of a wolf protecting her pup. She bent and wiped the blade off on Marshall's crotch.

"You will *never* come near me or mine again without permission. Do you understand?"

He just mumbled, holding his leg.

"I said, do you *understand?*"

"Yes, I understand."

Two Blankets turned and re-entered the longhouse.

RETRIBUTION

CHAPTER 14
FALL, 1862

TWO BLANKETS KNELT over Mira. She probed her little body and examined her eyes. "Are you sure you're all right? Do you hurt anywhere?"

"I think so, *Pike*. My side hurts. Why did he go crazy like that?"

She pulled aside the child's wraparound dress. There was a bruise along the ribs. She compressed these lightly. The bones did not seem to be cracked, but when Mira moaned, she left off pressing.

"I think you just need to rest. As to why he went crazy... sometimes there is no telling when a *whiteman* is involved."

Mira reached up and touched Two Blankets' face. She showed her mother bloodstained fingers to with a look of concern. *"Pike,* you have blood on your face."

"It is just a scratch, Mira. Now, you lay down, and I will clean myself up."

"I will." Mira climbed up onto the sleeping platform and pulled a fur over her.

Two Blankets pulled off her dress, wincing as she felt her own ribs move. *Her ribs might be good, but mine? I will be lucky if none are cracked.*

She probed the reddened area and winced. *That one I will have to watch. I will be multi-colored in a few days, but it will heal.*

Now, my face.

It too was red, and as she looked into the small mirror, she saw that Marshall's fist had cut her across the eyebrow. She dabbed at it with a damped cloth. The anger suffused her as she looked.

Aimee. *She* caused this.

Her hand reached down to where she usually carried the knife, then clenched on empty air. Her eyes as she looked at them in the mirror were cold and hard.

Aimee and I will meet over this.

She lay down next to Mira and pulled the fur over her.

I feel somewhat sad for this human, Aimee. Gray Wolf exposed a toothy grin.

As the afternoon wore on to early evening, Two Blankets roused herself. She pushed up on one elbow, and the pain put her right back down. Waiting a moment to get her strength up, she braced herself against the pain and pushed up. Her face throbbed, and her ribs ached badly.

She looked down at Mira. Her face had a scrape across it that she hadn't noticed before. This brought back her rage. She stood up shakily and grabbed the bar. Her legs refused to support her, then she forced them under her and straightened her back. She slipped her dress on over her head and noted the tear in the skirt. Over this, she tied on her belt knife. She pulled it once from the sheath, remembering the blood upon it, then pushed it back into the sheath.

"Mira, honey?"

"I am awake, *Pike.* You are dressed. Where you going?"

"I am going up to the Landing for a few minutes. I need to deal with a particular person. Can you stay here until I get back?"

"I can, but I would rather be with you."

Two Blankets thought it over for a minute. She looked at Mira, her little baby. She remembered how brave she had been. "You have been brave, a warrior today. You may choose."

"I will come. I will come and stand with *Pike.*"

"Let us put on your dress."

"And my bonnet, too. I want my bonnet."

Two Blankets nodded and tied the bonnet carefully beneath Mira's chin. "You look perfect."

"This bonnet was from *taz háma, Pike.* It is special."

"Yes, it is. Let us go now."

Together they marched toward the Landing. When they reached the porch, Two Blankets turned Mira to face her. The child looked up at her seriously. "Now, you must be a warrior today. Do you understand what that means?"

"I think so. I follow my war leader."

Two Blankets hugged Mira and nodded. She pushed open the door and entered. Inside, Delores Sue and Aimee sat at their usual table to the left. Most of the men in the camp were at the bar to the right. Conversation diminished, then faltered, then stopped entirely as everyone took in Mira's bruised face and Two Blankets' cut across her eyebrow.

She turned toward the table and walked deliberately.

Mira clambered up onto a chair. Delores Sue just stared in shock. "Oh, my, have you seen your face, Two Blankets?"

"Yes, I have seen it. I have a couple of cracked ribs that hurt, too. You can see Mira's bruised face. What you can't see are her ribs where Marshall kicked her across the room."

"Oh, are you all right, Mira?"

"Yes. I was just trying to help *Pike.*"

The whore looked from Mira to Two Blankets. "This is true?"

"Yes, he was going to kill me. He had already punched me in the face."

"This is intolerable. To my mind, no man should treat a woman so."

Aimee was carefully observing the conversation. "Well, that's not what I heard. I heard he was going to discipline you for sleeping with that Bayonne man, and that is why he had to slap you."

Two Blankets turned to Aimee. The cut over her eye was swollen and weeping blood. "Does this look like a slap to you? *Does it?*"

"If you deserved it, you can hardly expect a man to hold his temper."

"Do you, Delores Sue, or you Harry Everton, or you Ike, Samuel, any of you know where he got that idea? The idea that I was sleeping with *Monsieur* Bayonne? With the man, who is one of the last traders to trade with us on a regular basis? Do *any* of you know?"

They sat silently and let this thought brew. "I heard it from Aimee," said Harry Everton. "On the morning we tarred him."

Ike cleared his throat. "I heard it from Aimee, too. And now I'm wondering about what we did to that man."

Aimee looked from one to another. "You all saw how he treated her, kissing her fingers to greet her."

Two Blankets stepped around the table and pulled out the sheath knife. "You told Marshall that *Monsieur* Bayonne was down at my longhouse fucking me. *You* did that."

Aimee eyed the knife, but was refused to back down. "So what if I did? You were."

"You know I wasn't. You knew that I never did. He has never done anything other than been polite to me. Just as he has been polite to *you*. Do you know why he was at my longhouse?" She took another step, and the other woman recoiled. "He came there to give a bonnet to my daughter. Now, the only friend besides Delores Sue that I had here can never come back. We have lost his trade, his politeness, his news, *and* his friendship."

Aimee pushed her chair back and stood up. "I don't care."

"Just admit it is true, Aimee." In a quick stride, Two Blankets was right in front of her.

"I'll admit nothing." Aimee backed away a couple of steps. "You see how she is? Help me."

The men just looked at her, wondering what was going to happen next.

"Admit what you did." Two Blankets stepped closer. The knife tip flipped and cut the bodice of Aimee's dress from waist to throat. "You can see that I am crazy."

"All right! I admit it. I was jealous of how he treated you! Nice and sweet on you, he was."

Two Blankets flicked her knife, and the dress opened to expose her breasts. "You're *disgusting*. That is why you can't find a decent man. Don't you *ever* come near me. Don't you ever say my name or the name of my daughter. You work here. When I enter the Landing, you are to leave, immediately. Do you understand that?"

"You can't do that to me."

The knife sliced downward and split the front of the dress and petticoat off her, revealing her open-front drawers. Aimee drew the pieces together with trembling hands. She looked to the men at the bar, who only observed.

Money exchanged hands there and some muttering.

"I asked you something. Do you understand and agree?"

Aimee's eyes were huge and showed real fright now. Tears filled them as she finally surrendered. "All right, I agree."

She collapsed into a pool of cut fabric.

Two Blankets sheathed the knife. "Delores Sue, I am sorry to have disturbed your evening. Gentlemen. Mira, are you ready to go?"

"Yes, *Pike.*" Mira slid down from the chair and took Two Blanket's hand.

Walking together, they left the Landing.

"*Pike,* will we see *taz háma* again?" Mira fingered her bonnet. "I didn't get to thank him for my bonnet."

"I don't think so, darling. But he knows."

When they rose the next morning, she could barely get up at first, the pain in her ribs was so severe. Then, when she touched her face, she winced. She limped outside and made her morning's ablutions, then returned to the longhouse. One look at the animals made her remember Gilly. That brought a smile to her face for the moment, then a wave of sadness passed over her. What had happened to Gilly? Did he make it back East and get his enlistment? Was he even still alive?

She took a bucket and milked the cows. She found grain and fed the starving chickens and then the pigs. That was all she could do. She went back into the longhouse. Mira was still asleep, and she lay down on the furs, pulled one over the two of them and fell back into a deep sleep.

When she woke a few hours later, it was to Mira's nudging a plate under her nose. On it were some pieces of dried venison and some salmon. "*Pike,* you hungry?" A frown of worry creased her brows.

Two Blankets took the plate in one hand and her daughter up with her other arm. "Oh, sweet. You are so kind to me." She took a piece of venison and chewed it. "This is so good. Did you prepare it?"

Mira leaned into her hug, then pushed back. "You are so silly, *Pike*. You know I did not."

Two Blankets offered her daughter a piece of venison.

———————

AFTER THEY ATE and Two Blankets made tea, Mira played in the longhouse, and Two Blankets lay back in the sleeping furs. "If you need anything, Mira, wake me. I just need to rest this afternoon. I hurt a little bit still."

"All right, *Pike.* I be fine."

When she next woke, it was dark in the longhouse. Mira was lying next to her. She got up and built the fire back into flame. She made some raspberry tea and sat back on the furs to rest a bit. Her whole body hurt. She got the small piece of mirror and looked at her face.

"Well, I can see now why I hurt so much." Her face in the mirror was swollen across the cut, and the bruises were forming on her face. In another two days it would be worse, she knew from experience. Her eye would blacken, and the cut would begin to scar over even if she could prevent any infection.

She looked down at Mira, the one person in her life that could possibly make this suffering worthwhile, and smiled. Yes, Mira made the difference. All the difference.

She lay back down and fell asleep again.

The next day she decided it was time to visit the Landing. She dressed carefully and then asked Mira if she wanted to come.

"I don't want to act like I am afraid of going to the Landing. If you don't want to go because of your face, I understand."

"I am a warrior. I go." She stood for her mother to tie her bonnet.

Two Blankets combed out her hair, then dressed in her blue wool dress and strapped on her moccasins. Her knife was belted on over the dress where she could reach it if necessary.

They walked together to the Landing. "Now, Mira, listen to me. If I give you a hand signal like this, I want you to get out of there and come back the longhouse." She demonstrated the signal.

Mira mimed the signal. "I will, *Pike.*"

They entered the Landing. Two Blankets allowed her eyes to traverse the room. Several men were arguing next to the bar. Delores Sue and Aimee sat in their usual places. Aimee's eyes seemed to double in size at seeing her. She looked to the men for help and finding none, pushed back her chair and stood. Marshall was nowhere in sight. Perhaps he was laying down in his room. In an experiment, Two Blankets reached down and lifted the knife partway out of its sheath.

Aimee jumped back and headed for the stairs. Two Blankets smiled. Apparently, the appearance of a grin on her damaged face was enough to make Aimee run up the stairs.

"Oh, honey, your face." Delores Sue looked truly stricken. "Come here and sit down." She pulled out the chair. "You too, Mira. Come here, honey. Your face is all bruised up, too. Does it hurt bad?"

Mira went to Delores Sue and climbed up into her flounced lap. "Does not hurt bad. I am warrior."

"Yes, you are indeed." She touched the cut across Two Blankets' eyebrow. "I have some salve I'll bring over. You don't want an infection, do you?"

"No, mother Delores Sue, I do not. You are kind and my friend."

"I tell you, Two Blankets, I don't know if I can take it here anymore. It was pretty good when we first came her. The Landing was growing. Marshall was—well, he was Marshall. He was tolerable. Even when he wanted one of us, it weren't bad. Oh, my gosh, I'm sorry. I'm awful upset, I don't know what I'm talking about."

Two Blankets grasped Delores Sue's hand. "Believe me when I say it is all right. Marshall might be my husband, but he is not my lover. He never has been. I know you have to work for a living."

"Yes, well, it still ain't no excuse. Yes, I'm a whore. That just means I sell my body for money, and sometimes I have to give it away free to my boss. It's just the way it is. Anyway, as I was saying, I don't think I can take it here anymore. There just ain't enough trade here no more. The place is getting downright mean. I'm thinking of going back to Portland. Maybe even tomorrow. I'm sorry. I will miss you."

Tears were building in Two Blankets eyes. "Oh, Delores Sue. You are my only friend here, but I do understand completely."

"You will understand? You promise not to hate me?"

"I do mean it, and you have always been kind. I could never hate you. What about Aimee?"

"Oh, we ain't never been friends. Not like you and me are. Just two whores supporting each other in a hard place, if you know what I mean."

"I am sorry if I have made it more difficult for you, I really am. But I could not take anymore."

"No blame on you for that. It's been kind of amusing, watching her get some come back at her."

The next day, in mid-afternoon, when it was nearing time for the steamboat, Two Blankets saw Delores Sue approaching her longhouse. Her face was red as if she had been crying, and when she got closer, Two Blankets saw Delores Sue's eyes were red and her face blotchy.

"Oh, Delores Sue, I am so sad." She took the blonde woman in her arms and let her cry. When her sobbing finally settled into an occasional whimper, they looked into each other's eyes, brown into blue. There was recognition there and sadness, too.

"I hate the thought I am abandoning you, but I just can't take it here no more. I ain't brave like you."

"I am not brave. I have no choice. I cannot back down anymore."

"I know that. I think that takes courage. I am taking the paddle-wheeler back to Portland today. I've made money here, but even that's drying up. I just hope you will think of me sometimes."

"I will, Delores Sue. I will, I promise."

Two Blankets held her at arm's length. Then, both were interrupted by the steam boat's whistle.

"Goodbye, my friend."

"Goodbye, Delores Sue."

WHEN THE STEAMER pulled away from the dock and puffed off, churning downstream, Two Blankets felt the tug on her soul of another friend leaving her. For the next two weeks, she spent most of her days indoors as her bruises swelled, then subsided. The colors were horrid to look at, but by the time they appeared, most of the pain had left her. Mira also seemed to adapt, even quicker than Two Blankets. Her interest in everything around her subsumed any pain she might have felt. Two Blankets continued to make intermittent visits to the Landing, just to keep Aimee on her guard. Whenever she entered, the woman gave an alarmed start and practically ran up the stairs to her room, much to the amusement of the men. Two Blankets actually took some pleasure from her predicament, but tried to keep it in check.

One evening late, Two Blankets woke and had to pee. Very carefully, so as not to disturb Mira, she got up and pulled on her moccasins. Throwing a fur over her shoulders, she slipped outside. As she was squatting behind the midden pile, she looked about. All and everything was quiet at the Landing. Everyone at the bunkhouse was asleep, and indeed the Landing itself was dark. It was as if she could almost feel the whole encampment breathing.

As she got up and began walking back to the longhouse, she saw something dark near the dock. Then, she saw two men, dressed all in black. They even had dark scarves over their faces with only the eyes showing. She began to run to the longhouse to protect Mira, but then noticed that they were heading for the Landing, instead. She stopped suddenly. The two men reached the porch, then slipped inside. Two Blankets held very still. Then the two men emerged from the Landing carrying a struggling body.

Marshall.

As they neared the midden pile, she could see that his mouth was gagged and his eyes blindfolded. He struggled and kicked out his legs, and the shorter of the two men slapped him hard. Johnston gave out a moan and went limp. They crossed the bridge and headed for the forest alongside the creekside road. Fascinated, Two Blankets followed.

They reached the forest verge and left the road. Following the edge of the trees, they carried Marshall far enough that his cries couldn't be overheard.

When they stopped, Two Blankets ducked down.

Who were these men? She didn't care what they did to Marshall anymore, but why were they doing this?

The almost full moon came out from behind a cloud. The taller man pulled a knife. The moonlight glistened on the knife blade as it slit upwards and split Marshall's shirt. They pulled it off him. The knife hovered at his waistband a moment, and Marshall stood very still—very still, indeed, as pants and underclothes were cut off.

Now he stood naked against the tree. Ropes were tied about his wrists and feet. Then he was lifted up and jammed him upon a three-inch stub of a branch protruding from the tree. He wriggled at first, then stopped with a squirm and stilled. His hands were tied spread-eagled to the tree, and his legs likewise.

Two Blankets strained her ears to hear words. All she heard was, "Do you have the honey?"

A jar was opened, and honey was poured all over Marshal Johnston's body.

"You better hope it is only ants that find you, Johnston. You sure don't want to meet a bear out here."

She found that she had gradually stood up at this display and ducked down suddenly. The taller man looked in her direction. She was almost certain she had been seen, but he went back to his honey-painting. Finally, they stopped working and stood back. Satisfied, they turned and slipped away into the wood toward the Landing.

Stepped from her bush, Two Blankets approached Marshal quietly. His body was pale in the moonlight and sweating, despite the cold. He struggled against the ropes, then realized that every wriggle worked him down on the branchlet. She stepped on a branch, and it cracked. He pulled against his restraints. Grabbing up a stick from the ground, she used it to probe Marshall's body. The look of fear that contorted his face was satisfying, she had to admit. One last stroke down his chest forced him into a thrashing fit.

Two Blankets took one last look at Marshall Johnston and was satisfied. She turned and walked back into the woods.

At the longhouse, she checked on Mira, who had thrown her covers off. A smile and a sense of wonder suffused her face, and she pulled the fur back up to her chin. Silently, she took off her moccasins. She eased onto the sleeping pallet and pulled the furs up around her shoulders. It was a long while before she could sleep. She kept seeing the two figures, all dressed in black, working efficiently at their job of stripping Marshall.

She carried no doubt that they were the brothers Bayonne.

When she woke in the morning, she was pleased to see that she had awakened before Mira for a change. A couple of logs on the fire would warm the longhouse soon enough.

I was getting pretty lazy there for a while when my tiny daughter would beat me to it.

She crept out, milked the cows, and fed the critters. She did not like eggs, so she didn't bother with them. The milk she fed to the pigs, as that seemed like the best use for the horrid liquid.

As she went about her chores for the day, she kept an ear and an eye out for the Marshall search. At first, there was no stir. Then she noticed a group of men on the porch arguing or discussing. The men took off in several directions. The search was on, apparently. But as the day wore on to afternoon, he still had not been found. The thought of a bear, though satisfying, did bring an accompanying shiver. The only question was whether could she discover him and not give away the fact that she'd known where he was all along.

She picked up her gathering basket and asked Mira to accompany her. They picked along the roadside up into the forest, with the little girl investigating everything. Suddenly, Mira stopped and ran to her mother.

"*Pike,* what is *that?*"

"What, Mira?"

"There is a man in that tree."

Two Blankets looked and saw Marshall. He was slumped into his bonds. There seemed to be a stream of ants creeping up his calf to his stomach.

"Mira, can you run and get the men to help?"

"Yes, *Pike.* But *Pike?*"

"Yes, darling one?"

"*Pike,* do we want to help the man? He hurt us. I remember."

Two Blankets reached down and picked Mira up. "Let us look, and then we will decide."

"That is fair."

They stepped out of the brush and approached. Now that they were closer, Two Blankets could see that the ants had caused a rash all along his leg where they had crawled up. His other leg was swollen where she had stabbed it.

"So what do you think, Mira?"

Mira did not answer right away, which surprised Two Blankets. She realized that her daughter was seriously considering the question. "I think he has suffered enough to learn."

"I agree." Two Blankets set her upon the ground. "Run and tell Harry Everton if you can find him, or anyone else, if not."

"I will run and get help." Mira set off toward the Landing.

Soon Harry Everton, Ike, and Samuel arrived and took off the blindfold and gag from Marshall's eyes and mouth.

"Get me down, you bastards. Haven't any of you been looking for me?"

Harry Everton untied his arms and Samuel his legs, while Ike lifted him off the branchlet and eased him down.

"Careful, you son of a bitch or I'll shove a stick up your ass. See how you like it. It was those goddamn Bayonnes, I know it." Then he saw Two Blankets. "And it's *your* damned fault."

"I don't know what you are talking about, husband Marshall. Mira and I were just out gathering herbs and saw you. I sent her to run and get Harry."

"That's true, Marshall. Mira found me. We've been looking for you all day."

It's Bayonne. I just know it, and *she's* got something to do with it."

Harry Everton took a blanket and draped it over Johnston's shoulders. "Let's get you back to the Landing, Marshall."

"I want them Bayonnes." He tugged the blanket closer about his shoulders. "It ain't right they should treat me this way."

"Did you see anything? Or hear voices you could recognize again?"

"No, I didn't see any goddamn thing. They had me blindfolded. You know how them Bayonnes were, always talking right. That's how these were, talking all correct like."

"So, all we got is two men?" He looked to Johnston for confirmation.

Marshall nodded. "I was blindfolded. There could've been more. At least two."

"And they talked correct like?"

"That's what I said."

"That ain't much to go on, Marshall."

"What about mo...ti...*vay*...tion? We did tar that Frog."

"Well, we did do that. Wrongly, it appears. Aimee admits it."

"I want someone to pay for this. Ouch! My foot." Marshall hopped away from the stick that poked him. "Somebody's got to pay. I just don't know who or how."

Harry looked across at Samuel and Ike. "We could call the magistrate up here, but then he's going to open up the tarring. Not to mention the beating you gave Two Blankets. You might get away with that. Law's pretty lenient with how you treat your wife and her being Indian and all, but all on a whore's word? I'm thinking you better go careful there, Marshall."

Marshall turned on them. "Ain't nobody on my side here? You men know who you work for?"

Harry patted Marshall on the shoulder. "Let's get you back to the Landing. Get a drink or two in you. You're a lucky man there wasn't any bear out last night."

GILLY'S RETURN

CHAPTER 15
1863

THE LANDING SETTLED back into its winter routine. The war continued, but it seemed almost surreal. The casualty rate was enormous. What had begun as a mere three to six-month war settled into a continual bloodbath of men, materials, horses, and guns. The arguments among the few men left at the Landing were nightly, or at least, whenever news arrived and were vigorous if not violent.

Marshall limped about, frequently drunk, favoring his bad leg. He had no words for Two Blankets.

At least, he has no bad words for me. That is an improvement.

Indeed, his reservations regarding Two Blankets were almost as severe as Aimee's, who continued to act as if Two Blankets might drive a knife into her back at any moment. The whore's torment had long since become less than satisfactory, but on the whole, she judged it better than the alternative. Aimee had, at least, ceased talking about Two Blankets behind her back.

One afternoon in early May of 1863, the steamboat pulled into the dock. It was the rebuilt *Carrie Ladd*. On the bow was someone Two Blankets thought she recognized.

She stared at the man standing there.

"Now why do I think I recognize that man? Who could it be?"

He was somewhat slight of build and wore the worn blue of a Union uniform. Both he and the horse he was leading appeared tired to the bone.

"Worn, dusty, and tired. Looks like he was rode hard and put away wet." She spoke to Frank Millson who was walking by on his way to the sawmill after the dinner meal. "Do you recognize that man? I declare I should know him."

Frank turned toward the steamboat. He covered his eyes to block out the early afternoon sun. The man took off his cap and wiped his forehead. He turned toward them and shifted his weight. As he took that step, Two Blankets saw that he was leaning on a crutch and had a false leg.

"Why I'd say that that there is Gilly, Missus Two Blankets." He let out a hoot and waved his cap. "Gilly. Gilly." He began running toward the paddle wheeler. "Gilly!" His shout rang out.

"Mister Gilly. Oh, my goodness." Two Blankets walked almost like an automaton toward the steamboat.

Gilly led the horse down the gangplank. It was slow progress, as if his every step plainly hurt him. A thin mustache drew down over his lip. Two Blankets pulled up sharp within a few feet. The bitterness that pervaded his countenance was visible now. Was it bitterness, or was it physical pain? Two Blankets could not be sure.

"Gilly. So good to see you back. You got any news about the war?"

Gilly turned toward Frank, and the vague look became more focused. "You're Frank. Frank Millson?"

"Yes. Frank Millson. We all been wondering about you."

"You wanted to know about the war?" He hit his prosthetic with his crutch. "This here is all you need to know about the war, Frank."

He stepped down off the dock. "Missus Two Blankets. You don't know how many times I've thought about you and your kindness. It's what kept me going some nights when I had the nightmares."

Happiness and sadness surged within her, both at once. "I am glad you made it back. I am so thankful." Tears filled her eyes, and she hugged him.

"Well, *most* of me. I left my leg on the battlefield."

"It is always a celebration among my people when a warrior comes back."

Gilly brushed his fingertips along her scar. "Looks like you took a little damage yourself." His smile was kind.

"We have all taken some little hurt."

He dropped his reins over the hitching post at the Landing and stepped up onto the porch. Two Blankets saw the sweat of pain on his forehead but didn't say anything.

Inside were Aimee, Marshall, and Harry Everton. Aimee started to get up, and Two Blankets signaled her to sit. Harry moved to shake Gilly's hand. Then he sat down at the table.

"So, you come back." Marshall limped over and took Gilly's hand.

"You don't look much better than me, Marshall." Gilly lifted his prosthetic and rapped it with his crutch.

"Well, you know how women are." He gave Two Blankets a dark look. "Just a little family argument. Harry, get this man a drink. Hell, give us a glass and a bottle."

Harry poured Gilly a glass which he drank right down. He poured him another one and set the bottle down in front of him.

"Thank you, Harry."

"What happened? Last we heard, you was headed back to Pennsylvania."

"Oh, I made it to Pennsylvania, all right. Made it to Fort Laramie and took a flatboat down the Platte River to the Missouri. Down the Missouri to the Mississip'. Then I took a steamboat up the Mississip' and then up the Ohio River to Pennsylvania and joined up there. I got into the 11th regiment of Pennsylvania infantry because my brother was there. We trained a bit, marched a lot, and then went to war." He took another healthy drink, then drained his glass. "Our nickname was 'the Bloody Eleventh,' and we were so proud of our new uniforms and there was calls through the night you'd hear, 'the Bloody Eleventh, huzzah.' We was merged into I Corps, and in our first battle—Stone Mountain—we took only two wounded. That would be September 14, last year. Oh, my god, we was so proud and foolish."

His speech dropped off, and his eyes became distant. He shook himself. "Ah, yes, proud and foolish. Three days later we was at Antietam. The Union had some 80,000 men there, the Confederates less than 40,000. We was singing and shouting. We was so green. When the battle started, it was a bloodbath on both sides, more than 20,000 casualties, Union and Reb. A sixth of all the men that was there didn't walk away. Or walked away like me, but I was carried. The cannons never stopped that I could hear. I swear the bullets was like hail on a tin roof. The 11th Pennsylvania alone lost one hundred and thirty in one day. Almost thirty killed and ninety or so wounded. There was so many bullets flying, they flayed the bark from the trees."

The entire room was quiet as the men, Aimee, and Two Blankets adsorbed Gilly's news.

"Well, you can't say I didn't tell you not to go." Marshall poured more whiskey into Gilly's glass. "So, now what are you planning to do?"

Gilly caught the drift of what Marshall was saying. "I just came by to see my friends, Marshall."

"You got to understand, I ain't got no job here for half a man."

Gilly looked up at Marshall and stared with that distant stare he had now. "You know, Mister Marshall Johnston, I used to be afraid of you. I even respected you for what you done here at the Landing. I wanted to be a part of it." He laughed. "I don't know what I was thinking. That's the one good thing to come out of this." He tapped his prosthetic. "I can see what's important and what's not. My brothers-in-arms died at Antietam. You aren't a strong man, or a scary one. You're just a weak man playing at being strong."

Marshall's rage was building, but he checked it when he saw some support among the men. "You can spend the night here, then you'll have to move on."

Gilly pulled the pistol out he had strapped onto his right leg. "It is a funny thing, Marshall. You see this pistol here? I picked it up off a dead Johnnie Reb at Stone Mountain." He turned the cylinder. "The first man I killed there, I threw up. I ain't afeared to tell anyone that. The second, I didn't even look at. Gets so it don't make no difference. You just don't care no more, not much about your own life." He set the pistol on the table facing Marshall. "And you sure as hell don't care about any other man. It just don't matter anymore."

Gilly dropped his prosthetic leg to the ground with a thump. "With that kind of thanks for three years work here and the service to my country, I'd guess I'll be moving on." Slowly, he slid the pistol back into its holster.

Harry Everton stepped between the men. "Christ, Marshall, ain't you got any compassion or sense? There ain't no reason to push him on. Let him stay at least a few days."

"You against me, too, Harry?"

Harry leaned toward him and spoke in a whisper. "I ain't against you. I'm trying to save you. See how the men are looking at you and whispering."

Two Blankets got up and took Gilly by the arm. "If you want, you come down and stay at the longhouse as long as you want, Mister Gilly."

"Now, Missus Johnston, I don't want to be any cause for problems."

"Now, you wait a minute, Two Blankets. I demand—"

"You demand *nothing* from me, husband Marshall. I claim the longhouse as mine. You worried about someone taking advantage of me?" She looked at his leg. "I don't think so. You just want to control me. You send Harry or Ike or Samuel to come down and sleep there until Gilly has decided he is on his way."

"Thank you, Missus Johnston."

"Just call me Two Blankets. There is no Missus Johnston here today."

Together, with Two Blankets taking some of the weight off his prosthetic, they walked out of the Landing. They reached the longhouse, and Gilly eased down onto a seat beside the table. Two Blankets built up the fire and set a pot of water on to heat.

"Now, Gilly, you want something to eat. I've got a little venison stew."

"I'll tell you, Missus John..., Two Blankets, what I've been missing, and it ain't venison, though I thank you for that. I been missing salmon, fresh or dried. I don't care."

"Oh, we have salmon, and some *camas* cakes as well?"

"That would make me feel like I come home at last."

Two Blankets carved several steaks from the salmon she and Mira had caught that morning and skewered them. She set them against the fire to cook as well as some *camas* cakes from last night's meal to warm. She turned when she saw Ike come up with a bottle and a smile.

"Thought you might like some company, Gilly. Proper company like."

"Thank you, Ike." He took the bottle, took a drink, and wiped the mouth. He smiled. "This is more like the welcome I was expecting."

Mira came out of the longhouse, wiping the sleep from her eyes. "Gilly. Gilly, Gilly! That Gilly, *Pike.*" She ran to the man and hugged his leg. "What this?" She rapped on his prosthetic. Gilly eased the leg down and pulled up his pants leg for Mira's inspection.

"Oh, Mira, no. That's not polite."

Mira looked up. *"Pike,* his leg is wood. And it is hard, too."

Gilly leaned back, tears in his eyes. "It is all right, Two Blankets. It's just good to feel acceptance."

Two Blankets carved off several more steaks and placed them near the fire. Samuel, and then Harry Everton, showed themselves, each carrying a bottle and a glass. They shook hands with Gilly respectfully and soon there was an amiable gathering. When the salmon was cooked through, Two Blankets gathered them up on a wooden platter to serve. She didn't have forks or plates enough, but the men pulled out hunting knives and carved off chunks of the pink meat. The pile of *camas* cakes was as quickly consumed as Frank Milson, Kenny, and Arms the blacksmith arrived, followed a half hour later by Miller and Frederick.

Gilly had to repeat his war tale at least twice, and the men examined his revolver, a Grisworld & Gunnison copy of the 1851 Colt Navy revolver. When it came time to turn in, he found his horse brought down and stabled.

"You're welcome in my longhouse, Gilly." Two Blankets was not sure if she hoped he would accept or not.

"That's mighty kind, Two Blankets. If you've got a sleeping fur to spare, I think I'd rather bunk down here by the fire. I like seeing the stars, and it ain't cold on this...." He looked to Two Blankets. "...You still keeping track of the date on your calendar?"

"It's May 9, 1863, Mister Gilly. A Saturday, I believe."

He laughed without reservation for a change. Not a chuckle, but a deep belly-laugh.

Harry Everton turned to Gilly before he left. "I'm going to set a guard tonight, maybe as long as you're here. It's not like I expect you to take advantage of Two Blankets. *Nobody* takes advantage of Two Blankets. It's more for form than anything. Just wanted you to know."

"Thanks for your help, Mister Everton, sir. I do appreciate it."

They shook hands, and Harry left.

––––––––––

A FEW MORE days went by, until on May 13, Marshall decided he couldn't wait any longer. "I got to get back to my claims in Idaho City. Otherwise, I'll get there, and somebody else will be working them."

"Besides, as I understand it, there's a water problem there." Harry Everton spoke with authority.

"Damn right, Harry. The water runs out there in August, sometimes in late July, even. Then there ain't no more placer mining, and it shuts down. But you all expect me back before then."

Harry lifted his eyebrows, but that was all Marshall had to say.

"Keep things going while I'm gone." It was more of an order than a question. Harry nodded.

"I sure don't want to see Gilly here when I get back. He's been here long enough already."

"A few more days and he'll be in shape to move on, Mister Johnston. No harm done there. I put a guard on and no problems with Gilly. Now, do you want to drive cattle up there this year?" They put their heads together and sketched out what Marshall wanted done.

On May 15, Marshall was on board the Dalles-bound paddle-wheeler, and two days later, Gilly was ready to leave for Portland. Most in the camp were on the dock to see him off.

"I know you don't read, Gilly, but here's the name and address of a man I know. He might be able to put you to work until you get going again. Just ask for Mister Joe Ashton at The Happy Sailor, and he'll put you right."

"Thank you, Mister Everton." They shook hands.

Samuel shook hands with him. "If you think of being a bullwhacker try the yards on the edge of town and ask for Zeb Chance. He's my cousin. Tell him I sent you and despite your leg, I said you are twice any other man. 'Sides him and me, of course."

Two Blankets gave him a hug. "You are a warrior, and I will miss you."

Gilly looked her straight in the eyes. "You really mean that, don't you?"

"Of course I do, Warrior Gilly. I always say what I mean."

"You do at that. Goodbye, Two Blankets. I believe this is twice you've changed my life." The whistle from the *Carrie Ladd* signaled boarding, and Gilly led his horse onto the foredeck.

The next three months passed in routine tasks for Two Blankets. This appeared to be the pattern for her, short periods where someone or something demanded an exceptional response from her followed by periods of extreme routine. She was not sure which she liked better. Fortunately, it was in her nature to adapt and adapt she did.

She and Mira fished almost every day of the spring salmon run. This was serious business, and great fun for Mira, though she tried her best with her short fishing spear. When she had missed spearing her third fish and fallen in the water, she threw down her spear in disgust.

"I can't do it, *Pike*. All the salmon get away."

"Let us see if you can't catch one. First, you must pick the right rock."

"All rocks are not the same for fishing?"

"Oh, no. Come here now."

Mira hopped from rock to rock until she was next to her mother.

"You see here where the rock is undercut by the current? A good hiding place for a resting salmon."

"Yes, I see."

"Now, you must position yourself with your spear tip in the water."

"Like this, *Pike?*" Mira crouched holding her spear at the ready, the tip barely submerged.

"Now, the trick is that a fish appears in a position where she is not actually swimming. See how your spear seems to angle where it touches the water?"

Mira pushed the spear gently into the water and pulled it out. "I see now." She pushed the head back under the water.

"Now, we are very quiet and wait."

A salmon swam upstream and rested a moment under the rock before almost surfacing and swimming on.

Mira looked to Two Blankets, who nodded. She thrust her spear directly into the water. The spear struck the salmon's side and glanced off. The salmon thrashed and swam upstream in a hurry to get away.

"I did hit him, *Pike.* I did. I just need to spear at a little bit different... what is the word?"

"Angle. Yes, the next one you will get." She gave the child a hug, but Mira was already in her crouch waiting for the next salmon.

Two Blankets set her own spear down to watch. In a few more minutes, Mira speared the water again and this time hit solid flesh. She stepped behind her daughter and held to her waist. Mira fought the fish, then, at last, pulled a twenty-five-pound salmon from the water. The salmon was not happy, but Mira was—and that was what was important.

She smiled. "That is *táz názog,* Mira."

"It is *táz názog.*" The salmon gave a mighty thrash. *"Pike,* it is trying to get away."

Two Blankets put her hand on Mira's spear. "Let's get this salmon that you speared to shore."

Mira looked up at her mother with so much pride, it almost made Two Blankets tear up. Just keeping a hand on the spear, so they did not lose it, she allowed Mira to carry the cumbersome fish from rock to rock all the way to the riverbank.

MARSHALL STRIKES IT RICH

CHAPTER 16
FALL, 1863

TWO BLANKETS WAS harvesting the cattails with Mira when Marshall returned on the *Carrie Ladd*. She heard the whistle and looked up. The riverboat was looking a little tired these days, though she had only been functioning since 1859. Either the sinking and reconstruction the previous year or the hard work she had been put to, had not been kind to her.

She saw Marshall on the foredeck. Even from this distance, he looked excited. She gathered up her cattail stalks and began the walk back to the Landing. She dropped the bundle on her table and continued on reaching the Landing shortly after Marshall.

"Welcome back, Marshall." Harry Everton shook hands with Marshall Johnston. "How did it go in Idaho City?"

"Give me a drink, and I'll tell you. Idaho City is pretty amazing." One of the men brought his saddlebag, and they entered the Landing. "I've got a hard thirst. Haven't had a drink since The Dalles." Marshall laughed with such heart. Two Blankets had seldom, if ever, seen her husband in this kind of mood. "Pour Two Blankets a drink, too. I'm feeling so good, I ain't even mad at you anymore."

Two Blankets took a swallow of her drink. The other men from the camp were entering the Landing now, and she sat down.

"Idaho City is big now. You guys who drove the cattle up last year remember how big it was. Well now, there's about six thousand people just in Idaho City. It's the biggest town north of San Francisco. Hell, it's bigger than Portland or Seattle. There's some 25,000 to 70,000 people in the area. No one knows for sure, but Idaho City ain't the only town up there that's going like crazy. Hell, there's Centerville, Placerville, and Pioneerville. All of them is pretty big."

Marshall downed his drink and held out the glass for a refill. "I'm telling you fellers, you wouldn't believe it. Just in Idaho City, there must be two hundred fifty buildings. There's a dozen saloons at least and as many law offices. You got hotels there, and liveries and all the businesses needed to support a population that size, including butchers, grocers, and a dozen or more hotels."

Ike interrupted, "So there's a lot of businesses there. What about the gold? Was there gold there?"

Marshall grinned. "There's men last year who were making up to two hundred a day just panning. Now, that's a lot. Most ain't doing that good, but lots of 'em is making eight to twenty a day. In fact, if they can't make eight a day, they figure it ain't worth it." He pulled a pouch from his waistband. "You want to see some?"

"Oh, come on Marshall, you got our attention. Let's see it."

"All right. Take a look at this." Marshall poured out the pouch onto the bar. Most of the gold, shiny and as attractive as his story, was about the size of grains of corn. "Take a look at that, boys."

"Ain't that a beautiful sight. How much you figure that is?"

"Around two or three hundred dollars. Last year when I got there, I did get me a good claim—two in fact—and started panning. I made three or four thousand off of it. But you had to pack the dirt two or three hundred yards just to get to water. So I started buying up claims, especially when the creeks dried up. Last year I had a good twenty claims, all of 'em productive and I had men working them. Then the water dried up, everywhere 'cept for the Chinee. There was some fifteen hundred of them up there last year in Idaho City alone. Them boys know how to work with water. You ever met a Chinee?"

He looked about the group. A couple shook their heads yes and no.

"Well, you know they're yellow men, and most of 'em are little guys, no bigger than a white boy. But one thing they do is work together. They had water running through canals and across gullies in little streams enclosed by boards. I don't know what you call them."

"Aqueducts," said Harry Everton.

"Right, akkeducts. They might run water one or two miles to their sluice boxes and rockers. They was buying up claims that paid only two or three dollars a day. This year I bought up every claim I could find, even the poor ones, and then I sold them all to the Chinee, to one particular group of them. I cleared out of there with a fortune, and I'm sure those Chinee are making good on my old claims, too. Then, I went through and did it all again, poorer claims this time but still two dollar a day finds. So that Chinee group made out, and I sure did, too."

"Do you think there's still gold up there, Marshall?"

"Oh, I'm sure there is, but not for the panning. Most panning streams already got claims on them. There might be a year left. It was too much work for me though, hauling dirt on my back two hundred yards."

"Well, I do got to say, that there gold is beautiful, purely beautiful," Samuel said, holding the nugget up to the light.

"I even saw your friends up there, Two Blankets, the Bayonne brothers."

Two Blankets started at the reference to her name. "You did? How were they, the innocent Bayonne brothers?"

"Now, let's not get into that." Marshall chuckled, but he found little support for the beating of an innocent man. Some laughed with Marshall, others looked away as if ashamed of their participation. "It's a rough trip by wagon, but they got both theirs up there, and they was doing a brisk business. You'll pardon me for not going by to say hello." Marshall looked at her, it seemed, to see if she hadn't had some advance warning to his own beating.

"I am glad, then, husband Marshall."

"And the drive of cattle was well received. Samuel, you, Frank, and Kenny done a good job getting them up there."

Frank and Kenny slapped each other on the back. "It was a rough drive, but they sure sold fast. We'd hardly got there before every restaurant and butcher in town was there, all bidding against each other. We was only in town a couple hours, and then we was done."

"Well, I got to get me to Portland on tomorrow's boat, so I'm ready for a little comfort from my wife and some sleep."

Two Blankets quickly schooled her features, but she was sure Marshall had seen her surprise and dismay. "I will go and bathe then, husband Marshall."

"That'll be fine. You don't know how much I been missing you."

She got up and walked out of the Landing and headed for the stream. She could do this, she knew. She had done it many times. It was just that Marshall had not had any such interest in her since she became pregnant with Mira.

I know I can do this little thing. I know I can.

She bathed quickly and rinsed the cattail scrap from her hair. Then, she retreated to the longhouse and her wait for her husband. While there, she had to explain to Mira.

Surprisingly, little explanation was required.

"Mira, Mister Johnston is coming here soon, to use his husband's rights with me. It is not something I like, but it is an agreement I made when I married him."

Mira came over and patted her on the hand. "I understand, *Pike.*"

"When he comes, I want you to go outside. I don't think he will stay long, but don't come back until you see him leave. Do you understand?"

"Yes. When he comes, I leave. When he goes, I come back."

Two Blankets laughed. "You are a funny girl, and I love you."

They waited until evening. Two Blankets heard him first and gestured for Mira to leave. Marshall entered shortly thereafter. Two Blankets could see that he had drunk quite a bit by the way he walked.

That is no problem. I can usually manage him with a little drink in him.

White Mouse twittered in her ear. *He always worries me when he is like this.*

Gray Wolf got up, gave Two Blankets a nuzzle and walked to the door. *I cannot watch him do this to you. I know you can do it, but I'll be outside. He is not a wolf.*

"It is not a problem." She took a deep breath to steel herself. "Good evening, husband Marshall. It has been long since you have sought my sleeping furs."

"Huh? Oh, yes, it has. Well, I did think a lot about you this trip."

"You know I have never denied you the rights of a husband."

"You *did* stab me."

"I did, and I am not sorry. I would do it again if you hit me. Come over here and let us just see what you have got for me."

Marshall limped over to the furs and stood before her. She slowly unlaced his trousers and let them drop. His small organ stood stiffened in his drawers. When she stroked her hand across the thin fabric, he shivered. He pushed her back onto the sleeping furs. She fell back with her legs parted, and Marshall fell on top of her. Neither his customary period of erection nor his time away thinking about her lent him strength for the endeavor, which only lasted about two to three minutes. He wiggled his way in and thrashed for the couple of minutes required, then fell half-way across her.

Two Blankets did a quick calculation in her head. It was difficult with the distraction of Marshall laying across to recall the calendar. She finally came to the conclusion that she would have to visit the moon cycle hut in two days or so. This was a comfort. She was safe from the possibility—however remote—of his impregnating her.

She let him lay thus for a minute then gasped. "Husband Marshall, you must move if you want a live woman who is capable of doing that again."

Marshall slid off her onto his back. "I did need that. Oh, I did need that."

"Did you? Are you ready for a little more?" She reached down and stroked his spent organ. "Well, maybe not."

"Oh, that does feel good." His breath was husky.

"Let's see now what we can do, husband Marshall." She slid down until her face was just above his sex. It was indeed a tiny little thing. Dipping her head slightly, she took his whole organ and testicles into her mouth. One advantage of his having such a small *wootlat,* at least.

She mouthed him and soon felt his organ stir once again. Feeling him grow in my mouth gives me a sense of power.

This was odd. It had not been like this with Standing Bear, where all I wanted was to give myself over and feel him inside of me. Not like that at all, but a sense of power is something.

She continued suckling him. He was in truth no longer than her tongue. His hand grasped her hair, and he began thrusting.

This would be a problem if it were Standing Bear. I would be choking right now.

She allowed his testicles to fall and tightened her lips. Tight on the upstroke, then suck hard on the downstroke. He was able to last a little longer this time. She added a little twist to the downstroke. He arched his back, and his ejaculate seeped from between her lips.

It is a bit disgusting, but a small price to pay. It is easier to wash out my mouth than my tenino.

She rolled off of him. "I think I need a drink after that."

"I do, too. That was pretty damn good."

"For me, too, husband Marshall." She got up and fetched a bottle and a glass. Her first mouthful she swirled and spat into the fire pit unobserved. Then she took a real drink. The mediocre whiskey burned on the way down, but that was what she wanted.

Two Blankets poured a drink into the glass and handed it to Marshall. "Do you truly have to go into Portland tomorrow?"

He took the drink and downed it, then pulled up his drawers. "I do. I have business there. Important business."

"Oh, husband Marshall. Please allow me to do that." She tied the undergarments and pulled up his trousers, then buttoned them. "Will you be coming back, husband Marshall, before you leave?"

"I don't know if I can. I have a lot to do before tomorrow."

Careful. She didn't want to see him again tonight, but she couldn't let that out. Two Blankets pouted a little.

Don't overdo it, you fool.

"Well, I will see you as soon as you return then, perhaps. You can think about what is waiting for you, husband."

Marshall eased up on shaky legs. "I will do that, wife. You just be ready."

Two Blankets leaned back into the furs. "Oh, I will do that."

SALE OF THE LANDING

CHAPTER 17
FALL, 1863

SOMETIMES, WHEN LOOKING upon a scene which one had seen a hundred or a thousand times before, it just appears different. The reasons why this is so are not often apparent, only the truth of it.

This was how the Landing appeared to Two Blankets a couple of days after Marshall had left for Portland. Something had changed. She looked around the grounds and saw activity everywhere. She walked up to the Landing and noticed that the windows were clean for the first time since Gilly had gone off to war. The porch was also swept. Inside she found the bar clean and a man busy scrubbing the floor.

Harry Everton sat at the table, a cup of coffee at hand. He looked up from the sheaf of papers in his other hand.

"Harry, is the Landing going through a big cleaning?"

"Marshall's orders, Missus Johnston. Get the whole place cleaned up before he gets back."

"Well, I can't argue that it needed it, but do you have any idea why?"

"I do, Missus Johnston, but not one I would want spread around, and none of them good."

"I do have some interest in this, Harry. What do you suspect?"

He leaned back in his chair and thought for a moment. "Ah, I apologize. I been told not to tell anybody, but that doesn't include you. Even if it did, I think you'd have a right to know. I suspect we're about to see Mr. Alton Shales."

"For a new loan, or for a sale?"

"That's the question, ain't it?"

"Thank you, Harry. I won't spread any rumors." She retreated from the Landing and now when she walked back, she saw it with new eyes. Everything was being tidied up.

Shes went to the storehouse and began an inventory of which furs she would want to take, should it become necessary. She located about thirty and began moving them quietly to the longhouse.

When a new paddle-wheeler pulled up to the dock two weeks later, no one was surprised. Two Blankets saw Mr. Alton Shales on the foredeck, looking as crisp and dapper as usual. Marshall stood beside him, gesticulating at all his improvements.

The steamboat touched the dock, and the gangplank was run out. "You can see all the additions we've made, Mister Shales. We got a regular small city here. That we do."

"Let's be honest and call it a small village. I like your idea that it could be a regular stop for the *E.B. Baker,* though. I have shares in the People's Transportation Co."

"She's the fastest I ever been on, that's for certain."

"People don't like a monopoly, and she *is* the fastest. We'll see if the Oregon Steam Navigation Co. will compete. We already brought fares down to one dollar to The Dalles."

"Jaysus! Three years ago it was five dollars a head."

"Problem is, they own both rail portages at the cascades, but we'll see about that."

"Well, let's go on up to the Landing and celebrate a little. I got some whiskey with a label on it, just for this day." He shook the crate he carried, and the bottles rang out.

Shales twisted his mustache. "I say, Mister Johnston, are you trying to affect my judgment?"

"Naw, I tried that last time, remember? Found out you can drink as much as any man." Marshall laughed. "It is just an excuse to drink some good liquor."

Mr. Shales spent some three days at the Landing with his notebook and pen. There was little question that he was a dandy, from his top hat and pince-nez, to his brightly shined knee boots and crisply-pressed suit. Always there was his waxed mustache, which he was continually twisting.

"I like the red and blue paint, and the windows came out real nice."

"We're making a statement here. This ain't just a trading post. It's more like a tidy little town. Got me a blacksmith renting a building here, too." He waved his hand toward the shop. "Name's 'Arms' Olafson. He's been here five years."

"What's your main source of income now? Trade upstream or down?"

"Well, now, the Oregon trail trade has definitely dropped off, especially since the Barlow Road was complete."

"Yes, I figured that. We've seen the same in the Portland area."

"But recently we've seen a huge increase moving toward the gold fields. I been there myself, last year and this. Kinley, he's a tenant up on the plateau, drove a hundred head of cattle up to Idaho City both years."

"Hmm. I thought *you* drove those. Your men."

"Well, yeah, two of my men drove them up there. That's right. Now let's have a drink."

"Why do you want to get out of it now?" Shales' asked over their second drink. "I thought you were all fired up over this 'I got a town named after me' business."

"I done that, Shales. I want to get down to the Willamette, somewhere near Salem. I got some acreage there, and I might even try my hand at a little politicking. I've made out pretty good here."

The afternoon went in this fashion and the next two days followed in much the same light. Mr. Shales was exceedingly well-informed on the business of the Landing and the area. Occasionally, Marshall would get caught out, and eventually, he gave up trying to fool the man. Mr. Alton Shales was a dandy, no question about that, but Marshall was not misleading him on anything. If the *Tyee* was the best trader she had ever seen, Marshall and Shales ran close for second.

After two days, they came to some sort of bargain, and Two Blankets could tell just from Marshall's countenance that he was not entirely satisfied.

Ah, well, the best bargain is the one that leaves both parties a little unsatisfied. That is best.

Marshall had orders for her, as well. She was waiting at the dock to see Shales off on the *E.D. Baker*. The whistle blew, and the sternwheel churned in reverse into the current, and then the boat turned downstream and picked up speed.

"Well, that is that, as they say. Johnston's Landing is now Shales' Landing. Or Dandy's Landing, if he wants to call it that. Two Blankets, you got two weeks to pack up anything you want to take with you."

"With me to where? Where are we going?"

Marshall looked at her.

He likes the taste of this meal, I just know it.

Gray Wolf examined Marshall. *Yes, if you were a deer, he would be drooling about now.*

"Why, we're going to the Willamette. To Salem, my dear wife."

She couldn't help herself, "Salem? We are moving, husband Marshall?"

"Yep. You got two weeks to pack up anything you want to take with you. Anything from the longhouse."

Two Blankets, thinking of the furs already purloined from the storehouse. "And the storehouse, as well?"

"Yeah, I don't think Shales counted them furs. They'll be all rotted in another year, anyway. Anything else, just ask me."

"I will get started immediately, then, husband Marshall."

To say goodbye to a place that has been one's home for the last thirteen years is one of the most challenging things a person can do.

Two Blankets had been kidnapped at age ten and spent two years, first trying to escape, then accommodating herself to being a *mistshimus*. Then in 1854, she had been sold to Marshall Johnston as his wife. Although he had in no way been a good husband, the next three years had been among the best in her young life. She had made many friends among the Chinook and gained the respect of others, including the *Tyee*. Then the Chinook had had to leave and go to the reservation. Again, there were more goodbyes, this time to people she had grown to love and respect, and a new people to gain respect from. Finally, she had Gilly and Big Ed, who left for the Civil War. There were also Harry Everton, Ike, Samuel, and others.

She wandered the Landing in a daze, seeing the people she would soon be missing. The problem was this would be all of them. Every single one of them would no longer be a part of her life.

As she walked back up to the longhouse, Samuel crossed her path.

"Hello, Samuel."

"Hello, Missus Johnston."

"I just wanted to say that I will miss you when we are gone. You have been fair to me, and I appreciate it."

Samuel looked at her in curiosity. "I don't understand. Are you, are you going away someplace? Are you leaving Johnston's Landing? Does this have something to do with what happened to that Bayonne fellow?"

"No. Hadn't you heard? Johnston's Landing is being sold. That's why we are moving."

"Sold? Oh, son of a *bitch!* Sorry, Missus Two Blankets, this is the first I've heard about it. Oh, damn that man. I'm sorry. I will miss you, too. You have always been fair-minded. Please excuse me."

Samuel walked away cursing and punching his leg with his right hand.

So, he didn't know. Husband Marshall wasn't going to tell anyone. Two Blankets stood with her hands on her hips thinking.

White Mouse sat on top of her head. *Oh, I don't like it when she gets like this, Gray Wolf.*

Gray Wolf looked up at White Mouse, her liquid green eyes penetrating. *It is when she gets like this, White Mouse, that things get interesting.*

"Let's see what Ike has to say." Two Blankets glanced at the longhouse and saw Mira playing outside. She was standing on a log holding a spear. Then she would stab down with the spear and pull up a stuffed piece of leather designed to roughly resemble a salmon. She walked up and examined her daughter.

"Look, *Pike.* I caught *taz nazóg.*"

Two Blankets hefted the stuffed piece of leather. "It is a big one, too."

"Yes." Mira stood straight and tall.

"I am going out to tell Ike goodbye. Since we are leaving in two weeks. Did you know that?"

"I know we are leaving. I don't know why or if we are coming back."

"I don't know completely either. I just know we are going to Salem on the Willamette River."

"Is it as big as the *Nch'i-wána, Pike?*"

"I don't think any river is as big as the *Nch'i-wána.* We shall see, shall we? Do you want to come with me to see Ike?"

Mira stood very still, as she did when considering a proposition. Two Blankets waited patiently. "Yes, *Pike,* I will come."

Two Blankets nodded in as serious a manner as Mira's response.

"Let us look at the mill first." They started off walking toward the saw-mill. Two Blankets had not walked this way since the discussion between Marshall and Ike on the cutting during the spirit animal discussion. Ike had made considerable progress since then, Two Blankets could see by the bare trunks.

"They have cut a lot of trees, *Pike.* A very lot."

"They have, indeed. I hear the saw going. Do you?"

"Yes, *Pike,* I hear the saw."

Another two hundred yards and they came up on Ike. His back was to them, and he was covered with wood shavings and chips. They waited until he had finished his cut, then Two Blankets tapped him on the shoulder. Ike shut down the saw and turned to her.

Frank Milson waved and joined the group.

"Hello, Ike, and Frank, too."

"Hello, Missus Johnston and little Mira."

"Hello, Ike, and Frank, too." She repeated her mother's greeting.

"What can I do for you?"

Two Blankets paused, waiting for some reason.

"I'm sorry for the way we treated that there Mister Bayonne. We—" He looked down at the ground, ashamed she thought. "We got that all wrong. We didn't know, and I don't think we behaved proper like."

"It wasn't really your fault. Aimee set that up, and did it cleverly."

"Well, she might have set it up, but we sure did listen. So what can I do for you?"

"I just wanted to come by and say goodbye to you and to Frank. You have both been like friends to Mira and me for five years now, going on six I think."

"Goodbye?" His look was as questioning as Samuel's had been. "To both you and Mira?"

So, he had not known, either.

"Yes. We are moving to Salem. Marshall, Mira, and me are going."

"Is this a permanent move? Or just for a while?"

"It is permanent, I'm afraid. Marshall has sold the Landing, and we'll be going in two weeks. You have always been kind to us."

Ike just stood in silence for several tens of seconds. Then, he shook his head. "Well, we will miss you, Frank and me both. Two weeks. Damn. Damn. Damn."

He walked off swearing to himself.

"*Pike,* can I do the next one?"

"What do you mean, Mira?"

"Say goodbye and 'pologize. That way they feel bad at Mister Johnston. Is not that what we are doing?"

Two Blankets looked at her daughter with new eyes. Mira stood there waiting for an answer to what she thought was a real question.

If she thinks it is a real question, mayhap it is. Is that what I have been doing? Getting back at Marshall?

She smiled. They would have to try it Mira's way then. "Yes, my little one. You can do the next one."

Mira clapped her hands in front of her once. "Let's go find Mister Harry, then." Mira took her hand and in her most earnest mode led the way. Two Blankets let her lead.

When they got back to the Landing, they saw Harry Everton speaking with Samuel. Mira paused. "We must wait and talk in private," she said in a whisper.

When Samuel left—looking none too happy—they approached Everton with Mira still in the lead. Mira stopped in front of him and stood, her hands held clasped at her waist.

Harry turned to them. "Hello, Missus Johnston. Did you want something from me?"

"Hello, Harry. Mira has something to say to you." Two Blankets smiled her most ingratiating smile and nodded to her daughter.

"Um, all right." He squatted down on one knee until he was on her level. "What is it, Mira?"

Mira waited a moment to compose herself. "Mister Harry. I just wanted to thank you for being a friend to *Pike* and me for such a long time."

"Well, you and your mother have always been good friends to me, as well. I welcome your thanks." Thinking Mira was finished, he began to rise.

"Please wait. I am not done yet, Mister Harry."

He sank back onto his knee. "I'm sorry, little Mira."

"The second thing I want to say is we are very sad we will not see you anymore. We are moving in two weeks."

"Both of you? And Marshall, too?" He looked from Mira to Two Blankets.

"Yes. We are moving to Salem. Is that right, *Pike?* Salem?"

Two Blankets nodded.

"We are moving to our new home in Salem. I don't know if we will see you again." Mira moved closer to Harry and gave him a hug.

Harry stood up, holding Mira in his arms. Mira held him tight. "We will really miss you, and the Landing, too."

"I will miss you also, Mira. You and your mama."

"You are funny man. She is *Pike,* not *máma. Máma* is wife's brother's child."

"Your *Pike,* then. Thank you for being such an adult and telling me."

Mira pulled her head back and looked into his blue-gray eyes, set deep in his lined face. "Can I kiss you goodbye?"

Harry glanced at Two Blankets who nodded. "Why, yes. I believe I would like that."

Mira gave him a short kiss on the lips and then wiggled her legs until Harry put her down. He turned his attention to Two Blankets. "Thanks for giving me the forewarning, Missus Johnston."

"Please, call me Two Blankets."

"Two Blankets, then. I knew something was up, I just wasn't sure what. Let me know if you need any help getting ready, will you?"

"I will. We won't have much, but some help carrying down to the dock will be appreciated."

"Will do. Well, the day ain't getting any longer. I better be back at it. Goodbye and good luck. Somehow, I don't think you'll need any luck."

He turned away and strode across the yard.

"Did I do it right, *Pike?*"

"Oh, yes, you did, Mira. Better than I could have."

Suddenly Mira's face changed from serious to amused. *"Máma.* He called you my *máma.* That is funny."

"We will take a little rest, then go up to the Landing."

I wonder if Mira is right? How much of this is revenge and how much just a sadness at goodbye? Well, it is not as if I don't deserve some revenge.

Revenge did not feel as good. It did not sit so well on her stomach.

Entering the longhouse, Two Blankets lay down on the sleeping furs, and Mira joined her. She pulled the fur up over them, and Mira kicked off her section.

"Pike, it will be all right. We will find a way."

Two Blankets stroked Mira's hair and fell asleep with that thought.

She woke a few hours later and rose with a sense of determination. She dressed in her traditional dress and brushed her hair. Then she attended to Mira's clothing. Mira insisted on wearing her "Bayonne" bonnet.

"We are ready to go?"

"Yes, *Pike,* I am ready."

They walked up to the Landing. A couple of men were outside the bunkhouse, men Two Blankets did not recognize. They stepped up on the porch, and she turned to Mira.

"Mira, I want you to be very still when we are in the Landing. I suspect there will be some anger in there."

"All right, *Pike.* I will be the baby bird."

They walked in. Two Blankets got a cup of coffee and two bowls of stew from the ever-cooking pots on the stove and sat down. Aimee looked at her with nervous eyes, and Two Blankets signaled her to stay. Mira climbed up on a chair at the table and began eating. At the bar were Marshall, Ike, Samuel, and Harry.

"Now I'm telling you fellers, I was going to tell you."

"Marshall, you're saying after four years of work—and good work, loyal work—you weren't going to tell us until when? The day before you left? Christ, I thought I knew you." Ike thumped his fist on the bar for emphasis.

"I'm telling you now, ain't I? You're a sawyer. You work for me. You get the explanation I decide to give you."

"I just thought better of you, Marshall. Frank and I work for you for six years going on seven, and this is the treatment we get? I'll ask you this, was you ever going to tell us?"

Samuel said, "Or was you just going to wait for that Alton Shales dandy to tell us as you went off on the steamboat?"

"You fellers can leave any time you want. I don't owe you nothing."

"I want my pay through today, then. Right here. Right now," Ike said.

"Now? This your last day? Fine, here's your five dollars."

"And Frank's pay, too."

"And three dollars for Frank."

Samuel turned to Harry. "Did you know anything about this?"

"It's the first I've heard. I knew something was going on with that banker, Mister Shales. But a sale? No, I didn't know. Remember, I got a five percent stake in this little settlement. This don't do me any good either."

Samuel said to Marshall, "I want my pay, too. For me and Kenny."

"So, you're quitting, too?" He handed over the coins.

"Marshall, I'd wish you well, but I ain't got it in me. You're just a mean son of a bitch. So, instead, I'll wish you to get what you deserve." He turned to Harry Everton and held out his hand. "It has been an honor working with you, sir."

Harry clasped hands and shook. "My pleasure, Samuel. I could always depend on you and Kenny."

"We're going to head up to Idaho City. I'm sure they can use a bullwhacker there." He turned back to Marshall, looked him in the eyes, then spat at his feet and stomped out.

Harry took up a drink at the bar and swallowed it down. "Well, Marshall, one thing I can say about you. You sure know how to crap in the cradle."

"You saying this is my fault?"

"Not saying nothing about that. Just that we could sure have used those guys these next two weeks. If you'd have told them, we might still have them. Me, I ain't got much choice. With my five percent on the line, I gotta stay. I'll see you in the morning." He turned and exited the Landing, leaving Marshall alone at the bar.

"Come, Mira. Let us go back to the longhouse." She slid her chair back, and Mira climbed down off of her chair.

Marshall turned now to Two Blankets, a piece of his rage in his voice. "Two Blankets, did you tell them? Are you the one who betrayed me?"

Two Blankets stood slowly, her hand on her knife. Aimee saw the hand and backed off her chair and half up the stairs. "If you are speaking of 'Did I say goodbye to them?' then the answer is yes, and I did say we were leaving in two weeks. You did not say not to tell anyone, my husband Marshall."

"What if I had told you not to tell?"

"The answer to that is we will never know. Good evening, husband."

GOODBYES

CHAPTER 18
FALL, 1863

A FTER THE DRAMA at the Landing, Two Blankets felt a malaise creep over her. There was a euphoria that resulted from revenge, but there was a price as well. She wondered what she was going to do when they left this place, her home for so many years. What would happen with Mira as well? All she could do was wait it out.

Two nights later she felt so tired with worrying she went to bed early. When she woke the next morning, she noticed that Mira was not sleeping next to her. She got up from the furs, wrapped a sleeping fur about her shoulders, and looked about the longhouse. She couldn't see Mira. Stirring the fire into life, she called out. "Mira? Mira, where are you?"

Two Blankets opened the flap and looked out on the Landing. Wisps of fog drifted across the settlement. All was gray. Then she saw a tiny fire in the fire pit, and a small figure sitting cross-legged before it.

It was Mira, and she was sitting still, her breath a susurrus, with her eyes closed. Two Blankets sat next to her and let the fur rest on Mira's shoulders as well. She too slowed her breath following the pattern of in through the nose and out through the mouth, in through the nose and out through the mouth.

Finally, Mira shook herself and looked up at her mother. *"Pike,* I am glad you are here."

Two Blankets put her arm around the child. "What was it you were doing out here?"

"I was saying goodbye to one of the places I will miss."

"Can I do it, too? With you?'

"Yes, *Pike.*"

Two Blankets settled herself. "So, I sit like this?"

"Yes, *Pike,* but cross your legs."

"Like this?" Two Blankets crossed her legs. "Then what do I do?"

"We have this little fire. Take a little of the sacred moss and hold it up
like this."

Two Blankets imitated Mira's actions, holding the 'sacred moss' up to the
sky. "Like this?"

Mira glanced in Two Blankets direction. "Yes. Now hold it in each of the
four directions to the north, south, east, and west."

Two Blankets held the moss in each of the cardinal directions. "Yes,
and then?"

"Then you offer it to the fire." Mira tossed her piece of moss into the fire.
Two Blankets offered her piece to the fire, as well. "Then, you think about
all the happy times you had in this place. Like when we met here with *taz
háma, Monsieur* Bayonne."

"Ah, I see. Remember all the good meals we ate here?" Her inward smile
burst full-fledged upon her face.

"Why are you smiling, *Pike?*"

Two Blankets laughed. "I was thinking of Alton Shales. Once, before you
were born, he shot a grandfather elk. He was almighty proud of that kill. We
cooked him a huge steak from it that was so tough, he couldn't even eat it."

Mira thought for a moment. "Remember Gilly. I remember how hard he
tried to help you, how he counted the eggs every day and fed the pigs and
chickens and milked the cows."

"I had forgotten about that." She smiled.

"It was at the Landing that I got this." She pulled the tiny old bonnet from
inside her jacket. "From *Monsieur* Bayonne."

Two Blankets let her mind roam back in time. It was true. It was at the

Landing that *Monsieur* Bayonne had first given the tiny bonnet to Mira. "I remember that. But you were only two summers old then."

"I remember it, though. I do."

"I believe you." *It is strange, but I do believe her, she is so serious.*

"And then what do we do?"

"Then we thank the spirits and move on to another place."

They sat for a few more minutes, then Mira got up. "It is your turn to pick now, *Pike.* If you want to?"

"I do want to, and I pick—" she spun around "—the moon cycle hut."

"Good choice." Mira picked up a brand from the fire. "But, I don't have any more sacred moss."

"I have some sacred sage in the longhouse that I traded for. Will that work?"

Mira thought a bit. "Yes, the sacred sage should be very good."

Two Blankets went into the longhouse and got a little packet of sage. They walked together to the moon cycle hut. "I am happy you taught me this, my daughter. I was feeling so sad."

In the moon cycle hut, Mira built up a little fire from the brand, and they sat together. Two Blankets opened the paper packet of sage and handed some to Mira. Together they made the offering to the spirits of the north, the south, the east, and the west. Then they tossed the sage onto the fire.

The smell of the sage permeated the hut and her memories. As she closed her eyes, there were so many memories. They rushed at her, and she inhaled deeply.

"Pike, are you all right?" Mira petted her leg.

"Yes, Mira. It just surprised me a little. Did you know it was right here that you were born?"

"I did not. I came from your body right here?"

"Yes, you were so tiny and so perfect, my darling Mira. Delores Sue and Aimee helped me."

"Did it hurt?"

"Having a baby always hurts, but then the pain goes away. You can't remember it, and all you are left with is the gift."

"A *potlatch?"* Mira laughed. "I am a *potlatch."*

"Yes. A special *potlatch*. One I could never repay." Two Blankets mused on this for a little while. "It was here that I met my Nika, my first friend among the Chinook, though I didn't know it at the time. By the time I knew it, it was too late."

That is a sad memory. Nika came to womanhood in this hut only to have it stripped away before she could even consummate it. She remembered Nika's fall and her broken body on Two Blanket's first trip portaging the canoes up the *Nch'i-wána.*

"Too late, *Pike?*"

"It is too sad. I will tell you sometime. I became a woman right here, too."

"I remember once when you tried to contact the Gray Wolf here. We went to sleep, and when I woke up I saw you with her. You couldn't get back into your body, and she helped you. I smiled at her and petted her."

"I did not know that, my little one."

"Yes."

Over the following ten days Mira and Two Blankets said goodbye to numerous places about the Landing. Some were expected, such as the bathing pool where Mira remembered the baths she had had, and Two Blankets recalled the multitude of times she had washed after Marshall's visits to her sleeping furs. They also visited the fishing spot where so many salmon were caught. Mira acted out the *"great nazóg"* spearing expedition of her recent past, and Two Blankets thought of the many salmon she had speared there as well as the hundreds of times she had helped prepare salmon for the tribe. Mira even insisted that they say goodbye to the midden pile.

"Why do you want to say goodbye to the midden pile, Mira?"

"Of all the places we have visited, this midden pile might have the most memories. It has all the forgotten memories. The things we have forgotten and thrown away."

In this manner they went about, to the storehouse, the docks, the spot where Two Blankets did her tanning, until her mind was spinning with memory each time and each place she looked. They took a walk up to the plateau to celebrate the many times they had gathered *camas* root and other herbs. Mira looked about at the changes there. Mr. Zeke Kinley and his wife

Mary and their three children had wrought much from the landscape. His herd of cattle grazed across the expanse of the prairie, and his cabin showed the improvements of his continual work. Two more families had bought or rented land, and their cabins, though not as improved as Kinley's, showed in the distance.

Two Blankets thought as they sat in the *camas* field of the "great hunt," possibly one of the only times where Marshall had actually performed up to the expectations of his deal with the *Tyee* of the Chinook. He had actually surprised her in his efforts that time.

Amazing how strong some memories are if you give them a chance to come back.

You humans are shaped by memory, it seems. Gray Wolf rolled onto her back in the grass. *If you were a wolf, you would see that this grass is perfect for rolling in. It is not a memory. It is real.*

During this period of time, she also packed. Since she didn't know what she would be facing at their new home, Two Blankets also didn't know what to leave behind and what would be unavailable to her there.

"There is no one I know to ask. I know I should take all the herbs I can find right now, and my casket of *potlatch* gifts from the tribe, also."

She began with her herb collection and stacked all the bottles, jars, and packets outside her door. Then there were her rawhides, furs, and tanning tools, including what was left of the brain solution in its sealed jar. Two Blankets made a trip to the storehouse and made careful selections there. She found another twenty furs and a dozen hides to add to the thirty or so she had already taken and added them to the stack. She cleaned her clothes and Mira's and folded with care the two dresses she had bought from *Monsieur* Bayonne. She bundled them up and stacked them outside.

"Oh, my. This pile is getting rather large... but Marshall said pack what I needed."

Finally, she was down to her cooking supplies and tools. Her few cups, plates, bowls, and eating utensils, as well as the knives she had acquired, she packed as well as she could, rolling the utensils and knives carefully in a piece of canvas. Eventually, she sat on her sleeping furs, which would have to wait until the last day. She looked about the longhouse, and it now seemed empty, not empty of possessions but empty of the life it contained. Now, it was bare.

About midday, the *E.D. Baker* pulled in and released its passengers, which included Alton Shales and a couple of his men. Marshall met them and took them to the Landing. He was jubilant. Alton was less so but eager to complete the sale as well.

"How is your packing going, Mira? Do you need any help?"

"I am trying to bundle my clothes. Can you help and put your finger right here on the knot?"

Two Blankets put her finger on the binding and Mira tied it off. Mira put her *nazóg* spear through the lashing and carried it outside.

"I will need to rest a bit because tonight there is a place I must go—a special place—to say goodbye."

"Is it your Standing Bear place?"

"It is, but how did you know that?" Two Blankets searched her memory for anything she might have told Mira.

"I only know you loved him. And now he is at Warm Springs. And you cannot see him anymore."

"Yes, I did. And he is. And I cannot."

"I will lay down for a while with you, *Pike.*"

Two Blankets held out her arms and Mira joined her. Together they lay back on the furs.

When she rose later in the evening, Mira was there and ready to go. "I will go to the Standing Bear place with you."

They each took a sleeping fur, and Mira took her *nazóg* spear. There were few people about the Landing now, and they met no one along the road beside the creek. They walked quietly up the road until Two Blankets found the little rabbit trail, almost obscured beneath the loose branches and brush beside the road. Thirty feet along up the path, they came to the small clearing.

Mira looked about the small clearing. "This is a very pretty place, *Pike.*" She took a deep breath of the still, pungent air. "It is peaceful here."

Two Blankets found the small pile of stones she had placed here before and lay her fur down before it. She sat down and adjusted her position until she was comfortable. Mira sat beside her.

"Pike, why is this place special?"

Two Blankets looked down at her daughter. *It is a real question to her. She really wants to know, but how do I answer?*

"All right, I will try to explain it. There is one reason, the Standing Bear reason. That is private, and I won't explain that part. But the other part... Do you see those stones there? That is where your placenta is buried. That part is your part."

"What is a placenta?"

Now I feel like I am diving off a cliff with no bottom below me.

"When you were a tiny baby, as big as my fist and in my belly, you were very defenseless."

"I was that small when I was in your belly?" Mira was interested now and listening very carefully.

"Yes, you were and even smaller than that. All right. Now, imagine the coldest day in winter and you outside with no clothes. All you have is your favorite sleeping fur. What would you do?"

Mira held up her red fox fur. "Like this red fox? I would wrap up tight and cozy. Then I would be warm."

"Yes, exactly. There was a time when that fur would cover all of you. The placenta is like that, like a fur covering your whole body, even your face, so you will be warm and comfortable when you are in the belly of your mother."

Mira considered that. "I can see that then I would be warm in winter. But how would I breathe?"

"Ah. Well, that is the magic of the placenta. You have to remember, it is not a fur. That's just to show how it protects you. The placenta has a tube that goes right into your belly button, and it feeds you and gives you air, too, everything you need to live and grow."

"Into my belly button?" She opened her wrap and looked at it.

"Yes, your belly button used to be a part of me, my darling. When you came out between my legs, the placenta came out behind you. We waited a little while, then tied the cord off and cut it."

"That fur must have been all sticky and messy. I saw the pigs give birth."

"It was. That is why we buried it. But it was special, at least to me. Very special. It was part of you, and part of me."

"I understand... sort of." Mira ran her hand through the rocks in the little pile. She picked up a water-smoothed stone of almost black, dark green color spotted with blood-red that fit perfectly in her small hand. "May I have this to remember this place, *Pike?*"

Two Blankets felt a sense of relief that she had escaped any further questions. "That is a pretty one, and such an unusual color, too. May I see it?"

Mira handed the stone to her mother.

Two Blankets examined it. *So smooth and polished. The color, I don't recall seeing any this color near here.*

"Yes, of course, you may have it. Do not lose it. When you are finished with it, put it in the bag about your neck. It is special."

"It is special." Mira held it in her hand and rubbed it. She held it close to her face and tried to look through it. "Very special."

Two Blankets allowed her hand to stroke Mira's hair a few times. Then she dropped it back to her lap and "remembered" why she was here. The site of the burial of Mira's placenta was one, of course. Two Blankets thought she had taken care of that part. The other part was that this was one of her last memories of Standing Bear.

Oh, Standing Bear, what will I do with you? I cannot forget you, and I will not forget you. I promise that. When I remember you, I will try to just remember the good parts. But in some ways, they were all good, even the last time, when we created Mira. Can you see her? Or feel her? I do wish, sometimes, so much that you could know her. I vow to know her for you as well as for myself. To try to teach her as you would. She is exceeding brave sometimes. That is a part of her that reminds me so much of you, my dear, dear Standing Bear.

Tears began flowing down her face, but were they tears of joy or sadness? She didn't know and didn't care either. They were tears that came from him. That she did know. Her whole body shook with sobbing, and she lay down with her head in Mira's lap. Mira let her lay there and petted her hair with the stone in her hand.

"Oh, my darling. I am supposed to be comforting you, and here you are, stroking my brow."

"It is all right, *Pike.* You are here for me, and I am here for you. We will always help each other. This is your Standing Bear place. If you can feel it this strong, then it must be that he is here, too. He knows."

Two Blankets sat up and wiped her eyes and face. "That came as such a shock. Shall we go and finish packing?"

"Yes, *Pike.* Let us go." Mira patted Two Blankets on the hand. "I love you, *Pike.*" Then she hugged Two Blankets. They gathered up the sleeping furs and slipped out of the Standing Bear place and walked together in silence to the longhouse.

THE SACRED GROVE

TWO BLANKETS LOOKED at the pile of belongings sitting in front of the longhouse and sighed in despair. Though she could not know it, for sure, she could envision what Marshall would say.

He will say we can't take all this junk. We need crates, whiskey crates.

"Come, Mira. We need to get some crates."

They walked up to the Landing building and behind it. There were a hundred or more crates stacked back here, and some with bottles intact. Two Blankets fetched up three and Mira one and headed back to the longhouse. At the front of the Landing, she ran into Harry Everton.

"Hello, Missus Johnston."

"Two Blankets, please, Harry."

"Can I do anything to help out?"

"We do need some crates and perhaps someone to cart our supplies down to the dock. If you can spare someone?"

"I'll send down a couple of the men to help. They'll bring crates. A dozen?"

"Thank you, Harry. You have been awfully kind."

"Well, it ain't your fault how Marshall is behaving. You also have been a friend to me."

"Your friendship means much to me."

She turned away and carried her prizes off to the longhouse.

Together they packed the jars and bottles into the whiskey crates. When the men arrived, they made short work of transporting and stacking her supplies. Before she knew it all was stacked and tarped on the dock.

One of the men examined the job just finished. "Well, that'll do 'er."

"Thank you both. You have truly helped me, and I don't know why."

He looked embarrassed. "All of us feel pretty bad the way we treated that *Monsieur* Bayonne. You never gave us any trouble."

"The past is the past. There is nothing to be done for it now."

"Well, all the same. I really think it's us that owes you thanks, Missus Two Blankets."

―――――――

AS THE SUN dropped beneath the bluffs and evening approached, Two Blankets again gathered together a couple of sleeping furs. "I am going to the Sacred Grove to say goodbye to the Chinook people. I know you did not know any of them. If you do not wish to come along, I will understand."

Two Blankets again waited while Mira made her decision. Each serious question, like this one, seemed to require serious thought.

"If they were important to you, then they are important to me. I will come." She picked up her red fox fur and followed her mother out of the longhouse.

Walking towards the wood, Two Blankets noticed a flurry of activity about the Landing. Men were working at the dock, stacking crates, while others brought more from the Landing. The girls walked up the road toward the forest, then along the edge of it. When they reached the steam-powered portable sawmill, they turned toward the wood and followed a path into the grove.

At the edge of the Sacred Grove, Two Blankets stopped. "If we are to go farther in, we must disrobe, or we could stay here."

In answer, Mira began to remove her clothes and stack them carefully upon the ground. Two Blankets followed suit. They followed the path farther in, past the small canoe of the child that had drowned in that last year before the tribe moved to the Reservation. Two Blankets paused before the tree where Fire Stick's canoe had been temporarily raised before his removal to Warm Springs.

"I don't know what to do here, Mira. I didn't know any of these people except one child, but I feel a connection to them."

"Let us sit here, then, and ask the *weyekin* for help."

"That is a good idea."

Two Blankets spread the sleeping fur and sat. She assumed her meditative posture and Mira copied it.

"Oh, *weyekin*, I am *Nimi'ipuu*, but I do not know the word in Chinook. I know you have been here, guarding this land for the Chinook for age upon age. I am not a Chinook by birth, but they stole me from my family so long ago that I feel more than half-Chinook now. Now, all are gone except me and Mira, and tomorrow I will be gone as well. Then there will be no one honoring you. Only the *whitemans* will be here. That is why I am here."

"*Pike*, just sit and listen. You are trying too hard."

This little person is very smart. Sit and listen. Sit and listen. White Mouse chittered in her ear.

Gray Wolf lifted her ears. *Sometimes action is required. Sometimes 'Do Nothing' is all one can do.*

She sat back and quietly listened. She heard the river first, then the caw of a crow. Then she heard a humming singsong voice coming from next to her. She cracked her eyes a bit and glanced to her right. Mira was rocking from side to side and singing in a strange non-language. It was hypnotic, and she began singing in counterpoint.

She heard the soughing of the wind blowing through the trees and the scraping of the limbs, a kind of sawing sound. Several birds seemed to join in with their own calls. The ripple of the stream added its own song.

Two Blankets stopped singing and began listening in earnest. She thought she heard a small chirruping coming from her shoulder. Glancing down she saw that White Mouse had her eyes closed and was swaying back and forth with her mouth open, and a small cry emitting from her mouth. Gray Wolf opened her mouth, and a mournful cry escaped from deep within her.

Two Blankets closed her eyes and sang again. Not with words. Only with sound and feeling.

It was not a song at all, but an atonal rhythm. It continued with the help of some other strange beings, help from the *weyekin* it seemed. Somewhere in the background was the cry of a big cat and then the huff of a bear. A crying that sounded almost like a woman screaming. That would be a red fox. All of these and more joined in. It continued for a period, though Two Blankets could not tell how long. Then it slowly tapered off and finally ceased. She opened her eyes and looked down at Mira. Mira's eyes opened and looked into hers.

"Mira, you are so smart. I think we have been answered."

"Yes, *Pike,* I do, too."

"Shall we go home?" She began to get up and gather the furs together.

"Yes. I am cold."

They walked out of the grove, put on their clothes, and walked to the longhouse.

A NEW LIFE

CHAPTER 20
FALL, 1863

TWO BLANKETS PACKED up her sleeping furs and took a last look at the longhouse. It was empty now, and she had already said all the goodbyes to the Landing she was ever going to.

When the *E.D. Baker* pulled in that afternoon, headed downstream, everyone hurried to the dock. As soon as the gangplank was run out, a crew of the steamboat's stevedores hastened to load their pile of cargo. In fifteen minutes the crates that had taken hours to organize and stack was piled on the foredeck, and they were being beckoned aboard.

Out on the river, another riverboat tooted its whistle and passed them. The *E.D. Baker* blew a signal of its own and began backing away. Two Blankets and Mira hurried aboard, followed by Marshall, who led his horse and mule.

The paddle-wheeler backed into the current with a great thrashing of the paddle wheel. The black smoke belched out of the single tall smokestack.

Marshall moved to the port side rail. "That's the *Wilson G. Hunt.* There'll be a race now."

"Why would there be a race, husband Marshall?"

"Two reasons. First is they run for another company, the gawds-be-damned Oregon Steam Navigation Company. The O.S.N. has had a monopoly on this river for far too long. They even own both portages up at the Cascades. Second, anytime you get two similar boats together, like now, there's a race."

"Pike, this is a big boat. A *really* big boat." Mira seemed interested in everything new. "Can I look at the back of the boat, at the big wheel?"

"Just be careful, Mira. Be very careful. We don't know what will be dangerous here. I will come back with you."

They walked back along the port side, picking their way past sacks and crates of cargo. When they reached the stern, Two Blankets looked upstream, but the Landing, or Bent Creek camp as it had been known in Chinook times, was already obscured by a bluff.

The paddle wheel was huge, at least twenty feet in diameter, and ran all the way across the stern. The noise was oppressive, the chuffing of the smokestack, the creaking of the drive, and the thrashing of the stern wheel.

"Pike, isn't it amazing. It is like riding on the back of a great beast."

A little further on, they saw a waterfall of immense height. As they came up on it, one man walked up and said, "That there is Multnomah falls, one of the tallest falls in these here United States."

"Ah, Mira, I know a story of these falls. Let us go forward, and I will tell you. "They walked toward the bow of the boat, looking at the beautiful tall falls.

"Once, several lifetimes ago, there was a great *Tyee* of the Chinook or the Wasco people who was named Multonomah."

"How long ago is several lifetimes, *Pike?*"

"Bone Rattler, the ancient shamaness that I knew, said her teacher knew him, and her teacher was very old, as well. Multonomah had a daughter who he loved very much. Just as I love you. She was very beautiful, so he arranged a marriage with a young warrior of the neighboring Clatsop tribe. He was a very handsome warrior and she was not opposed to the match. There was much feasting, and a *potlatch* like no one had seen for years. The feasting and gift giving lasted for days and days. But then a sickness came over the tribe."

"What happened then, *Pike?*"

"The chief called on all his medicine men and old council members, but no one knew what to do. Finally, an old man came down from the mountains, older than anyone in the tribe. He told the council that when his father was a very old man, he had told him that a time would come when everyone in the tribe would die unless a maiden who was also the daughter of a *Tyee* was to climb to the top of a high cliff above the river and throw herself off to make the Great Spirits happy with them again. The *Tyee* called all the young maidens together, and after seeing them said to his clan, 'Prepare yourselves to die like warriors. I will not ask this of any maiden of this tribe.'"

"I am not sure I like this story."

"It is a sad story, very sad, my Mira."

"The sickness stayed in the village, and many more people died. The daughter of the High *Tyee* wondered if she should be the one to jump off the cliff, but she really cared for her warrior. Finally, a few days later she saw that he was now sick. She cooled his face and left him a bowl of water. Then she slipped from the village and began climbing the path to the cliff above the village. All night and all day she climbed until she reached the top. She stood on the edge of the cliff and called to the Great Spirit, 'You are angry with my people. If I sacrifice myself will you take away this sickness quickly? Show me a token in the night sky to give me an answer.'"

"Did the Great Spirit show her?"

"Just then the moon rose above the trees, just across the river. Right over there." Two Blankets pointed north across the river. "She knew it was her sign, and she threw herself off the high cliff. The next morning, all those people who expected to die during the night woke up alive and there was much rejoicing. But the young warrior, her betrothed, ran up asking for the maiden. They looked about and did not find her. Then they climbed up the path and found her body on the rocks. The warrior picked up her body, and the *Tyee* called out to the Great Spirit, 'Show us a token that my daughter's sacrifice has been accepted." As they watched, first a spray of water that was silvery-white broke over the rocks high up, then floated down in a mist to the pool by their feet. That is the story about how the falls were formed."

"That is a very sad story, *Pike*."

"Yes, it is."

"Pike, Pike. Look at that." Mira jumped up and hung on the railing.

Two Blankets looked up from her musing story. Just off the port bow was a second steamship. This was a side-wheeler. It must be the *Wilson G. Hunt,* and the *E.D. Baker* was gaining slowly.

Two Blankets and Mira walked up to the bow to observe. A crowd of men was on the foredeck and several had bottles with them. An air of drunken joviality surrounded them.

"We're gaining on them, yes we are."

"There's another foot. God damn O.S.N. bastards."

"Let's hear it for the People's Transportation Company. You O.S.N. bastards. Huzzah. *Huzzah."* Some of the men joined in the cheer. Others took it as a toast and lifted their bottles.

The *E.D. Baker* gained a couple more feet on the *Wilson G. Hunt,* then three more. Now the side wheel of the *Hunt* was beside the bow of the *Baker.* The *Hunt* swung a few feet toward the *Baker,* which had to slow and pull away to starboard. One man flung an empty whiskey bottle at the churning wheel and was loudly congratulated. Another bottle flew across. The current seemed to favor the *Wilson G. Hunt,* and she gained back what she had lost. Suddenly, the *Baker's* bow swerved across the stern of the *Wilson G. Hunt,* and she quickly made up the lost ground. The men crowded over onto the starboard side, jeering and cursing. *The Baker* passed the paddle wheel then amidships of the *Hunt* on the starboard side. The men crowded around Two Blankets now.

"Captain Hakes fooled 'em. We've got the current now."

"Why does it make a difference?" Two Blankets asked.

"Well, little lady, if you look ahead, Portland is just around that next bend. We're in the current now and will be inside at the turn around the bar. If you could see the docks, there'll be maybe fifty wagons and two-wheeled carts lined up to take cargo. We get there first, we get the first wagons. The second boat may have to wait an hour or two to begin unloading."

The *E.D. Baker* docked in Portland ten minutes before the *Wilson G. Hunt,* to much cheering from those aboard the *Baker.* Cargo was lifted by block and tackle up to the docks and waiting wagons. When one was filled with goods, it moved off with a cracking of the driver's whip, and another took its place.

Meanwhile, a steam scow had pulled up and tied off to the *E.D. Baker's* bow. Marshall went to the port side and talked with the men on the scow.

"What is it, husband Marshall? We aren't unloading to the wagons?"

"No, I arranged for this scow when I was last here. They'll run us up to Oregon City. It'll be faster and cheaper."

Men from the scow began loading Marshall's goods onto the scow. With them working, and several stevedores from the dock, they soon had all his and Two Blanket's supplies and stores loaded. Two Blankets carried her Warm Springs casket, and she and Mira walked the gangplank to the little scow. Marshall paid the stevedores. He brought his horse forward. The horse took one look at the water and the gangplank, neighed fearfully, and reared at the passage. Marshall covered the head of his horse with a coat and quietened her. As he talked to her softly, she became accepting and docile. Then softly he led her down the gangplank. The mule followed dutifully.

"That man sure knows his horses," a stevedore said appreciatively.

"He does." Two Blankets, herself was somewhat amazed. "Horses, guns, and whiskey." Then she and Mira followed Marshall down the gangplank.

Two of the crew released and coiled the lines, and they were off up the Willamette River.

Two Blankets held tight to Mira's hand, since there were no guard rails on the scow. It pulled away from the Baker and churned off upstream. They passed the *Wilson G. Hunt,* which was just now tied and waiting for wagons. The captain was on the dock, eight feet above them, arguing with the boss of the stevedores, apparently trying to get some help for his ship. She could not hear them, other than loud voices, but she could see the captain waving his arms and the boss shrugging his shoulders.

Beyond this, along the dock were a couple of smaller steamboats, then she saw two great sailing ships. Their tall masts and furled sails were like nothing she had ever seen before. Then they were away from the dock area and moving upstream on the Willamette. Portland seemed to her to be a very large town, though it only contained about 4,000 people at the time.

"Husband Marshall, what are those white things in the streets of Portland?"

Marshall glanced up irritated, then laughed. "Them's the stumps. They call Portland 'Stumptown.' Town's growing so fast they don't get time to remove the stumps, they just paint them white. That way the wagons don't hit them."

Under her breath, she said, *"Whitemans are very strange."*

In less than two hours they pulled over to the east bank. This was just a small village, but Two Blankets could see the reason. Just upstream, she could see Willamette falls, a drop in the river of some forty feet running all the way across the river, some 1,500 feet.

Though it was approaching evening, five wagons were waiting for them. The wagon drivers would not be involved in the loading process, but each wagon carried a stevedore, and they quickly had the wagons loaded. Marshall paid off the scow captain, tied his horse to the wagon, and climbed up onto the lead wagon. Two Blankets climbed up onto the seat of the second wagon with Mira by her side.

"Pike, do we have any food? I am hungry."

Two Blankets thought back. They hadn't eaten all day—events had been so exciting going on one after another. She reached back and brought up her basket. "I am sorry, Mira. We have been so busy, I hadn't thought about food. Let us see, shall we?"

Mira looked into the basket. "Do we have any smoked salmon?"

"I am sure we do. Sir, would you like a little salmon?"

The driver seemed surprised that she spoke English so well. Then he apparently absorbed that as fact. "Yes, ma'am. I would, if you have some extra."

Two Blankets handed the driver a chunk of salmon and a *camas* cake. Then she gave a piece to Mira and took one for herself.

"This is the portage around the falls?"

"Thank you, ma'am, for the salmon. Some of the best I've ever had. Used to be there was a portage on both sides, but West Linn got wiped out in the flood of '61. It's only a mile or so."

They continued on the bumpy road. "That there is Oregon City. Has about a thousand folks. We're headed above the falls to Canemah. It's a smaller town, but it does have a couple of inns, for the overnights, the people waiting for the upstream run. You'll be on the *Relief* and head out tomorrow."

Shortly thereafter they saw the *Relief* and soon had their cargo unloaded to the sternwheeler. When all was shifted to the deck of the steamship, Marshall indicated the town.

"We'll spend the night up in Canemah. Then we got to be down here by dawn." He hurried on, forcing Two Blankets to pick up Mira and run after him. Crossing the dirt street, he entered the establishment and greeted the bartender like an old friend. The bartender gave Two Blankets a key and directed her up the stairs to her room.

Two Blankets remained where she was.

The bartender turned to Marshall. "Your squaw want something?"

Marshall smiled slyly. "That'd be my wife, barkeep. So, I'd say you should address her as such."

"What would it be you'd want, Missus—"

"That'd be Johnston," said Marshall.

"Yes, well what can I do for you, Missus Johnston?"

Marshall smiled and turned back to his whiskey.

"Excuse me, sir, but my daughter and I would like a meal. Is there some food ready now or must we wait?"

Two of the men standing near chuckled. "She speaks better English than you do, Johansen."

He looked at her crossly and indicated the pot on the central stove. "There. Pot on stove. And bread, too." Then he went back to his conversation with Marshall.

Two Blankets examined the pot, then took two bowls of the soup and some bread, and she and Mira climbed the stairs to their room. The stairs and railing were raw and unpainted, as were the walls in the small room. Entering the room, she looked about. There was a rope bedstead with a mattress made of a straw-stuffed bag, a small window, and a chair. A couple of grass stuffed pillows lay on the mattress and also a couple of blankets. Two Blankets set down her casket. Squatting down on the floor she tasted her stew.

"Well, the stew is edible. Not good, but it will do."

She and Mira ate the stew in what quiet the room allowed. Two Blankets checked the bed. As she pulled back the blanket, a myriad of small black bugs scurried to escape the sunlight. She pulled the top blanket, shook it out carefully over the bed and spread it on the floor in the corner.

"Let's sleep on the floor, Mira. I don't like that bed."

"All right, *Pike.*" They lay down on the blanket, and Two Blankets held Mira to her body.

Everything is so strange in this whiteman's *world. I am afraid I have made a mistake. But I don't know what I would have done.*

White Mouse was a faded image of her normal self and only chittered. Gray Wolf also looked thinner than usual. *It is hard to be strong in a* whiteman's *place where no one believes in you.*

You have chosen your path. You must stay on it, at least for now.

Late that night Marshall entered the room. Two Blankets stirred and looked up. The smell of whiskey was on him.

"Husband Marshall. There are bugs—"

He threw himself down on the bed.

"—on the bed."

A snore escaped his mouth almost immediately.

Two Blankets smiled and closed her eyes.

————

A BANG ON the door and a voice announced the next morning, "Steamer's leaving in thirty minutes!"

Two Blankets raised herself stiffly to one elbow. Mira stirred, then woke completely.

"*Pike,* where are we?"

Two Blankets stroked Mira's hair. "Shush. It is all right. Remember the sternwheeler and the River Willamette?"

"Yes, I remember. I forgot where I was."

The sound of Marshall erupting from the bed startled Two Blankets.

"Oh, god damn it. There are bugs in this bed." He shook his arms and pulled off his shirt. "I hate bedbugs."

The three of them hurried from the hotel with Marshall scratching. They reached the sternwheeler and Marshall went to check his horse and mule. Men were gathering in small groups on the bank and on the boat, smoking, drinking, or just plain talking. Within another half hour, the boat was loaded and they were headed upstream.

Two Blankets noticed Mira squeezing her legs together. She picked her up and began searching for a toilet. Finding one on the outside edge of the boat, she sat Mira down.

"This will be fun, Mira. You can look down and see the river."

When both had finished, they climbed up to the upper deck and sat, legs dangling over the edge forward of the helm. For every ten minutes, or hour, or three hours that she watched the green water pass beneath the hull. For every ten feet, or mile that she watched the bank drift into the past, she felt a distancing from her past and her home. Yes, this was a beautiful river and probably much beloved by its former inhabitants. Who used to live here? She thought she had heard they were the Kalapuyan people. Once they had been great traders with the Chinook and Nez Perce, and some 15,000 strong. Now, they were all gone. So the Kalapuyan might have loved this river, fished and hunted here, lived and danced, were born and died here. But it wasn't the *Nch'i-wána*. For one thing, it wasn't nearly as wide. It didn't have the feeling of carrying all to the sea before it. Two Blankets was certain this river could be angry, but not on the scale of the *Nch'i-wána*. This was a country of open grasslands with the occasional grove of great oak trees or stand of conifers.

When, along the banks, some farmers gathered with a wagonload of goods to take up to Salem, or some farmer wanted to get off, the steamer would blow its whistle and nose into the bank. As soon as they were aboard, or had departed, the *Relief* would blow her whistle and proceed upstream. This was the only time when the brownish-black smoke, sparks and small bits of glowing bark would overwhelm Mira and Two Blankets as they huddled next to the wheelhouse. As soon as they reached the current, they would be off again.

When they saw the men below eating sandwiches handed out by the crew, Two Blankets and Mira headed down below to get a lunch themselves.

Meat, bread, and cheese and a cup of coffee was the standard lunch. It was simple fare but they were very hungry and ate every bit placed before them. They watched the river turn before them until finally, Salem appeared, a small town of some 1,500 people. Though not large by *whiteman's* standards, all of them seemed to be out working at the same time.

The *Relief* blew her whistle, and she nosed into a dock. Already, there was the stand of wagons waiting ready to unload. Two Blankets and Mira slipped down the narrow stairs and worked their way forward. If she knew Marshall at all well, he would have a set of wagons waiting for him, probably the wagons in front. As it turned out, it wasn't the first wagon or the second that waited for Marshall, but the third, fourth, fifth, and sixth.

Two Blankets chuckled. *Well, I was close enough.*

Soon enough, they were on their way with the horse and mule following by lead. They moved away from the river then turned right on a rough road.

"This here be Ferry Street," the driver said.

Two Blankets could see the ferry waiting at the end of the road. The wagon bumped up onto the ferry and pulled up to the bow. The second pulled up parallel, followed by the other two and Marshall's horse and mule. All were tied down, and the men began poling out into the river, which was only a couple hundred feet wide at this point. On the other side, the tie downs were released, and the wagons rolled off onto the muddy bank. The wagon driver clucked to his team, and they bumped off. Up on the bank, they turned left and followed a track parallel to the river for a piece. Soon they came to a wide creek and turned right and followed it for a good mile.

In the near distance, Two Blankets saw a house. It was brightly painted white, with green shutters and had a steep roof with what looked like a large attic or possibly an attic room. The wagons pulled up and stopped in front of it.

Why are we stopping here, I wonder?

Marshall jumped down off his wagon and spoke to his driver, who started unloading. "Well, Two Blankets. What do you think?"

"I do not understand, husband Marshall. What do I think?"

"What do you think about the house. This is our new home. Beautiful, ain't it?"

Two Blankets looked again at the house. Situated in a grove of oaks, it had a porch running all the way along two sides. Two large windows on the left were faced with curtains and one on the right. A large whitewashed barn was off behind it to the right, and she could hear the stream gurgling as it ran behind the house.

"*Pike*, is this our new home? Can I go in? It looks real pretty."

"You go right on ahead, Elizabeth," Marshall said. "Your room is upstairs."

Mira ran up to the porch and opened the door, leaving it open. Two Blankets could see a stair climbing up. Its banister was a polished and carved wood, and carpet runners ran up the stair.

"It's beautiful, Marshall. When? How did you get it?"

"Well, I got this here house and the six hundred forty acre land grant about a year ago. The man who built it for his wife died in the flood of '61. You heard about that at Canenah. She decided not to come west. Then I got my own three hundred twenty acre land grant up the creek for about four hundred dollars. Pretty sweet deal, eh."

The window opened from upstairs, and Mira poked her head out. "*Pike*, you have to see my room. Come up here! It is so beautiful, with a bed and roses on the wallpaper."

Two Blankets just stood there as her goods were unloaded onto the porch.

White Mouse chittered. *This is going to be hard, really difficult.*

She stroked her soft white hair.

Gray wolf stood and examined the house. *There may be fat mice*—White Mouse gave her a half-scared, half-dirty look—*rats to hunt in the barn.*

"*Pike*, come look, please."

Darlings, you are both right. This meat is going to be really hard to chew. There is nothing we can do but accept at this point.

"I am coming, Mira."

She climbed the steps to begin her new life far from the *Nimi'ipuu*, the Chinook, and the *Nch'i-wána.*

R. L. ADARE HAS been writing since he was a teenager. Taking a major in linguistics at university, his interest in anthropology and language development has frequently played a part in his writing. While studying linguistics he also took a minor in German, so he could read Hesse in the original as well as obtain a teaching credential. He has taught for ten years after having been an accountant for thirty-five. Along the way, he and his wife owned a kite shop on the Oregon coast for ten years and lived on a thirty-six-foot sailboat for ten years, which they sailed down the coast from Seattle to Monterey.

Among his favorite thousand authors are Zane Grey, Herman Hesse, D. H. Lawrence, C. J. Cherryh, Lawrence Durrell, Ursula Le Guin, Anne McCaffrey, Kurt Vonnegut, Jacqueline Cleary, and Diana Gabaldon.

He has been published in *Wings, Pass the Hemlock, The Whale Song Quarterly, Ariel Chart, The Wyrd, Saddlebag Dispatches* and *Cobra Lily*. He lives with his wife of 35 years and their manx cat, Pixie, in South-western Oregon.